"You are uncomm... o-
served William. "Wh... e
you so poor an opini... ex?
I am of the belief th... who has had her
hopes blighted could overlook the indisputable fact
that a woman as desirable as she is beautiful must
attract the notice of gentlemen wherever she might
be."

"Good heavens! Will Powell, paying me compliments?" quipped Felicity. "The highwayman's pistol
has indeed addled your wits, it would seem."

William, who had not failed to detect the hint of
brittleness in her lilting tone, sharply narrowed his
gaze. "Addled? Why?" he demanded. "Because I
pointed out the obvious?"

"You will pardon me if it has not been obvious in
the past that you have ever found me in the least
attractive," Felicity countered.

Will was all too keenly aware of the enticing picture
Felicity made, gowned in white sprigged muslin, a
white straw beehive bonnet with green ribbons tied
in a bow beneath her chin, her cheeks slightly flushed
and her eyes sparkling with what he greatly suspected
to be hurt mingled with proud resentment. He
caught her wrist.

"The truth is, Lady Felicity Talbot," he growled,
"you are a cursedly attractive woman, and you know
it."

And then, in the next instant, he kissed her.

A NOBLE HEART

Sara Blayne

Zebra Books
Kensington Publishing Corp.
http://www.zebrabooks.com

ZEBRA BOOKS are published by

Kensington Publishing Corp.
850 Third Avenue
New York, NY 10022

First Printing: July, 2000
10 9 8 7 6 5 4 3 2 1

Printed in the United States of America

To Christine and Richard with love and the wish that their marriage will ever be blessed with happiness, love, and romance.

One

It came to him through a thick, impenetrable haze that, though seldom one to be in his cups, he must have dipped rather deeply the night before. Indeed, considering the size of the headache pounding in his skull, not to mention the dryness of his mouth, which suggested an advanced state of dehydration, he must have been rather more than just three sheets to the wind. He must have bloody well spliced the main brace!

A low groan burst through his lips. The devil, he thought. A drunken spree might explain his nagging headache and the nausea in his stomach, but hardly the extreme pressure on his chest, like a great weight pressing him down against the bed, making movement impossible and breathing a matter of great effort.

He was aware of a rising sense of panic engendered by the dread suspicion that, in a state of extreme inebriation, he must have sustained some sort of paralytic injury, when his senses were assaulted by a decidedly unpleasant aroma, like stale breath in the face, followed almost immediately by the indignity of a wet, slurping tongue applied in an upward motion encompassing his nose to the center of his forehead—which served at last to bring him wholly and irrevocably awake.

His eyes flew open, and he found himself staring in stunned disbelief into the unlovely aspect of a pink tongue draped over large, ivory canine teeth amidst an impenetrable mop of thick white hair in which there appeared an unnerving lack of discernible eyes—all at exceedingly close range.

The dog, for so it was (something of a cross between an Old English Sheep Dog and a Great Dane, speculated its hapless victim, dragging in a belabored breath), gave every impression of exultation at discovering the human returned to the land of the living, a sentiment it immediately expressed in a resounding yelp of appreciation, which did little to alleviate the man's pounding headache.

"Yes, no doubt I am happy to see you, too," agreed that worthy in exceedingly dry accents. "I might point out, however, that it is bad manners to perch on the chest of an acquaintance you have only just met, let alone pin him to the bed by the shoulders. If you wish a burgeoning friendship, I suggest you remove yourself from my person immediately."

The dog, far from demonstrating any noticeable inclination to adhere to that well-meant advice, instead gave vent to a lengthy and vociferous rebuttal, which had the immediate effect of eliciting a hurried tattoo of footsteps along the corridor beyond the open door.

"Goliath!" pronounced a horrified feminine voice from the doorway. "You wicked dog! Get down from there at once!"

The newcomer, sweeping into the room, gave the immediate impression of youthful energy coupled with grim determination, as she grabbed the dog by the scruff of the neck and attempted to haul the creature bodily to the floor—to little effect.

Goliath, apparently overjoyed at what he perceived as a glorious new game, gave a bark of delight and, in an attempt to further express his pleasure with an ecstatic wagging of his practically nonexistent tail, set his entire hind end to shaking—to the detriment of the human beneath him.

"You dreadful creature, *enough!*" declared the determined beauty, bracing her heels and giving a mighty tug, which brought the dog, sliding and scrambling, at last off the bed, not to mention off the sorely beset man in it. "Do not expect any rabbit stew for you tonight, you bad dog." An imperative arm shot out, a stern index finger indicating the open exit. "*Out,* before I have Chester tether you in the stables."

Goliath, convinced at last of his own perfidy and taking advantage of the opportunity to escape his mistress's unmistakable displeasure, gave a gleeful bound through the door and, skidding around the corner, vanished. In the sudden silence of the room, the dog's thumping footfalls could be heard retreating down the hall and presumably down the stairs as well.

"My lord, I do beg your pardon for Goliath," exclaimed the beauty, crossing directly to the bedside. "He is actually a sweet, lovable creature when one gets to know him. As it happens, this has always been Bertie's room, and I daresay Goliath stole up here thinking to find his old master. I pray he did you no injury."

"Only to my dignity," replied his lordship, suffering a peculiar light-headedness as he looked up into the breathtakingly lovely face bent solicitously over his. "Where am I? Have I died and gone to heaven?"

His inquiry, the product of his sudden flightiness, elicited a wry gleam of a smile from lips that, full and enticingly sweet, seemed most distractingly designed for kissing. "Hardly, my lord, though it was a near thing. Pray lie still," added his angelic benefactor, firmly pressing him back against the pillows as he made ineffectually to shove himself up into a sitting position. "You have been quite ill and must not try yet to exert yourself."

"Egad," he groaned, glad enough to collapse in the bed. He clenched his eyes against the spinning of the room. "I am weak as a bloody kitten. How long—?"

His eyes flew open in horrified disbelief at the answer.

"Six days, my lord, and as many nights. Indeed, you lay so long in insensibility, we quite feared for your recovery."

"Six days?" gasped his sorely beset lordship, too stunned by that revelation to voice any other questions for the moment, a circumstance which seemed to afford the vision of beauty some little relief. The crease that had etched itself between her eyebrows at discovering her patient besieged by Goliath smoothed away as it became clear to her that his lordship did not appear on the verge of a sharp decline because of the unfortunate mishap.

"It is a wonder you are alive at all," his ministering angel pointed out with an odd hardening of the lips, which had a curiously chastening effect that he found less than gratifying.

Indeed, his lordship's temper, not to mention the persistent throbbing in his skull, had hardly been improved by the discovery that he had no memory of how he came to be in such unprepossessing surrounds. Not that the room was unpleasant, with its lace curtains floating on a gentle breeze issuing from an open window or with the scent of lilacs wafting from a freshly picked bouquet set on a stand by his bedside, for it was not. Certainly there was no denying that the sudden appearance of the young beauty with glorious brown hair and lovely eyes, made singularly arresting by a glow of concern in their golden brown depths, had served to lend to the simplicity of the chamber an elegance it previously lacked.

But who the devil was she? And how had he come to be in what had once been "Bertie's" bedroom? he could not but wonder as the intriguing female sat on the edge of the bed and laid the back of her hand against the side of his face with what would seem a total lack of self-consciousness that bordered on the familiar.

"Thank heavens the shock of Goliath's assault has not brought on a return of the fever," she observed with seeming heartfelt relief, "and the wound appears not to have suffered from the experience, though perhaps I should have a look at it. How do you feel, my lord?"

"As if I have a thousand toothaches in my skull," growled his lordship, tinglingly aware of her nimble fingers reaching to undo the bandage that he only then became aware was bound about his forehead. It was on the tip of his tongue to demand to know the nature of the wound to which she had referred and which obviously had more than a little to do with not a few of his persistent discomforts. Only, her infinitely gentle touch served quite thoroughly to distract him.

"Thank heaven," breathed his ministering angel some moments later with a great deal of satisfaction, "the wound is none the worse for your ordeal with Goliath. No doubt you will be glad to know it is well

on the mend. I daresay the scar will hardly be noticeable. It will, at any rate, be easily concealed beneath
your hair."

"Excellent. It would seem I have a great deal for
which to be grateful," murmured his lordship, who,
lost in the spell of her nearness and her fingers moving over his temple as she tenderly cleansed the
wound and re-bound it in fresh bandages kept for
that purpose on the bedstand, could not bring himself to do more than lie quiescent while he watched
her from beneath heavily drooping eyelids.

Dressed in a morning gown of rose-colored sarcenet, she was a remarkably beautiful woman, who,
past the first blush of youth, perhaps (beyond the age
of coming out, but no more than four and twenty,
surely, he thought), yet exuded a youthful glow and
vibrant energy that really was quite captivating. Of
average height, she was hardly in the current fashion
of the petite, pleasingly plump, blond beauty who
gave the impression of helplessness and fragility.
Quite the contrary, not only was she slender, with a
willowy waist and small but well-rounded bosom, all
of which he found strangely appealing, but, as she
leaned over him, intent upon her task, he could not
but note that the slender arms, emerging from beneath short puffed sleeves, were pleasingly firm and
that the small, shapely hands were infinitely capable.

In spite of the ivory perfection of her skin, which
showed an imperviousness to the sun's harmful influence, she was obviously a female given to athletic
pursuits. Her rich, brown hair, shot through with
golden highlights, was worn in short curls, which
framed a heart-shaped face made distinctive by the
wide, full mouth given to laughter, the delightful
flash of a dimple in either cheek, and a long, straight
nose and prominent cheekbones.

She was a veritable angel of perfection, he decided, inhaling the sweet scent of her—lavender, he thought, and rosemary. Indeed, her tender ministrations were having a decidedly salubrious effect on his ruffled temper, not to mention the pounding of his headache. He was, in fact, acutely aware of being lulled into a delicious state of torpid contentment attended by a daydream in which his angel fitted herself neatly into his arms and offered up her tantalizing lips to receive his kiss—when suddenly the mood was shattered.

"I do wish you would stop staring at me as if you had never seen me before," declared his ministering angel with an unwonted sharpness. Bolting unexpectedly to her feet, she favored him with a glorious blaze of anger. " 'A great deal to be grateful for,' my lord? Faith, what an understatement. You haven't the least idea how fortunate you are. And you are far from being out of the briers yet. Oh, I should gladly beat some sense into that head of yours if I thought it would do the least good. How *could* you have placed yourself so foolishly at risk, and for what?" she demanded, leaving little doubt that she thought him a hopeless case. "What in the world possessed you to forget who and what you are for something that was not worth risking a single hair on your head?"

It was only then, as he searched for a means of answering her, that he felt the world seem suddenly to tilt and turn. Indeed, he had the dreadful sensation that an abyss had opened up beneath him, plunging him into a spinning void. Then, as from a very great distance, he heard someone call out to him and felt strong hands clasp his arms and bring him, reeling, back again.

His angel's face swam into focus, the brown orbs huge and dark against the sudden pallor of her complexion.

"I fear, my dear girl," he said slowly, his eyes mirroring the awful blankness he felt inside, "that I have indeed so thoroughly forgotten who and what I am that I not only cannot tell you why I should have done it, but I have not the least idea *what* it is that I have done. I beg your pardon if I have been staring at you in an uncivil manner. The truth is, however, I do not have the least idea who you are. Indeed, I cannot even recall my own name."

Felicity Talbot regarded her patient with no little astonishment. *She* knew perfectly well who he was. She, after all, had been hopelessly in love with him since she was ten. It was, in fact, the curse of her life that her brother Bertram had chosen to bring his closest friend home from school for the holidays when she had just entered that gawky stage her mama used to call the age at which nobody loves one save for one's own mama and papa. Certainly, that had been true in the case of her brother's friend, who had promptly adopted her as a sister to add to his brood of four female siblings for whom he entertained an unshakable brotherly affection.

It was as if he had never really looked at her again, she reflected ruefully. Certainly, he had never for a moment altered in his attitude of easy camaraderie toward her, any more than he had ceased to take her for granted, the way one was wont to take for granted a childhood pet for whom one has continued to entertain a sentimental attachment long after one has ceased, save for an occasional pat on the head, to pay any heed to it. And then, just when she might have caught his attention, something catastrophic had happened to forever blight her hopes.

It had been the bitter drop in her cup that the year

before her own come-out, just when she had grown most satisfactorily into her arms and legs, he had met and instantly lost his heart to her Cousin Zenoria, who, a year older than Felicity, had ever been as fickle as she was petite, blond and beautiful.

He was William Powell, Viscount Lethridge, heir to the Earl of Bancroft; and less than a sc'ennight ago he had wounded the Marquess of Shelby, perhaps mortally, in a duel over the Lady Zenoria.

The insane fool! she thought, a lump rising to her throat at the thought of what he had risked for the honor of a woman who did not even know the meaning of the word.

A mist clouded her vision at sight of the hopelessly blank expression in his eyes. Damn him! Even as a youth of seventeen, he had been marvelous to look upon with his crisp blond hair, laughing blue eyes, and the boyish lop-sided grin that had had the peculiar effect of making her feel wondrously warm inside. To her chagrin, she discovered that his mature aspect, in spite of, or perhaps because of, its lean, hard masculinity made even more so by its six-day growth of beard, was a deal more disturbing to her physical and emotional well-being than had been that of the youth who had captured her heart thirteen years before.

Inexplicably, she suffered a pang at sight of the lines about the stern, handsome lips. The lines had not been there two years ago when last she had seen him, though the marvelous eyes had already even then taken on the flinty aspect that served as an impenetrable shield behind which her dear Will, once so open and full of fun, had learned to conceal his innermost feelings and thoughts. That fine, noble-hearted youth must surely be gone forever.

Now there would ever be Lethridge, a man with a reputation for being dangerous, a man who had fought a duel with a hardened rakeshame over a woman and won.

Zenoria had done that to him, Felicity mused darkly. Zenoria and her vain, fickle heart, which, not satisfied with the love of one true man, must make a conquest of every male who had the misfortune to come into her sphere of influence.

Lethridge, who had always been admired and respected by his peers as a right 'un, a bruising rider and top-of-the-trees sawyer, a man as handy with a pair of fives as he was with a pistol and sword, a Corinthian, was hardly blind to the faults of the woman who had long ago won his heart. More was the pity, Felicity thought. No matter how often Zenoria flung her suitors in his face, no matter how blatantly she demonstrated her unwillingness to commit herself to marriage, Lethridge never failed to come to her rescue whenever she found herself in the lurch. It was as if he could not help himself.

A plague on the man! she thought uncharitably, feeling her heart beating beneath her breast with alarming velocity. As the only daughter of the Duke of Breverton, she had dreamed of one day winning Lethridge away from her cousin. Foolishly, she had even refused several advantageous offers of marriage while she waited for the maddening nobleman to take notice that she had grown into a woman considered by some to be a beauty in her own right. But no more, she told herself. As a confirmed spinster of three and twenty, she had long since given over any such vain, foolish hopes. And if occasionally she felt her life was just a trifle empty, she quickly reminded herself that she had espoused a worthy cause peculiarly suited to her unique position. Possessed of a more than moderate competence and the independence enjoyed by few of her female contemporaries, she had found fulfillment, even a measure of contentment, working to improve the lives of destitute women. She had, in fact, almost succeeded in putting Lethridge entirely out of her mind, if not out of her heart.

Oh, *why* had her brother Bertram ruined everything by showing up on the doorstep of her country cottage in Kent with the wounded and unconscious viscount in tow? she wondered irritably. She could hardly have turned them away, she told herself defensively, not when Lethridge had appeared so alarmingly pale and uncharacteristically vulnerable. Faith, whom was she trying to fool? she thought wryly. She had never before known such fear as swept over her at sight of William Powell, unconscious, a bloodied bandage tied about his head. She had not hesitated to take him in, nor had she spared herself nursing him through six days and nights of fever and delirium. Mrs. Morseby, her housekeeper of long-standing, had finally been brought to remonstrate with Felicity, saying her mistress would be of no use to anyone, let alone his lordship, if she wore herself to a state of collapse.

It was only with a deal of reluctance that Felicity had at last been prevailed upon to allow the housekeeper and, occasionally, Annabel Jones, the young guest at Primrose Cottage, to relieve her in the sickroom for a few hours at a time. She had slept the sleep of exhaustion, only to awaken each day with the fear that word would arrive that Shelby had perished of his wounds. The marquess's death would mean exile for Lethridge and heartbreak for his remarkable family, but most especially for his youngest sister Josephine, who had become in recent years particularly dear to Felicity. However, word had not arrived, and now Lethridge was awake, his memory erased by the bullet that had creased his head.

The devil take him! she fumed, well aware that once

he was in possession of all the facts, he would undoubtedly do something infinitely foolish, like bolt from his bed and out of her house out of some mistaken notion of honor. It would be just like him to insist on returning to London when he had hardly the strength to lift his head, let alone withstand a carriage ride that would very likely bring on a recurrence of the fever or worse. She had not worried over him and tended to his most intimate needs day and night for nearly a se'ennight only to have him fling her efforts all away on some stupid sense of pride or, more unpalatable still, out of the compulsion to see the woman who had been the cause of his present difficulties.

It simply was not to be thought of, even had it not been imperative to keep him hidden away until Bertie returned with news of Shelby's fate. She must keep Lethridge in the dark, and yet she must tell him something. She really could not bear to see him in his present anguish.

"I daresay it is little wonder that you have lost your memory," she said somewhat tartly at last, compelled to ease the terrible blankness from his eyes. "After all, you received a crease to the skull that must have jumbled what few brains you have. As it happens, I am Lady Felicity Talbot, and you are William Powell, Viscount Lethridge—my cousin," she added, turning away to hide the telltale blush that stung her cheeks at that final utterance, a patent lie meant to give the semblance of propriety to what could only be considered a compromising situation.

"William Powell," repeated his lordship, a deep furrow etching itself between his eyebrows. "Viscount Lethridge." With a hint of impatience, he shook his head. "It does not ring a bell, I fear. And you say I am your cousin?"

"My cousin once removed, as it were," Felicity confirmed, crossing her fingers behind her back. "We have been the very best of friends since we were children. I should even go so far as to say you and Bertie are as close as brothers, of which you possess two, Timothy and Thomas. Your father, as it happens, is the Earl of Bancroft. Your home is Greensward in the North Yorks. Surely you must remember Greensward?"

Helplessly, Lethridge shook his head, his blue eyes rueful. "No. Absurd, is it not? I cannot seem to recall anything before I awakened to Goliath's tender ministrations only a few moments ago." He lifted his gaze to Felicity's. "You still have not told me how I came to be here, or where 'here' is, for that matter."

"My poor Will," exclaimed Felicity, reverting to the familiar address she had been used to employ in an earlier time when the youthful Viscount Lethridge had taught her how to bait a hook and cast a fishing line. Impulsively, she sat on the edge of the bed. "You *are* in a bad way if you cannot remember Greensward, or Primrose Cottage, for that matter. You are in Kent, near Faversham. As a boy, you were used to come here often over the holidays to hunt pheasant with Bertie. You were, in fact, on your way to spend a day or two with us, when you had the misfortune to be held up by highwaymen. With your usual reckless abandon, you resisted; and, though you managed to drive off the blackguards, you were wounded."

"Ah, yes, the wound," murmured Lethridge, gingerly touching his fingers to the bandage. "And—er—Bertie, where is he? Surely, he did not suffer at the hands of the villains."

"Fortunately, Bertie was here with me," Felicity answered, wondering at the depths of her newfound depravity. Faith, how easily the lies poured from her lips! "When you failed to put in an appearance with your usual punctuality, Bertie went out to look for you. He found you lying in a crumpled heap by the road, your curricle and team a short distance away. He brought you home, and now he has gone to Greensward to inform your mama and papa what has happened and to reassure them that you are receiving the best of care. And that is all there is to it," Felicity ended, her unaccustomed flight of fancy having come up hard against her eminently practical nature, which warned that too many lies, besides being difficult to remember, must inevitably become hopelessly entangled. "Now you should rest, while I go and fetch your broth to you."

All there was to it? thought William, who had an entire lifetime to fill in, not to mention an aching sense of emptiness, which the young beauty, his self-avowed kinswoman, seemed curiously able to hold at bay.

"No, wait." Lethridge's hand curled about her wrist, preventing her from rising. "I have not the least desire for broth, and, as it happens, there is a great deal more I should like to know. Pray do not go just yet."

Felicity, who was hard put to conceal the involuntary leap of her pulse beneath his touch, indeed, who felt she must escape the viscount's unsettling proximity very soon if she wished not to betray herself to him, steeled herself to meet his gaze with a calm composure she was far from feeling.

"I fear it will have to wait, my dearest Will," she said gently but firmly, disengaging her hand. "You are far from recovered from the fever, let alone your wound. If you are to rebuild your strength, you must have nourishment."

"And I suppose you do not intend to indulge me until I have drunk all your demmed broth, is that it?" demanded her patient with a wry twist of his handsome lips.

"I do not," Felicity confirmed, withdrawing to the door. There she paused to look back at him. "Try not to fret, Will. No doubt, with rest, everything will come back to you. In the meantime, you must concentrate merely on getting well again. You might try to think of this as a holiday."

His angel of mercy gave him a last, fleeting smile before whisking around the corner and out of sight.

"A holiday, good God," he groaned, sinking back against the pillows. *A holiday from what?* he wondered, trying to force himself to remember. But no matter how hard he tried, he simply could not break through the blank wall that separated his present reality from a past that eluded him.

At last, his head pounding with the effort to make some sense of the thing that had happened to him, he shoved himself up and, flinging aside the bedcovers, swung his legs over the side of the bed. It required all of his strength, not to mention his considerable willpower, to push himself to his feet. For a seeming eternity, he stood, his head reeling and sweat pouring over his body under the borrowed nightshirt that was too small for his tall frame, before at last he staggered across the room to the dressing table. Leaning his hands against the edge of the table, he peered in perplexity at his image in the looking glass.

"William Powell, Viscount Lethridge," he murmured, recognizing the face staring back at him, but unable to attach the name to it. "Heir to the Earl of Bancroft, whose home is Greensward in the North Yorks." Hellsfire, it meant *nothing* to him! None of it. Miss Talbot might have been talking about someone of whom he had never heard, for all the impression it made on him. Indeed, she could be making it all up out of thin air, and he would not have known the difference.

Almost instantly, the image of another face, one remarkable for the vivacity of its lovely features, not the least of which were golden brown eyes that had the disconcerting propensity to glow with compassion one moment only to sparkle gloriously with anger the next, obtruded itself into his reeling consciousness.

He could not recall ever having seen a more fascinating woman. Hellsfire, she was the *only* woman he could recall at the moment, and what a woman she was! It seemed utterly inconceivable that he could ever have forgotten her or, indeed, that, having known her, he should have been contented with a relationship based solely on friendship. She was the sort of idealized woman a man dreamed of finding one day, but never really believed that he would.

Besides being possessed of a singular beauty that must draw eyes wherever she went, she presented the arresting impression of a sweet, fiery nature of the sort to arouse a man's primitive urges to possess and protect. More telling still, there lay beneath that delectably feminine exterior an unmistakable, quiet sort of strength that reminded him of someone, though, for the life of him, he could not think who it might be. Certainly, Miss Talbot was one of those rare creatures who would meet any sort of crisis with a characteristic calm capability. She had already demonstrated that much. After all, how many females of refinement would have taken in a wounded man and then cared for him as he lay, helpless and unaware, in his sickbed? He did not have to have command of his memory to know that was hardly the accepted thing for an unmarried female who laid claims to being the daughter of a duke. Indeed, in the norm it was not to be thought of for any gently born female.

Why, then, had she done it? he wondered, finding a great deal about the young beauty that provoked his curiosity.

He had not failed to detect a subtle change in his angel's demeanor in the wake of the unnerving discovery that he was bereft of all sense of who he was. There had arisen an immediate tension in the air, which was attended by a nervousness in her manner, evidenced by a tendency to look away when she was speaking. This from a female who previously had behaved toward him with a total lack of self-awareness that bordered on the familiar! he reflected, recalling the blaze of anger that had lent fire to her eyes only moments before his telling revelation. She had spoken to him in a manner that would be acceptable only between persons who enjoyed the intimacy of a long friendship. She had, after all, accused him of having a shortage of brains, he remembered with a wry twist of the lips.

Afterwards, though she had not hesitated to refer to him as her "dearest Will" and despite the fact that she had evidenced toward him a sincere concern for his well-being, he could not be mistaken in thinking he detected a certain restraint in her manner toward him that had not been there before. Added to that was the matter of her curiously abrupt conclusion to the interview, along with the sense that she wished nothing more than to remove herself from his presence.

A highwayman's bullet may have cost him his memory, but it had not served to impair either his instincts or his ability to reason; and both of these faculties told him that Lady Felicity Talbot was keeping something from him. Perhaps it was nothing more than the discomfort of a failed affair of the heart. It occurred to him that the beautiful Felicity might have rejected a suit from him, perhaps because she felt she could not feel for him anything other than a friendly affection. Certainly, that would explain her sudden reticence—the dread of having to relive an uncomfortable scene of rejection. Strangely, the thought was not one conducive to comfort.

If only he could remember, he thought, his glance, half wild, searching for some clue, something to jog his memory. His eyes came to rest on a gentleman's personal items laid neatly out on the dressing table—a well-healed leather purse, a penknife, a gold watch and fob, a solitaire diamond pin, all of which undoubtedly should have been familiar but, maddeningly, were not.

His attention was drawn to an exquisitely wrought walnut box, which would seem to evoke a dread fascination. It, alone of all the things on the dressing table, struck a strange chord of memory. Knowing what he would find within, he reached to open the lid.

The brace of dueling pistols shone a dull blue against the red velvet lining. The checkered grips were plain, the octagonal barrels of exaggerated length designed to give the duelist the greatest possible advantage against the nervous jerk of an arm at the moment of firing. William knew without trying that the point would be true. He knew, too, the feel of the grip in the palm of the hand.

Deliberately, he lifted his gaze to probe the eyes in the mirror. "William Powell," he said again. "Who the devil are you?"

Two

"Not in Town? Will? But that is preposterous. What do you mean, he is nowhere to be found?" demanded Florence, the Marchioness of Leighton, of her elder sister Lucy, who had the further distinction of being the Duchess of Lathrop. "It is the middle of the Season. And Will promised he would be available for Mama and Papa's anniversary celebration. It is only a few weeks away, Lucy. He is supposed to make certain the new travel coach is ready on time."

"And so it will be, Flo," Lucy replied, her flaming red hair glinting sparks in the sunlight filtering through the bay window. Her gray-green eyes, which had the arresting quality of changing colors with her mood, were just now clouded with worry, the color of the mist on the moors. "Lathrop will see to that. I believe the more significant problem is the nature of Will's absence."

"The nature of Will's absence? Why, whatever do you mean?" queried Flo, who, the acknowledged beauty of the family, was fair-haired and blue-eyed like all the Powell siblings with the exception of Lucy, a throwback to her father's Irish grandmama. Leaning forward, Flo set the tea server on its tray. "You say that as if you think some ill has befallen him."

"Good grief, Flo," interjected Francine, the Countess of Ransome and the third of the Powell sisters, flopping down on the caffoy-upholstered sofa with a characteristic hoydenish lack of elegance in sharp contrast to her three more self-possessed sisters. "Surely you must be aware of the rumors going the rounds."

"If you mean the thing about the Marquess of Shelby, I choose not to give them any credence," Florence answered with a careless shrug of a shoulder that belied the resentful flash of her blue- violet eyes, a reaction that Francine had a special knack for eliciting from her older sister. "Leighton has assured me that there is not a shred of truth to any of them."

"Leighton *would,*" asserted Francine, rolling her eyes meaningfully at Josephine, the youngest of the four sisters assembled in the marchioness's private sitting room. "He would say anything to protect you from something he considered too disturbing for your delicate sensibilities."

"That is not altogether fair, Francie," Josephine, the Countess of Ravenaugh, gently chided before Florence could give vent to those delicate sensibilities. "Ravenaugh went out of his way to keep *me* from hearing the rumors. If it were not for the fact that Tom can keep nothing from his dearest wife, I daresay I should be in the dark as well. Lady Juliana came to me only yesterday evening with the news that Shelby was on the threshold of death's door, and all because the marquess boasted he had enjoyed Lady Zenoria's favors. How very like Will to take it upon himself to defend a lady's name, even one who has gone out of her way to cast doubt on it. Will has always had a noble heart. In that, I daresay he is most like Papa."

"Oh, indeed," countered Francie with characteristic acerbity. "His *heart* is noble. It is, however, his reason that is in question. I cannot think Papa would do anything so foolish as to take to the field of honor over a female who had made a habit of flinging her contempt in his face. Rather than risk his life, not to mention his reputation, in a duel, Papa would counsel Lady Zenoria to practice restraint and the marquess to wed the lady in all haste."

"But then Papa's case is hardly comparable to Will's," Lucy pointed out with her usual calm good sense. "After all, Papa fell in love with Mama when they were only children, and in all these years he has never even looked at another woman."

"Lucy is right," Josephine interjected. "One must take into account the fact that Will apparently loves Lady Zenoria. I have had to accept it, little as I like it. After all, he has resisted our every effort to engage his interests elsewhere. If he could not be made to see that Lady Felicity Talbot is the ideal match for him, then he must indeed be enamored of her cousin. And all of you know as well as I that love defies all reason."

"Pooh!" exclaimed Francie, wrinkling her nose in comical disgust. "*True* love may defy all reason, but what Will is suffering is a lethal dose of infatuation, and if someone does not come up with a cure for it, we may lose the heir to Greensward, or, almost as untenable, be forced to welcome Lady Zenoria as the future Countess of Bancroft."

"Lady Zenoria the mistress of Greensward! Good heavens," gasped Florence, her lovely face expressive of horror. "Surely things are not so desperate as that."

"I am afraid Francie is perfectly in the right of it," Lucy concurred quite soberly. "At the moment, the future of Greensward hangs on a thread. Lathrop has confided in me that the betting books are running heavily in favor of Shelby cutting his stick before the week is out."

"Will actually met Shelby in a duel?" Florence said with the air of one who, stunned at the revelation, had not quite yet grasped the significance of events being discussed around her.

"Will not only met Shelby in a duel, he has perhaps fatally wounded him," Francie stated for her elder sister's clarification. "Worse, rumor has it that Will may have been wounded as well, which is why Lucy has called us all here today."

This announcement, far from having the desired effect of bringing Florence up to date on the matter that crucially concerned them all, appeared dangerously close instead to sending the marchioness into an immediate swoon.

"Will wounded! Oh, merciful heaven." Going an alarming shade of mother-of-pearl, Flo clasped a hand to her bosom.

"Florence Anne Marie, don't you dare enact a Cheltenham tragedy," said Lucy, setting her teacup aside in order to bracingly clasp her sister by the shoulders.

"Faith, I *told* you we should not bring her in on this," Francie declared, screwing her face up in disgust. "Now that we have, however, we might as well ring for the smelling salts."

"Hush, Francie," scolded Lucy, as close to being out of all patience with her impulsive younger sister as she had ever been. "This is all your fault. You might have broken the news to her with a little more delicacy. You knew very well what would be her probable reaction to simply blurting it out."

Francie who, far from knowing what it was to be possessed of delicate sensibilities, had been accused by her mama of having none, and who, indeed, was the undisputed daredevil of the family, yet had the grace to look chagrined at her beloved eldest sister's stern set-down. "You are right, of course, Lucy," she admitted wryly. "I should have known better than to spring it on Flo all at once. Having reached the ripe old age of six and twenty, I should have learned a few social graces by now. I begin to think I am quite hopeless. I do beg your pardon, Flo."

"It is all because Ransome indulges you to excess," declared Flo, who, under Lucy's firm grip, no longer resembled one on the verge of a sharp decline. "You are a countess now, and the mother of three young hopefuls. It is time you ceased to behave like an indisciplined hoyden."

"Excellent," applauded Francie, her infectious grin breaking forth. "You must not be afraid to open the budget. A good venting of the spleen is just what you need."

"Really, Francie," scolded Josephine, struggling not to give in to a burble of mirth. In spite of the gravity of the situation that had brought them all together, Francie had ever had the faculty for making her laugh. "You are deliberately trying to bait Flo, when you know how little it will serve. Pray try and behave yourself."

"This from the runt of the litter," exclaimed Francie, making a comical face at the youngest of the Earl of Bancroft's daughters. "Having a husband and family of her own certainly has made a difference in our sickly Jo. She was never used to rip up at me."

"Fiddle!" retorted Josephine, her lovely eyes dancing. "I may have been of a sickly constitution growing up, but I have never been a pansy."

"No, not a pansy," agreed Francie with a wry grimace. "As I recall, you had the happy knack of appealing to my conscience."

"Of which I am quite sure you had none,"
Florence interjected, straightening up and smoothing her skirts. "Thank you, dearest Lucy. I am quite
recovered now. Indeed, you may be certain I shall
not succumb to weakness again. I am ready to hear
all the sordid details."

"Are you quite certain, Flo?" queried Lucy, observing that her sister's cheeks had yet to lose their pallor.
"This is not one of my romantical novels of adventure
and intrigue. It is quite real, and it concerns our
brother Will. If you had rather not be made a party
to it, I am sure we shall all understand."

At this intimation that she was not equal to sharing
in a family crisis that her sisters were apparently gird-
ing up to meet, Florence visibly stiffened in her seat.

"I shall not go off again. I promise," she said, gazing round at the other three with a determined set
to her chin. "Pray, let us get on with it. Tell me everything."

"That's the thing, old girl," applauded Francie,
patting the marchioness on the shoulder. "We Powells always stand buff in the face of adversity."

"For heaven's sake, Francie," retorted Flo, ever
quick tinder to Francie's spark of incorrigibility. "I
may be nine and twenty, but I am hardly an 'old girl.'
Pray do not call me one."

Francie, observing with no little satisfaction the
color that flooded Florence's face, was unwontedly
quick to tender her apology for a remark that was as
uncalled for as it was inappropriate.

"Splendid," Lucy commented dryly, observing
Francie with a knowing eye. Obviously, the little
malapert had deliberately baited Flo for the express
purpose of stimulating just such a response. With her
blood flowing, Florence had not the look of a wilting
violet, but displayed the steely glint of a Powell ready

to do battle. "I suggest we begin by bringing Flo up to snuff on events that took place some six days ago, after which we shall all put our heads together to determine what to do to resolve the situation. Now, who wishes to be the one to tell Flo what we know about the unfortunate incident?"

It was quickly and unanimously decided that Lucy herself, who, the author of numerous popular Romance novels, was a master at telling stories, should be the one to perform that office. The eldest of the Powell sisters began with the events leading up to the fateful meeting at dawn between the Earl of Bancroft's heir and the Marquess of Shelby.

Reports varied, but it was generally agreed that the most reliable account was the one given by Lady Windholm, who had it from Mrs. Brockhurst, who heard it from her modiste, Mme. Duprey, who just happened to have been fitting Lady Zenoria with a scandalously indecent Roman tunic gown of transparent rose Persian silk, slit up the side to well above the knee, when Mr. Llewellyn of the Essex Llewellyns burst in on the Lady Zenoria with the news that Lethridge had apparently deliberately forced a confrontation with the Marquess of Shelby the night before in the Goldfinch, Ransome's private gaming club. Before the modiste could be dismissed, Llewellyn had related that Lethridge, giving the appearance of one in his cups, had engaged the marquess in a rubber of piquet for pound points.

"Then I daresay Shelby's purse is a deal lighter," Flo was moved to comment with every appearance of supreme confidence. "Will was always Papa's most apt pupil in games of chance, and you know how Papa always insisted that, if any one of us undertook to learn any sort of game, especially one involving mathematics, we must master every possible strategy involved in it. I should be very greatly surprised if Will has ever met his match at piquet. Still, it is curious. Will has never been the sort to risk the family fortune in gaming."

"Very astute of you, Flo," observed Josephine in her gentle manner. "It is very unlike Will to indulge in a high-stakes game of any sort, and even more so ever to be seen in his cups. How much less like him to lose heavily at a game that is like child's play to him."

Josephine, having delivered that pronouncement, could feel her sisters tense in anticipation of Florence's probable reaction. Whatever they had expected, however, it was not to hear a distinctly unladylike snort from the prim and proper marchioness.

"But that is absurd," Florence declared with perfect aplomb. "Obviously, it was all a sham. Will had some ulterior purpose in what he was doing, you may be sure of it. He may have lost all sense of reason where Lady Zenoria is concerned, but he is hardly a fool."

"That would seem a contradiction in terms," Lucy observed dryly, a green glint of amusement flickering behind the gray mist of her eyes. "However, I believe it is precisely to the point. Will most definitely *was* up to something. He was, in fact, setting the marquess up for a fall, and he carried it off brilliantly. I believe even Papa would be impressed with Will's strategy. Having convinced everyone that he was incapacitated with drink, Will allowed himself to be drawn into a high-stakes game in which he lost steadily—until Shelby, believing he had a goose for the plucking, grew inordinately careless. He allowed Will to catch him marking the cards."

"It was simply splendid!" broke in Francie, her face lit with admiration. "Suddenly, without warning,

Will shoots out his hand and catches Shelby in the act of nocking the ace of spades with a thumbnail. Then, cool as you please, Will drawls, 'You really should not have tried fuzzing the cards on me, my lord marquess, especially when it was so clumsily done. I have always known you were a cheat and a liar, and now I have irrefutable proof. It is, in fact, my considered opinion that your lucrative career as a Captain Sharp has come to a sudden and ignominious end.' "

"Will said that?" said Josephine, who had not heard that part of the story in quite that detail.

"Ransome quoted it to me verbatim," Francie was quick to affirm to the others. "You may be certain that he was inordinately pleased by it, too. Will saved him from having to show Shelby up for what he is. You know Ransome will not have a cheat in his house. And now that he has a family, he is not quite so quick to jump into the breach as he once was. Thank heavens. The last thing I should ever wish is to have Ransome engaging in a duel with a professional duelist."

"And yet that is exactly what Will has done," Lucy pointed out. "Naturally, Shelby did not hesitate to call him out, or Will to accept the challenge. It was the whole point of the exercise, after all—to provoke the marquess into a duel that did not involve Lady Zenoria. There is no doubt, however, that everything Will did was motivated by Shelby's boast that he had enjoyed the lady's favors."

"Dear me, I cannot think what is worse," Josephine exclaimed softly, her delicate features grave with worry, "that Shelby may die and Will be forced into exile, or that we do not know where Will is or how badly he may have been hurt."

"Can we be certain that Will was wounded?" asked Florence, hoping against hope. "Perhaps he has only done the sensible thing and gone into hiding until it is seen which way the wind lies with Shelby."

"I'm afraid not, Flo," Lucy replied gravely. "Lathrop and Ransome tried to talk Will out of the wretched business—to no avail. Still, they arrived at Will's lodgings in the Black Bull in time to encounter Lord Esterbrook and Mr. Grantham as they left. Although Will would divulge nothing of what had passed between him and the gentlemen, who were obviously serving as Shelby's seconds, Lathrop does not doubt they were there to complete the arrangements for the duel."

"Faith, if Ransome and Lathrop *knew* the arrangements had just been made," interrupted Florence, "then why did they not simply restrain Will, forcibly if necessary, from making the appointment? It would have saved everyone a deal of trouble and worry."

"I believe," Lucy made haste to answer before Francie, who had fairly snapped to attention, could leap to her beloved Ransome's defense, not to mention that of Lucy's own Lathrop who, of all Francie's brothers-in-law, was her favorite, "you know the answer to that as well as the rest of us, Flo. It was a matter of honor, and both Lathrop and Ransome were once soldiers. You could hardly expect them to go against their soldier's code."

"I suppose not," conceded Florence, recalling somewhat belatedly, perhaps, that Lathrop had sacrificed his military career to engage in just such an affair of honor. But then, he had done so to save the life of the young lieutenant who had won the heart of Lathrop's beloved sister Roxanne, and that was a deal different from Will's foolishly flinging all caution to the wind over a female who had done nothing to deserve such a sacrifice. She could not but think that Lathrop and Ransome could have done something to stop Will from pursuing such a feckless course.

"They met the next day at dawn on Finchley Common," Lucy continued. "Lathrop has since learned from Lord Esterbrook that Felicity's brother Bertram and Mr. Jerome French served as Will's seconds. Unfortunately, both gentlemen, along with Will, seem to have dropped off the face of the earth. Neither has been to his lodgings since the fateful event."

"And Will?" Florence queried, a hand straying to her palpitating heart. "What had Lord Esterbrook to say about our brother?"

Lucy answered with a curious glint in her eye. "With no little persuasion, Lord Esterbrook was further brought to reveal that Will was struck down by the marquess's shot. He could not testify as to the severity of the wound. Only that Will was carried off the field of battle. I'm afraid Lathrop and Ransome were unable to obtain anything further from the man."

"I daresay he had nothing further to tell," opined Francie, recalling Ransome's bruised knuckles with a grim smile. "Which leaves us in the unwelcome position of knowing only that Will was wounded, and all because Shelby had the poor taste to boast about something everyone already knew. Damn Will! I could throttle him for putting us all through this."

"For once I am in complete agreement with you," declared Florence, who in the norm would have brought her sister to task for using language clearly unsuited to a lady of refinement. "Unfortunately, it is hardly to the point when we haven't the least idea where to find him."

"Oh, but I daresay we do," quietly offered Josephine, earning the instant attention of everyone present. "It would seem natural to assume, after all, that Will has been carried to a place of safety by his seconds and, perhaps more importantly, to someone who would be willing and able to minister to his wound. Since they are both bachelors with living parents, we can rule out the possibility that they have taken Will to their respective homes."

"Heavens, yes," agreed Francie. "Had they done, you may be sure the Duke of Breverton would immediately have informed our parents of Will's circumstances, as would have the Right Reverend Thaddeus French and his wife. Jo is right. But then, where does that leave us?"

"In the position of having eliminated at least two possibilities," Lucy replied. "And on the way to coming up with others, if I know Jo. Obviously, Mr. French and Lord Bertram are the most logical links to Will's whereabouts."

"I daresay they are our only means of discovering where he is," Josephine said, her lovely brow furrowed in concentration. "Since we cannot find them to demand where they have transported him, then we must rely on logic. I daresay they must have taken into consideration the need for secrecy, which would mean someplace somewhat remote and yet not too far removed from London. One must hope, after all, that Mr. French and Lord Bertram are sensible enough to realize the danger in transporting a wounded man over any great distance."

"And it could not be just any place," Lucy pointed out, "but one in which they knew resided the sort of care Will required. A doctor, perhaps, or one versed, at the very least, in ministering to the sick."

"Or perhaps only someone who they knew cared enough for Will to take him in and see to his needs," Florence postulated, thinking of a time when she had stood vigilance at her dearest Leighton's bedside and how close he had come to death's door.

"Surely you are not suggesting they took him to Lady Zenoria!" said Francie, no little taken aback by what must be a patently absurd notion.

"Really, Francie," Florence countered, greatly offended. "I wish you will not persist in thinking of me as a fool. I said someone who *cared* for Will. Lady Zenoria, I doubt not, is incapable of caring for anyone but herself."

"Well, then, if not Lady Zenoria, then who would you suggest?" demanded Francie, hands on hips. "Will has made it plain to every female who might have entertained any sort of affection for him that he is blind to everyone except Lady Zenoria. Our last hope for him was Lady Felicity, and even she has finally seen the futility of thinking to attract his notice. She has not made an appearance in Society for the past two years. Indeed, it is my understanding she has become a permanent recluse in the country."

"On the contrary," demurred Josephine, who, the same age as Lady Felicity, had felt, upon their having been introduced some five years previously, an immediate affinity for the other woman. "She has merely turned her attention to other pursuits. I happened to run into her some six months ago at the lending library where she was doing research on some sort of project that had captured her interest. I believe I have never seen her so excited. Unfortunately, her mama, the duchess, was waiting for her, and there was not time for her to say more than that her days were happily occupied and that she would make a point to let me know all about herself as soon as she had finished setting up housekeeping on her own. I deeply regret that I did not make an effort to call on her before my last confinement. I have, I fear, lost touch with her. And since Breverton and the duchess are presumably unaware of Bertie's involvement in the duel, I hesitate to contact them in order to inquire where we should find Lady Felicity."

"If she has set up housekeeping on her own, I cannot think it can matter now whether we find her or not," Florence offered. "Her brother would hardly choose to compromise his own sister by installing Will in her household. It would be unthinkable."

"I daresay Flo is right," said Francie, her eyes sparkling with mischief. "A pity. It might have been the ideal solution to our problem."

"Yes, but hardly the sort of thing one would wish on Lady Felicity," countered Josephine, smiling wryly. "Just think of the scandal."

"Scandals of that sort are easily wrapped in clean linen," Lucy pointed out. "It takes only a special license and a wedding. On the other hand, you may be sure Will would never be a party to anything that would jeopardize Lady Felicity's reputation. He has always looked on her as another sister, and you know how fiercely protective he is of us. No, I fear we must rule Lady Felicity out."

"Then who is left to us?" queried Florence, clearly reluctant to abandon her theory that Will must presently reside with a female who cared for him. "I believe Mr. French has only two brothers, both bachelors."

"I daresay, then, it must be someone of whom we are totally unaware," Francie theorized, her brow puckered in cogitation of how little they actually knew of their oldest brother's pursuits or his most intimate friends since the seven Powell siblings had all dispersed from Greensward to take up the threads of their own, separate lives. "I suggest we must begin by inquiring into Will's circle of acquaintances. I do not know about the rest of you, but I have been so involved with my own life that I have been sadly remiss in keeping up with Will's. Not that he ever invited speculation. He has always been one to keep to himself."

"I daresay that is only to be expected of the oldest son," observed Lucy, who was also feeling a twinge of guilt for having allowed a distance to grow between herself and Will without her having even been aware of it. "Papa always depended upon Will to learn the running of the estate. It will all be his one day, after all, and you know how Papa feels about duty and one's obligation to the land and its tenants, not to mention pride in one's birthright. It is one of the reasons Greensward continues to be prosperous when many another, larger holding has been tossed down the River Tick."

"Which brings us back to the question of where to begin our search for the missing heir," Florence reminded them. "Need I mention that we must be discreet in our inquiries? The last thing we should wish is to have word of the duel and its uncertain outcome reach Greensward. There would seem to be little point in worrying Mama and Papa until there is some news as to Will's probable whereabouts."

"For once I agree with Flo," Francie asserted, surprising everyone, but Flo most of all. "They have been so looking forward to their anniversary celebration to be followed by their visit to the South of France. It would seem a shame to put a pall on all their plans just when Papa has finally persuaded Mama that we can all rub along without her for a few weeks."

"Perhaps," Josephine murmured doubtfully. "On the other hand, I think we should consider the distinct possibility that they will both be furious with us for keeping them in the dark."

"Josephine is right. They will be terribly disappointed if they find out we knew about the duel and did not tell them," Lucy affirmed. "And you will all admit they are perfectly capable of dealing with even this sort of crisis. Heaven knows it will not be the first time one of their brood has courted disaster. Still, I think we might wait just a little while longer. Perhaps we shall be fortunate enough in the next few days to learn something about Will that will provide them some peace of mind."

It was quickly agreed that Lucy was in the right of things and that it would be perfectly acceptable to allow the earl and Lady Bancroft to remain in ignorance of their eldest offspring's peccadillo at least for the time being.

"Well, then, if that is settled," Francie broke in in her usual impulsive manner, "I suggest we begin our search at once. You may be sure Lathrop and Ransome are already employing their considerable resources to discover what they can. It is up to us to explore the possibilities Jo has presented. I, for one, am going to pay a morning call on the Right Reverend French and his wife. I daresay they might have some notion where their son has gone."

"You will do no such thing, Francie," Lucy hastily objected.

"Indeed, I should not advise it," Jo said in support of her oldest sister. "I daresay they have no inkling that Jerome is not in his usual haunts, in which case it is doubtful you would learn anything from them. You would only alarm them, and that is the last thing we should wish if we are to keep a lid on things."

"But I disagree," Francie objected. "I doubt not there are any number of things I might learn, such as who Jerome's intimates are and if one of them might happen to have a hunting lodge tucked away somewhere not too distant from the city. You may be sure I should comport myself in such a manner as not to give myself away. I am not such a chuckle-head."

"No, but you obviously have not thought the thing through," Lucy persisted. "After all, you are hardly accustomed to calling on the Right Reverend French and his wife. It would undoubtedly be thought more than a little odd should Lady Ransome suddenly present herself at their doorstep. No, it simply will not do, Francie."

"No, it will not," agreed Florence, a peculiar gleam in her eye. "On the other hand, it would not be thought in the least strange were the Marchioness of Leighton to make such a call. As it happens, the vicar at Oaks has expressed a desire to retire from his parish, which means we shall need a replacement. Who better to ask to suggest a candidate than the Bishop of Exeter?"

"I daresay there *could* be no one better," concurred Lucy, suddenly smiling. "In fact, I think you should call on the bishop without delay. The rest of us will wait to hear what you discover. In the meantime, we shall all keep our ears open. There undoubtedly will be a great deal to be learned simply by attending the social events to which we all receive invitations on a daily basis. It is time the Powell sisters once again took an active part in the Season."

"And past time we took an active interest in Will," Josephine observed soberly. "Who would ever have thought Will, who has always been the most dutiful of all the Powell brood, would have landed himself in such a bumblebroth?"

"It is always the ones of whom you would least expect it," Florence replied sagely.

"Pooh," retorted Francie. "It is always the strong, silent ones, the ones who tend to keep everything inside. One never knows what to expect from them because it is impossible to know *what* is going on inside their heads."

"We should have known," Josephine stated flatly. "We are his family. We should have been the ones to know where he might have gone. Now, all we can do is hope he is receiving the best of care."

"No doubt we may comfort ourselves," offered Florence, "with the knowledge that Will has always been well able to look after himself. I daresay he will send us word of his whereabouts before long. After all, he is hardly the sort to forget there are loved ones who will be greatly concerned about him."

Three

Felicity Talbot glanced up from the alfresco nunch-
eon of pigeon pie, boiled eggs, paper-thin ham,
thickly sliced bread, cheese and an array of dried
fruits she had just finished arranging on the square
of cloth spread out on the ground. Instantly, she
stilled as her gaze came to rest on Lethridge, lying
propped on one elbow on his side, his eyes, unseeing,
on the blade of grass he was twirling between a thumb
and forefinger.

Felicity's heart went out to him in spite of all her
best efforts to keep that unruly organ under a tight
rein. How unlike the keen, purposeful Will she had
always known was this silent, brooding man! "You are
doing it again," she observed.

Lethridge's singularly blue eyes swept up to meet
hers.

"I beg your pardon?"

"Frowning, my dearest Will," Felicity answered,
her smile wry, chiding him. "You know very well this
outing was to take your mind off your troubles for a
while. I must say, you are not very flattering. It is your
first excursion out of the house, and it is a perfectly
lovely day. You might at least try to enjoy yourself just
a little."

Will, thus brought to a realization that he had in-

deed been poor company for the past several minutes, returned Felicity's smile with a rueful grin of
his own.

"You are right, of course. I'm afraid I was wool-
gathering," he admitted. "I was trying to recall ever
having been here before. You would think a place as
lovely as this would . . ." He stopped, filled with a
sense of the hopelessness of it all.

The devil, he thought. No matter how hard he tried,
he could not make the sweeping hills, resplendent
with blossoming cherry orchards and burgeoning
beechwoods, appear in the least familiar, any more
than he could dredge up the smallest detail from his
damnably elusive past. It was as if his life had begun
only four days ago, when he had awakened to Goliath
on his chest and the beautiful Felicity bending over
him. And as if it were not enough that his own iden-
tity remained maddeningly unattainable, he reflected, taking in the provocative picture of Felicity
Talbot observing him with her all-too-discerning
eyes, but he must be acutely aware that this cursedly
sweet, fiery young beauty continued to be a complete
puzzle to him.

Who was she, really? he pondered. And why had
she taken him in and cared for him? Somehow he
could not make himself believe she was acting purely
out of altruistic motives. In spite of her unflagging
sympathy and kindness, her seeming willingness to
share any number of tidbits about his family—he had
six siblings of whom he had not the slightest memory,
egad!—he yet had the nagging suspicion that she was
deliberately keeping things from him. Still, he reminded himself, she was here, and she had saved his
life. If nothing else, she should have earned his trust.

Deliberately, he shook off any feelings of unrest.
"But no matter." Flinging the blade of grass away, he

sat up. "This looks a sumptuous repast, and I, I confess, am devilishly sharp set."

"An excellent sign that you are improving," observed Felicity, relieved to see the terrible blank look recede behind the cheerful mask he had assumed, even if it was only for her sake. She reached to fill a plate for his lordship. "If we are to make the trek back to the cottage, you will need your strength."

"Kind of you to remind me," observed Will with a grimace.

Felicity gave vent to a burble of laughter. "I did try to warn you you were not quite up to a walk just yet, but you would come."

"As much as I enjoy being cared for by a beautiful woman," William replied, "I cannot remain an invalid forever. My family must be worried. If they cannot come to me, then I must go to them. Perhaps seeing them will help me to remember."

"I am sure of it, Will," said Felicity, turning her face away to conceal a by now familiar queasiness of guilt at the string of falsehoods she had been forced to concoct to keep Lethridge satisfied. She did not doubt that Lady Bancroft would not care in the least to discover she was kept at home tending to the earl, who unfortunately was an elderly recluse too feeble to withstand the rigors of travel. As for the robust Earl of Bancroft, she dared not contemplate what *he* would think of it! "On the other hand, you must not torment yourself with what cannot be helped. Your parents have been assured of your well-being. There would hardly be any sense in leaving here before you are fit again, now would there?"

"No, I don't suppose there would," William conceded, unable to deny the wisdom of her advice.

The truth was he was deucedly weak after his bout with the fever, and his head yet throbbed with a dull ache, a constant reminder that he was far from being himself again. Bloody hell, it had taken nearly all of his pitifully small store of inner reserves to walk the hundred yards to the edge of the spinney. It was humiliating to acknowledge even to himself that, had he not had the girl's slender strength on which to lean, it was doubtful he would have made it beyond the French doors leading out into the garden. As it was, panting and sweating from his meager efforts, he had dropped gratefully to the ground upon reaching their objective, the low knoll overlooking the silvery glint of the Swale in the distance. Still, he had made it, and, if he were ever to get his strength back, he must make the attempt again on the morrow.

"Are you always so eminently sensible, Lady Felicity?" he queried, accepting the plate laden with victuals.

"As a matter of fact, I consider myself to be a wholly sensible female," Felicity answered, filling Lethridge's goblet with wine. "A view that, unfortunately, is not shared by my mama and papa. *They* believe I am foolish and hopelessly headstrong, as would be any gently born female who refused four advantageous offers of marriage and who must now be thought of as being clearly beyond her last prayers."

"Gammon," scoffed William, plainly incredulous at such an absurdity. "You may be beyond the first blush of youth, perhaps, but by no stretch of the imagination are you beyond your last prayers. Do not try and tell me there are not any number of eligible *partis* eager to change your single state, for I promise I shan't believe you."

"Oh, any number." Felicity laughed, balancing a plate on her knees. "Not only am I the sole daughter of the Duke of Breverton, after all, but I am in possession of a not insubstantial fortune of my own. You may be sure I should have a surfeit of admirers were I not happily ensconced in the country."

"You are uncommonly cynical, Miss Talbot," observed William, closely studying her lovely countenance. "What, I wonder, occurred to give you so poor an opinion of the members of my sex? I am of the belief that only one who has had her hopes blighted could overlook the indisputable fact that a woman as desirable as she is beautiful must attract the notice of gentlemen wherever she might be."

"Good heavens! Will Powell, paying me compliments?" quipped Felicity, averting her gaze that he might not see the flash of consternation in her eyes. *The devil,* she thought. He *would* see her as reasonably well to look upon—*now,* when he was deprived of all memory of the beautiful Zenoria and when her own highly developed sense of integrity would not permit her to take advantage of his vulnerability. Faith, it really was too bad of him! "The highwayman's pistol ball has indeed addled your wits, it would seem."

William, who had not failed to detect the hint of brittleness in her lilting tone, sharply narrowed his gaze. *Good God, what was this?* he wondered. "Addled? Why?" he demanded. "Because I pointed out the obvious?"

"You will pardon me if it has not been obvious in the past that you have ever found me in the least attractive," Felicity countered, knowing she was on dangerous ground but unable to stop herself. "It is, after all, hardly the sort of thing I am accustomed to hearing from you. 'Brat' is more like, or 'hoyden' or 'malapert.' Not precisely terms to turn a girl's head, you will agree." Leaning forward, she reached for a wedge of cheese.

"No, but apropos, I daresay," Will retorted darkly.

All too keenly aware of the enticing picture she made, gowned in white sprigged muslin, a white straw beehive bonnet with green ribbons tied in a bow beneath her chin, her cheeks slightly flushed and her eyes sparkling with what he greatly suspected to be hurt mingled with proud resentment—he caught her wrist.

"The truth is, Lady Felicity Talbot," he growled, "you are a cursedly attractive woman, and you know it."

The next instant, he kissed her.

Felicity stiffened, her eyes widening in startled surprise.

It was only a fleeting kiss, no more than a brushing of lips. Strange that it should render her tingling and breathless.

Then, just as precipitously, he released her.

The rogue, she thought, ruefully aware that her heart was behaving in a most reprehensible manner beneath her breast. It was not as if she had not been kissed before, she sternly reminded herself. There had been Thaddeus Wilcox when she was only nine and he ten, and Sir Andrew Parks, a great deal older, who at a masquerade ball had mistaken her for his "niece," or so he had claimed. And then, too, this time she *had* been taken wholly unprepared, and this time it *was* William Powell who had done the kissing.

Resisting the urge to cover the telltale beating of her traitorous heart with her hand, Felicity arched a haughty eyebrow in her best imitation of Lady Zenoria, her cousin.

"And what was that supposed to prove, my lord?" she queried, for all the world as if he had not just shaken her to her foundations.

Will, nearly as surprised as she at his ungentlemanly breach of conduct, could only marvel at his hitherto unsuspected propensity for giving into irresistible impulses. Worse, despite knowing that he had behaved badly toward a gently born female who had the further distinction of having succored and cared for him when he was in need, he was acutely aware that he felt not the smallest remorse. On the contrary, he had enjoyed it immensely; indeed, he regretted only that the stolen kiss had been of such short duration. In truth, had that been all for which he had to berate himself, he would not now be experiencing a damnably uncomfortable sensation of guilt.

The fact was, however, he had been only half serious when he accused Lady Felicity of displaying all the signs of one disappointed in love. Her reaction, unfortunately, had given him the distinct impression that he had hit far too close to the truth. Worse, he had been given to strongly suspect *he* was the culprit who had blighted her hopes! At the very least, it seemed all too clear to him that he had sometime in the past behaved toward her in a manner that had been something less than exemplary.

Hellsfire! he groaned to himself. What sort of man was he?

Lady Felicity, however, was waiting for an answer, and, even if he was the worst sort of cad, he could not apologize for having made a point that needed to be made. If anything, it would seem he had been given a second chance to put things right with her. Surely he had owed her that much at least.

"Perhaps only that I am something less than a gentleman for taking advantage of a woman who has treated me with kindness." He released her wrist and leaned back, suddenly weary. "But then, perhaps that is only what you might have expected from me." Running a hand through his hair, he laughed and shook his head. "It would seem I find myself at a singular disadvantage. Absurd, is it not? You look at me and see a man you have known practically all of your life. I, unfortunately, haven't the faintest notion what sort of man that is."

The silence that stretched between them would seem indisputable evidence that she considered him precisely the sort to take undue advantage of a female. Indeed, he could not but wonder that her brother Bertie had allowed such a one to be left in his sister's care, Will was darkly reflecting, when the touch of Felicity's palm cradling the side of his face startled him out of his unrewarding reverie.

"I cannot allow you to entertain any doubts concerning your character," she stated firmly, her gaze unwavering on his. "Listen to me, my friend. You are William Powell, Viscount Lethridge, a gentleman of honor and nobility, a man of sterling reputation, a loving son and brother, and a true and excellent friend. You are, in short, one of the finest men I have ever known. That does not mean, however, that you are not infuriatingly arrogant, bullheaded, obtuse, and utterly reprehensible for thinking you might kiss me whenever you feel like it. Indeed, I—I wish you will not. You must see, after all, that it would complicate matters that are already . . . well," she faltered, suddenly and acutely aware of the dazzling blue of his eyes on hers, "well—*com*plicated," she finished lamely and felt, to her dismay, a hot rush of blood to her cheeks. Hastily she dropped her hand. "I'm afraid," she continued, drawing herself up in her most dignified manner, "while I may choose to overlook your indiscretion this time, next time I may not be so disposed."

"Shall you not?" murmured Will, the pressure casing from his chest ever so little. Egad, but she was magnificent! He could still feel the tender warmth of her hand upon his cheek; indeed, he could not but thrill to her sweet words of assurance that he was not the cad his hasty action would seem to have branded him. She was all generosity, was Lady Felicity Talbot. More than that, she was infinitely adorable. "That would, of course, presume there is to be a 'next time,'" he observed, a slight twitch at the corners of his lips belying the blandness of his expression. "A possibility that I deem not in the least remote, since I confess I derived a deal of enjoyment from this, my very first kiss."

"Your first—!" Felicity exclaimed in patent disbelief, only immediately to break off in confusion as the meaning of his assertion sank home. "But of course it would be, since you cannot remember any other. Not that I can be certain there have been others," she hastened to assure him. "I mean, after all, it is not the sort of thing you would choose to confide in a female acquaintance. But naturally I assumed . . ." Suddenly she broke off whatever she had been about to say. "Devil!" she exclaimed at sight of the gleam of unholy amusement in his compelling orbs. "You are roasting me."

"Not at all," he demurred, odiously giving vent to a chuckle, a deep, vibrant sound that had a wholly unsettling effect on her physical and emotional well-being. "You are, for all practical purposes, the only woman I have ever kissed, and I shall not play the hypocrite and deny that I found the experience wholly enlightening. I daresay it is inevitable I shall be revisited by temptation. In which case, I should naturally accept whatever punishment you might deem appropriate to the occasion, for I do assure you an assault on those lovely lips would be well worth it."

"Do you?" murmured Felicity, with a peculiar gravity previously lacking in her demeanor. She searched his face with shadowed eyes. "I should be careful what I did were I you, Will Powell. You might come one day to regret it."

The devil he would, thought Will, his eyebrows fairly snapping together over the bridge of his nose. Now, what was that supposed to mean? Though the words might be so construed, they had not the sound of a threat. A warning, then? he pondered, but of what?

It was on the tip of Will's tongue to demand an explanation, but Goliath regrettably chose just then to come bounding out of the cherry orchard in apparent glee at having found them. Will, conscious of vague feelings of dissatisfaction, leaned back to watch the fun as Felicity, laughing and scolding, was hard put to ward off the dog's assault in time to save the remains of their repast; and regrettably the moment was irretrievably lost.

Felicity, who could only be grateful for Goliath's timely interruption, was careful after that to steer the talk away from dangerous waters, and William, more weary than he cared to admit, was contented to let matters rest for the time being. Consequently, the remainder of their outing was passed in small pleasantries and merriment at Goliath's antics.

The walk home was accomplished in slow, easy stages with Goliath for once pleased to trot a few paces ahead of his mistress and the man leaning for support against her slender form.

At least, Will comforted his bruised male pride, there was something to be said for finding, clasped to one's side, an alluring female whose figure conformed most satisfactorily to his larger, masculine frame. He did not doubt he would have been the envy of any number of the members of his sex. Lady Felicity was a demmed attractive woman—*and* a cursedly elusive one, he reminded himself, well aware that she had erected an impenetrable barrier of banter and merriment between them.

Why she should seem so determined to distract him from pursuing the threads of their earlier conversation was more than curious. It was a bloody enigma. A pall of mystery, in fact, seemed to hang over the cottage and all of its inhabitants, from Mrs. Morseby, the dour-faced housekeeper, to Chester Huggins, the scarred and misshapen groundskeeper and sometimes groom, he was to reflect some moments later as they approached near enough to the house to espy the somehow forlorn figure of Miss Annabel Jones standing at her customary solitary post on the balcony. He did not have to see the young woman's strangely sad, pinched features to know she was staring out over the downs to the Swale. She spent the greatest portion of her waking hours doing little else. Felicity's rather vague explanation for what he privately considered Miss Jones's morbid fascination, that someone the young woman had dearly loved was recently lost at sea, he found just a trifle romantical and reeking not a little of sentimentalism.

Miss Jones, had she truly lost someone, would be better occupied immersing herself in matters that concerned the living than wasting away over something that, while possibly tragic, could not be changed. But then, perhaps he was the sort who was peculiarly lacking in the finer sensibilities, Will sardonically reflected. In which case he might very well be insensitive to the sufferings of others. Still, whatever he was, he could not dismiss the feeling that

Miss Jones simply was not the sort to pine excessively
over the death of a loved one. Far from displaying
signs of a weepy disposition, the vague images he had
of her caring for him in the sickroom gave the impression of a cool competence. Nor would he have
judged her to be the sort of female used to sentimen-
talizing the less pleasant facets of life. A female of
the lower orders, she had about her the aura of a
woman who had been made to experience more than
a few of life's vicissitudes. She was obviously a survi-
vor, one who in the norm would display a mettlesome
disposition.

No, with Miss Annabel Jones, as with everyone else
at Primrose Cottage, there was something that did
not quite ring true.

It had seemed obvious at Will's first emergence
from the sickroom that he was regarded as something
less than a welcome houseguest, an impression that
had hardly been dispelled by Mrs. Morseby's demeanor toward him.

"So you're awake, milord," had been her first
words to him when she came to change his bed
linen. "And none too soon. A week's a long time
for a fine lord like yourself to be away from London.
I expect you'll be a mite anxious to be getting back
as soon as ever you're on your feet again."

In spite of the respectful trappings of that singular
speech, he had received the distinct impression that
the housekeeper was wishing him at Jericho. At first
he had attributed Mrs. Morseby's brusque manner as
indicative of something she held against him from
his unremembered past, but lately he had begun to
think that she would have treated any uninvited
houseguest with similar disapprobation. Indeed, he
had begun to suspect it was not himself that she be-
grudged, but the presence of any outsider at Prim-

rose Cottage. Why? he wondered, frowning as he caught sight of Mrs. Morseby's somber aspect peering down at him from an upstairs window.

Instantly the housekeeper drew back, allowing the lace curtain to fall into place, but William had the distinct sensation that she was there yet, watching his progress with Lady Felicity, whom she seemed devoted to looking after like an aging hen with but a single chick in the nest.

He could not but find such a notion more than a little odd. Lady Felicity, after all, was not only a woman of wealth and position, but she resided under the Duke of Breverton's not insignificant mantle of protection. Will found it difficult to imagine anything that would call for Mrs. Morseby's dour vigilance. Surely she did not entertain the suspicion that he meant to make off with her mistress. The idea was preposterous. A man would have to be a fool to incur the wrath of the Duke of Breverton, not to mention that of the Marquess of Rutherford, the lady's eldest brother. Rutherford was slow tinder, hard to ignite, but once brought to a flame, he was the very devil in a fight.

A faint smile touched William's lips at an image of the marquess in a flame because someone had tested the genial Rutherford's patience too far in a foolish prank.

Abruptly he halted, struck by the significance of that brief flash of memory. The image had been quite distinct: a man whom he knew positively to be the Marquess of Rutherford charging at the perpetrator of the stunt like an enraged bull. But charging after whom? thought William, struggling to hold on to the fragment. Bloody hell! It was like trying to hold on to the fading remnants of a dream upon awakening, and just as useless.

"William!" Felicity's voice, sharp with concern, brought him, reeling, back to the present. "Will, what is it? You went suddenly as white as a sheet."

"No, did I?" Feeling helplessness and frustration wash over him, he shook his head. "It was nothing—only that for a moment I almost remembered something. An image of Rutherford in a stew. Silly, is it not? The image was quite distinct, but separate from anything with any real meaning. He is your brother. I know that much at least, and that it is highly doubtful he would be in the least pleased to discover a gentleman in residence with his unmarried sister. I should go, Felicity. Now. Before you are thoroughly compromised."

"But that is impossible, Will," declared Felicity, who could only receive this determination with considerable alarm, indeed, who saw all of her painstaking plans to prevent just such an event unraveling before her. "Indeed, it is out of the question. You are hardly fit to make your way upstairs, let alone embark on a journey. Besides, you are making a great deal out of nothing. Rutherford would hardly take exception to your presence here." Helplessly, she glanced away. "Why should he? You and I are cousins, after all."

"Once removed, as it were," William did not hesitate to remind her. "Kissing cousins, if one might be so bold."

"Yes, but we have already established that *you* may not," Felicity retorted, her cheeks flaming, nonetheless. "You will stay until you are quite recovered, Will Powell. You may be certain Rutherford would insist upon it, as do I."

It was on William's lips to reply that, weak or not, he was perfectly able to remove to an inn in Faversham until he was stronger. Only, Goliath chose that very moment to give vent to a low, menacing growl, savage enough to raise the hairs on the nape of Will's neck.

"Now, what the devil," he uttered, turning to look for the source of the dog's displeasure.

He was met by the sight of a strapping, well-knit fellow, somewhat above average height and attired in a top hat, a plain coat of good quality fabric though of a rather poor cut, loose trousers, and silver-buckled shoes that would seem to denote a man of some substance but inferior degree. A tradesman, perhaps, thought Will, whose initial impression of the bold-cut features topped by coal black hair and made remarkable by eyes of a particularly gelid green was of the order to make Will wish he were not weak as a bloody kitten. It was Will's considered opinion that, if the man were a tradesman, his was not the sort of trade that would prosper in the light of day, a judgment that was only reinforced by the perception that Lady Felicity had, for the barest instant, gone suddenly quite rigid.

She recovered almost immediately. Will, however, was acutely aware of a distinct change in her as she nodded coolly at the stranger, who was lounging insolently with one elbow propped atop the ironwork gate.

"Mr. Josiah Steed," she pronounced in well-modulated accents that, to one well couched in the polite manners of Society, would have left little doubt Lady Felicity Talbot was on her mettle. The stranger, however, appeared singularly unmoved, William grimly noted. Carefully removing his arm from Felicity's shoulders, Will straightened.

With a smile that noticeably failed to ease the chill from his eyes, Steed lifted his hat.

"A good day to you, Miss Talbot," he replied. "And

a fine day it is, too—for a picnic." His gaze speculative on the lady's tall companion, Steed set the hat back in place at a jaunty angle. "Saw the two of you at the edge of the spinney as I topped the hill. Heard you had a houseguest, Miss Talbot. Only, word was you had a woman staying at the cottage." The chill green eyes returned to Felicity. "It would appear rumor was a mite mistaken."

Felicity's lips parted to inform her uninvited caller that she had not the slightest interest in what rumors were circulating in the neighborhood, when she was silenced by Lethridge, his voice steely edged beneath its velvet softness.

"I suggest it is you who are mistaken—Mr. Steed, is it?" drawled Will, marveling at the effrontery of the fellow.

Felicity, who had no illusions as to what Steed was or of what he was capable, felt her heart suddenly sink.

"At your service, gov'nor." The rogue smiled, bowing in such a manner as might have smacked of the unctuous had the gesture not been so patently insolent. "Begging your pardon, but mistaken in what manner, gov'nor?"

"In presuming to accost a lady," Will did not hesitate to inform the fellow.

"Dear God—" groaned Felicity under her breath.

Will ignored the slender hand that clutched at his sleeve. "If you have some business at Primrose Cottage, Mr. Steed, you will address yourself to me. Do I make myself clear?"

The insolent grin faded from Steed's face, to be replaced by a look of malicious cunning, which could not but strike Will as singular indeed.

"Clear enough, gov. In fact, I'd say you've been more than plainspoken. There's some that might tell you that's not always a healthy thing in these parts, especially"—Steed's eyes shifted to Lady Felicity with a significance that was hardly lost on Will—"for the meddling sort. You can ask Zachary Trent about that."

Felicity's gaze never wavered from Steed's, though inside she felt a hard fist close on her vitals. Fortunately, Lethridge seemed not to notice.

"I'm afraid I haven't the pleasure of this Mr. Trent's acquaintance," she managed coolly enough, though she was aware of a hollow feeling of dread somewhere in the pit of her stomach.

"Haven't you, ma'am?" queried Steed, his tone, not to mention his look, clearly disbelieving.

Beside Felicity, Will only just refrained from landing the villain a facer. Mr. Steed, it would seem, Will grimly reflected, was of a distinctly case-hardened lot to demonstrate so little dread of his betters. Who the devil was he, and what purpose had he here with Lady Felicity? Whatever it might be, at least the rogue was made aware that the women of Primrose Cottage were not unprotected.

"Miss Talbot has made herself plain on that point," observed Will with chilling deliberation. "Furthermore, as it appears you *have* no business here, my cousin and I shall not detain you further. My dear?" he added, presenting his arm to Felicity.

Felicity, torn between resentment at Lethridge's assumption of command in a situation about which he had no knowledge and relief at having been masterfully spared what could only have proven an uncomfortable scene, was given little choice but to comply. It would hardly have served, after all, to present a divided front at this point.

Still, she was aware of a growing dissatisfaction with

William Powell as, obediently, she placed her hand in the crook of his elbow.

"Good-bye, Mr. Steed," she said, allowing Lethridge to lead her away. "Goliath, come."

Will, having terminated what he had sensed was a potentially dangerous meeting, was not sure what he expected upon achieving the safety of the Blue Salon. Certainly it was not, as soon as the door was closed behind them, to have Felicity turn on him with glorious, flashing eyes.

"That was well done, my lord," the lady uttered scathingly. "I suppose you think to have my congratulations."

"For dealing with an obvious bounder?" returned the viscount, elevating a single, incredulous eyebrow. "I hardly think so. I beg your pardon, Miss Talbot. Was the fellow a friend of yours?"

"Pray do not be absurd," Felicity snapped. "You know very well he was not."

"Well, then." Will eloquently spread his palms. "I fail to see what has put you in a pother."

Felicity, having deposited the picnic basket without ceremony on the sideboard, reached up to tug at the ribbons to her bonnet. "I am *not* in a pother, and the truth is you haven't the slightest notion of what you have done."

"But it is patent, is it not?" countered Lethridge, intrigued by the twin spots of color in the lady's cheeks. "I was giving the rogue a lesson in manners."

"On the contrary, Will Powell," Felicity fired back at him. "You were incurring the enmity of a man who would think nothing of killing us all as we lie in our beds. What in heaven's name gave you the notion I should welcome your interference in something that is none of your concern?"

"But you are mistaken, surely." Will's lip curled

sardonically. "It is my concern, both as a gentleman and your kinsman, when a man as dangerous as you say Steed is has the temerity to accost a lady in my protection. Should he be so unwise as to present himself again in similar circumstances, you may be certain I shall not hesitate to instruct him by more forceful means of persuasion."

Felicity paled, seeing before her the Will Powell of old. Even weakened by his wound and the fever, he had not hesitated to stand between her and danger, nor would he in future. It was all because of his wretched code of honor, the same sense of nobility that had prompted him to fight a duel over a woman who did not love him! A noted Corinthian, Viscount Lethridge was more than a match for the likes of Josiah Steed. In his present state, however, Will Powell stood not a chance in such a fight as that must be.

Faith, what a coil she had got herself in! She dared not tell Will what Steed had been doing loitering outside her gate. Nor could she disabuse his lordship of the notion that he was in any way responsible for her safety, not without revealing the compromising nature of Steed's presence at Primrose Cottage.

Oh, why the devil did not Bertie return with news of Shelby? Her fabrication of lies was fast assuming unwieldy proportions that must inevitably come toppling down around her, and then how was she to keep Lethridge safely hidden until he was himself again? How was she to keep him safe from Josiah Steed and the dangerous mission she had undertaken?

The answer was that she could not if he were ever to find out what she was about.

Four

"You must not be afraid to tell me the truth, Annabel," declared Felicity some little time later in her private study. Turning from the window, she leaned her hands on the oak writing table and earnestly faced the girl who was standing, taut and pale, before her. "Can you be quite certain he did not see you?"

The girl's thin features paled even more, if that were possible, Felicity grimly noted.

"Truly, m'lady, I slipped inside as soon as ever I saw his lordship lookin' up at me. Mr. Steed never laid eyes on me. I'm most certain of it."

"Then we may be grateful *some* good has apparently come from this," Felicity said, dropping with no little relief into the chair at the desk. "Steed has heard rumors of a houseguest at Primrose. Encountering his lordship in my company may serve to cast some confusion over matters. At the very least, he will think twice before showing his face here again. In the meantime, I think it would be better if you refrained in future from strolling on the terrace. I'm afraid you will have to limit yourself to the rose garden for your daily outing."

Annabel's eyes, like deep blue pools, appeared too large for her face as they rose to regard Felicity with a troubled intensity. Nervously she twisted her hands in the folds of her dress.

"Pray forgive me, Lady Felicity. I never dreamed he would come looking for me at Primrose Cottage. You're taking a frightful chance, hiding me away like this. I wouldn't want to do naught that might bring *him* down on us. He's a devil, Lady Felicity, that wouldn't stop at anything to have his way."

"I am well aware of Mr. Steed's reputation for ruthlessness," said Felicity with an impatient wave of the hand. "Which is why you must take care not to be seen. As long as he only suspects you *might* be here, we should be safe enough. He is unlikely to force himself into the house on a mere suspicion, especially now that he knows his lordship is in residence."

"If you say so," said Annabel, clearly entertaining some little doubt on that particular matter. "But, beggin' your pardon, m'lady, how long do you think I can stay shut up in your house? You've been kinder than I'd any right to expect, but it can't go on forever. What about Meggie? I'm dying inside not knowin' . . ." Here Annabel's voice broke, and, overcome with some powerful emotion, she buried her face in her hands.

Instantly, Felicity came to her feet and, rounding the desk, clasped the young woman to her breast.

"Softly, child," she murmured, though Annabel could not have been more than four years Felicity's junior. "We will find Meggie, I promise. I expect word any day now. Zachary Trent is most determined to help. He will not fail us. You must believe that."

Mention of Zachary Trent seemed to work a positive influence on the distraught girl. Lifting her head, she gazed at her benefactress with something approaching a fierce expression.

"I do believe in Captain Trent," she said on a shuddering breath, "when he's not drinking. He said he'd help, and he will. Only, I pray it doesn't come too late. If something was to happen to Meggie, I couldn't bear it, m'lady. I'd not want to go on living."

"Nonsense. Nothing is going to happen to Meggie. Steed will not harm her so long as he believes he can use her to break you to his will. You must not give up hope, Annabel."

"I—I'll try, m'lady. Only, it eats on me so. The notion that I might be the cause of harm to Meggie, and to you and everyone who's been so good to me. You hadn't ought to've taken me in. I ought not to have let you."

"Now, that is outside of enough, Annabel," declared Felicity, giving Annabel a small shake. "You were hardly in any case to do anything else. You cannot have forgotten what he did to you."

"No, I couldn't ever forget that," agreed the girl with a shudder. "But it doesn't matter. There isn't a law in the land or a man who'd say Steed wasn't in his just rights for what he done. The truth is, m'lady, I'll never be free of him till one or both of us be dead."

The girl had spoken the simple truth, Felicity knew with a mingling of anger and despair. It would have been true even for a female of wealth and position, and would remain so until women were given the same rights under the law as men, a possibility that seemed far-fetched in the extreme, thought Felicity, gazing at the fair-haired, delicately wrought Annabel with a familiar sense of hopelessness. And yet there must be *something* that could be done to save Annabel from Steed's brutal disposition.

Sternly, she quelled a shudder at the memory of Annabel as she had been two months ago upon their first meeting. Broken and bruised, the savage marks of a man's hands about her white, slender throat, the child had lain all but lifeless, a pitiful creature too sunk into pain and dejection to do more than stare dully up at Felicity out of blackened eyes, half swollen shut. How Annabel had found the strength to make her way to Primrose Cottage, where, she had heard, the mistress of the house had a reputation for helping women in need, was beyond Felicity's comprehension. But somehow she had done it, and, once there, she had found a fierce if unexpected protectress in the only daughter of the Duke of Breverton.

Had Felicity been a man , she would not have hesitated to exact a terrible payment from the brute who had savaged the girl. As it was, there had been no recourse but to keep Annabel hidden. If Steed knew where to find her, he would not hesitate to come and take her away—and the law would be on his side.

It mattered not a whit that Steed's reputation for being a river pirate and a smuggler was common knowledge among the local inhabitants. He would be well within his rights to demand the return of his wife!

"You must try not to think of the worst, Annabel," she said at last, summoning a smile that was meant to be bracing. "We will find a solution, I promise you. Until then, pray stay out of sight. Captain Trent will contact us soon, I am sure of it."

"Yes, m'lady." Dipping a curtsy, the girl turned to leave, only to pause with her hand on the door handle. "I can't ever thank you enough, Lady Felicity, for all you're doing for me." She flashed an eloquent look over one shoulder at Felicity. "I never dreamed there could be some 'un like you in the world."

The next instant Annabel was gone, and Felicity was left staring at the door that had closed in the wake of the girl's passing.

"Dear God," she groaned, sinking down once more in the chair. Annabel had made her out to be some sort of saint. The poor child could not have been further from the truth. Felicity was all too aware of how empty her words of comfort to Annabel had been. She had not the smallest assurance that Trent would make an appearance, let alone bring word of Meggie's whereabouts. She could not even be certain after today that Trent was still alive!

In spite of herself, Felicity could not but think that would be a poor payment even for the young rogue who, captain of a small schooner, claimed to ply an honest trade along the coast of England. Felicity had more than a vague suspicion that Trent was not averse to doing a bit of smuggling or anything else shady that would put the jangle of gold in his purse. Worse, he was given to drink and had a reputation for fighting and carousing—hardly the sort to inspire a great deal of confidence, reflected Felicity, recalling to mind the less than respectable image of the schooner's captain in the dingy light of a boat lantern upon their one and only meeting at the docks below the fisherman's cottage. Neither, from his first unceremonious words to her, had she trusted his motives.

"Your man Huggins tells me you're looking for someone to do a little nosing around for you," he had announced without preamble. "Says you'll pay handsomely. I've never been one to turn down a lucrative offer, ma'am. Only show me the color of your gold, and I'm your man."

"I sincerely doubt that you are anyone's man, Captain Trent," Felicity had retorted, eyeing the hard, unshaven visage with scant approval. He was young for one who prided himself on being captain of his own ship; indeed, he could not have been much above two and twenty. Further, there had been an air

of recklessness about the slouched figure, a boat
cloak slung carelessly back over one shoulder, that
she had not trusted—until, that was, she had detailed
the plight of the young woman who resided in her
care.

"I wish you to see if you can discover where the
villain is keeping the girl, but it must be done discreetly. If Steed were to find out what we are about,
he would—"

"Steed! Josiah Steed?"

The name had slashed through the stillness of the
night, disturbed only by the quiet lapping of the
waves against the shore, and Felicity had been struck
by Trent's suddenly taut form looming over her, his
eyes glinting pale sparks in the lantern light.

"You say the woman was beaten to within an inch
of her life. The bloody devil. I'll have his heart for
this. And the wench. She will recover?"

"She has recovered, physically. Her hurts have
healed. It is her spirit that concerns me. She is wasting away with grief and worry."

"Over the girl, Meggie." He had pulled away so
that Felicity could no longer clearly see his face. "Aye,
she would. The cursed brat means everything to her.
Well, you can tell her to stop worrying. Tell her
Zachary Trent will find her Meggie for her."

Sternly, Felicity schooled her features not to reveal
her bestartlement at his vehemence, not to mention
the fact that he knew about whom she was talking
without her ever having revealed Annabel's name.
Indeed, she had suddenly very much suspected that
gold would not be the prime motivating factor behind Trent's offer to help. While the thought was one
to bring her a measure of confidence that Trent
would do as he promised, it had also served to occasion her some misapprehension. Trent, after all,

demonstrated a hotheaded nature. It would hardly do to have him taking matters into his own hands.

"Splendid," Felicity had said somewhat acerbically. "And when and if you do uncover something, Captain, you will send word to me. I will not have Meggie put unnecessarily in harm's way. Once we know where she is, I shall make whatever arrangements are necessary. Is that understood?"

"Begging your pardon, ma'am, but now that you mention it, I don't understand you at all," countered the captain, coming around to face Felicity. "Why should a fine lady like yourself put herself out for a poor creature like Annabel? It hardly makes sense, now does it?"

"No more than why a young man who obviously has had at least a measure of schooling and undoubtedly comes from a good home should be pursuing a livelihood in the seamier environs of the lower Thames. I do not suppose you care to explain that to me, Captain? Or how it is that you are obviously personally acquainted with Annabel, for that matter."

She was awarded a white flash of teeth for those astute observations. "No, ma'am. As it happens, I prefer not to discuss my past. As for Annabel, we go back a long way. She helped save my life once upon a time. I expect I owe her something for that."

"And you, one must hope, are the sort to repay your debts," Felicity said with a pointed look. "As am I. Here is a purse to defray your costs, Captain. There will be more when you have something of merit to report. I shall expect word from you in the next few days. I believe I need not remind you that time is of the essence."

Trent, she noted with a keen prick of interest, hesitated for the barest fraction of a second before taking the purse and hefting it in his hand. "Time?" Once more he grinned, a devil-may-dare sort of grin that had the effect of bringing Felicity's doubts crowding back, stronger than ever. "You may be certain I shan't waste a moment spreading this around in the right places. Good evening to you, ma'am. It has been a real pleasure to meet you. If I were you, I shouldn't tarry overlong. See that she doesn't, Huggins. The docks are no place for a lady like her."

He had turned, and then, with a swirl of his boat cloak, vanished into the mists—and very likely from their lives, mused Felicity ruefully.

"Five days," she proclaimed to the empty room. "A plague on the rogue. If Steed has not done him in, I shall be tempted to do it. No doubt he is only now sleeping off a very fine drunken carousal. Faith, how could I have been such a fool as to give him the purse *before* he had some news to offer?"

Really, it was outside of enough. Things were not going at all the way she could wish. And what if Steed had put a period to the captain? Unprincipled rogue or not, she would never be able to forgive herself if she had been the cause of his losing his life. Her every instinct told her that Steed had only been baiting her. He could not possibly have known about her arrangement with Trent. No one but herself, Annabel, and Huggins had been privy to it. And Trent himself, of course. She very seriously doubted that the captain would have been so remiss as to tell Steed about it, or anyone else, for that matter. Whatever he was, Trent was no one's fool.

No, she told herself. Steed could not have known anything for a certainty. No doubt Trent, in spreading the money around in order to garner tidbits of information, had earned Steed's attention. The pirate, putting two and two together, or in this case Felicity's openly determined efforts to help destitute women, the rumors that the duke's daughter was harboring a mysterious houseguest, and Trent's sudden unprecedented interest in the river pirate's missing wife, coupled with the captain's unusually generous purse, had led Steed to Primrose Cottage that afternoon to discover what he could.

What he had discovered was, not his errant wife, but a gentleman who had not hesitated to put him in his place.

Faith, it was not enough that she had the captain's uncertain fate to cut up her existence along with everything else on her already crowded plate, but she now had to worry that Steed would see fit to take his rancor out on Lethridge, who was hardly in any case to defend himself.

Felicity suffered a queasy sensation at the memory of the confrontation between the viscount and Josiah Steed. She experienced all over again the shock of turning to discover the river pirate lounging against her garden gate for all the world as if he owned the place. The resulting clash of wills had been inevitable from the first moment the two men had laid eyes on one another.

A plague on Steed and William Powell's code of honor for giving her one more thing to worry about!

Steed was the last person she had expected that day, especially since she'd been more than a little distracted at the time. Faith, not only had she been unsettled at Will's unexpected flash of memory, but only an hour previous to Steed's unwelcome appearance, she had come dangerously close to revealing far too much of her feelings to Will!

What the devil was the matter with her? It seemed that she simply could not keep a tight rein on her tongue, not to mention her emotions, where William Powell was concerned. But then, he had always had the effect on her of making her feel giddy as a school-girl, when all she had ever wanted was for him to see her as a woman. It was the height of irony that now, when he at last was giving every appearance of a man drawn to her feminine charms, she must not only resist his overtures and the responses of her own unruly emotions, but she must do all in her power to discourage the very thing that had been her heart's desire for almost as long as she could remember!

How he would detest her were she to give in to the promptings of her heart while he was at the singular disadvantage of having lost his memory! It was bad enough that she had been forced to create a web of deception to keep him safe until he was himself again. She simply could not bear the thought of how he would look at her were he to regain his memory only to discover she had willingly allowed him to do what he would never have done had he been in his right mind. Nor would she have cared to have him come to love her under such demeaning circumstances. It would have been a lie, like all the others she had concocted the past few days. She, after all, knew very well that his heart really belonged to Zenoria.

No, she must simply take care never to let her guard down whenever she was in the unsettling proximity of William Powell. He wielded far too potent an influence over her emotions, not to mention her instincts for self-preservation. She hardly trusted herself where Will Powell was concerned, obviously with good reason, she thought, flushing hotly at the memory of his lips brushing against hers.

Furious at her unseemly reaction to the mere memory of that stolen assault on her lips, she bolted from the chair and began furiously to pace. The devil, she fumed. *Why* had he kissed her? It was really too bad of him, especially in light of the fact that he had all but declared that in future he was likely to assault her lips on any number of occasions without the slightest provocation. To her chagrin, she felt an unwitting thrill course through her from the top of her head to the tips of her toes at the mere thought of such an ungentlemanly breach of conduct. Nor was it in the least comforting to acknowledge to herself that, had it not been for the singular circumstances that must constrain her, she would not have felt the smallest maidenly qualms at such a prospect. On the contrary, she did not doubt that she would gladly have conspired limitless opportunities for just such pleasurable indiscretions.

This was an acknowledgment that was hardly conducive to self-congratulations. On the contrary, she could only berate herself for the worst sort of a fool. William Powell had never felt anything for her, save for a careless affection of the kind reserved for the younger sister of a close friend. Had she any pride at all, she would long since have given over any thought of winning any deeper regard from him. Obviously, she was seriously lacking in the most elemental self-respect to even be tempted to take advantage of the peculiar situation in which she found herself. And yet she was tempted, more than she could ever have thought possible before Bertie had arrived on her doorstep with the wounded viscount, so much so, in fact, that she did not see how she could go on with the charade she had created.

Still, she must go on, she sternly reminded herself. She was left with no other choice, especially now that Will had thrown the gauntlet down in the face of a member of that notorious band of Gentlemen who would think nothing of slitting the throat of anyone who had the misfortune to incur their enmity. While she had been willing to take that risk upon herself for the sake of Meggie and Annabel, she could hardly have wished such a thing for Will, who had not had the smallest inkling of the sort of man with whom he was dealing. Not that it would have stopped him had he known, she reflected wryly. Will Powell would still have stepped between her and the notorious Steed without the slightest regard for self. It was hardly in his nature to do otherwise.

He was, after all, a Powell; and the Powells were a noble breed in the truest sense of the word. Damn him! The last thing she could wish was to have him die for her.

She was interrupted in her unrewarding ruminations by the hall clock chiming the hour of five and, reminded that the dinner bell must soon sound, hurried to her room to change. Irritated to find that she was paying special attention to her appearance, even going so far as to waste precious time discarding one gown in favor of another, far more attractive creation, she at last flung out of the room in disgust.

Really, she must get a grip on herself, she mused, and, with the certainty that Lethridge was already there before her, was made immediately aware of a quickening of her pulse rate as she came to the open door to the drawing room.

Nor did it help in the least upon entering to be met with the sight of Will Powell, one elbow propped along the mantelpiece, his lean, handsome profile somber as he gazed unseeing into the fire.

Faith, how splendid he was to look upon! she thought, taking in the tall masculine figure. Even in the absence of his manservant and constrained by a wardrobe necessarily limited to what Bertie had hurriedly been able to fling in a valise and a bandbox, he presented an elegant appearance. The funereal black of the Wellington Frock, drawn slightly in at the waist with a horizontal dart, served superbly to accentuate his broad-shouldered, lean-hipped build, as did the black pantaloons buttoned tight to the ankles. His neck cloth, arranged in the Osbaldiston, was tied to perfection, and his half boots shone with a black, uncanny sheen. He was in all ways but one the Lethridge who was considered a nonesuch, a Corinthian, and an arbiter of fashion, and that one dearth was that he had no memory of who and what he was. No doubt instinct and training had prevailed when it came to dressing himself with the immaculate perfection for which he was well known, she reflected. Then, taking a deep breath, she strode purposefully forward.

"Pray do forgive me," she said, patently oblivious of the striking image of grace and beauty she herself presented dressed to the nines in her red gros de Naples evening dress with the new high waist, the neckline edged with a ruff, and the round skirt with a broad border of artificial flowers. With her short, artfully disheveled curls parted in the middle à la Titus, she was a vision of bewitching loveliness. Smiling, she proffered her hand to the viscount. "I fear I have kept you waiting."

Her feminine charms, however, were hardly lost on Lethridge, who was sardonically aware that the mere sight of her was enough to make the blood run, fast, in his veins. "If you have, it was well worth the wait." Lifting Felicity's hand, he saluted her knuckles. "You are looking particularly lovely this evening."

Straightening, he suddenly frowned, his gaze narrowing sharply on her finely wrought features.

"A-am I?" Felicity faltered and glanced away from his pointed stare. In dismay, she felt her heart absurdly pounding.

"What is it, my girl?" William demanded. "Something is troubling you. And pray do not try and deny it."

"But I don't deny it." Felicity laughed wryly and pulled away that he might not read too much in her eyes. "As it happens, I am suffering a slight headache, brought on, no doubt, by that dreadful man, Steed. Can you blame me?" She gave a slight shudder that was not entirely feigned. "Huggins assures me Steed is a free-trader, not to mention a river pirate. Can you imagine that? And he had the nerve to brace me practically at my front door. Is it any wonder that I am a trifle unnerved?"

"I daresay it would be marvelous only if you were *not* considerably shaken," agreed William with only the hint of irony. He, after all, recalled all too well the lady's remarkable composure in Mr. Steed's unsavory presence. Lady Felicity might have been trembling inside, but she had demonstrated a cool outward demeanor in the face of danger that might have put to shame many a male of his acquaintance. But then, he had come to expect little else from this remarkable female who was proving to be as maddeningly intriguing as she was irresistible.

Still, Will was not in the least surprised to discover that Steed was a member of one of the numerous bands of Gentlemen who plied their nefarious trade up and down England's coasts. He had known at once that the man was as sinister as he was impertinent. Will did, however, find a great deal that was puzzling in Felicity's present behavior. She was hardly the sort, after all, to launch into a stream of confidences that gave the impression of feminine vulnerability, especially in light of the scolding she had given him earlier on this very same subject.

He was damned if he did not believe the little minx

was trying to fling dust in his eyes, and it behooved
him to discover why. "I was a trifle unnerved myself,"
he admitted, crossing to a grog tray on which resided
a decanter of port and another of brandy for his lordship's pleasure. "I'm afraid I was hardly in any case
to take on Mr. Steed had the villain decided to press
the issue."

"Precisely my point, Will," agreed Felicity, relieved
that he had been so easily diverted from his original
train of thought. The last thing she could wish was
to have to endure a Spanish Inquisition from
Lethridge at this particular time. She was far too distracted by his disturbing proximity to fabricate a new
string of lies. "It was patently foolish for you to invite
a contretemps with Steed. You might easily have been
injured, or worse. In either case, I should never have
forgiven myself."

"It would hardly have been your fault," Lethridge
pointed out, filling a glass with port. "It has been
some time since I left off my shortcoats. You may be
certain I should take full responsibility for my own
actions."

"Oh, indeed," said Felicity, already fully aware of
his highly developed sense of integrity. "That would
hardly change the fact, however, that you placed yourself in peril out of the mistaken notion that I required
your protection. I am perfectly capable of dealing
with Mr. Steed on my own, thank you very much."

"Which is why, of course, you are suffering the
headache," Lethridge was odiously quick to point
out. "I'm afraid, Felicity, you cannot have it both
ways. Either you are frightened of the man, or you
are not."

"Well, of course I am frightened of him," Felicity
declared, her face reddening at the neat trap he had
laid for her. "That does not mean, however, that I

cannot deal with him. I have been taking care of myself for a very long time now. I hardly need you or anyone else to manage my affairs for me."

It was a mistake. She knew it as soon as she blurted it out. Indeed, she would have given anything if she could snatch back those final words. Lethridge, she noted, had hardly blinked an eye at that last, hasty admission. Still, she fancied she read the hard leap of triumph in his heavy-lidded eyes.

"It would seem I was mistaken," he drawled, eyeing her over the glass he raised to his lips. "Mr. Steed apparently did have a purpose in accosting you at your gate. If you are involved in some way with him, my dear, you must be fully aware that he will be back again. In which case, I suggest that you and your entire household are at risk. Now, why do you not simply tell me what the devil the man was doing here? Somehow I cannot think you have taken up smuggling. You are hardly in the habit of imbibing French brandy, and you certainly are not in need of a means of supplementing your already sizable income. What, I wonder, does that leave?"

"It leaves me marveling at your flight of fancy, my lord," retorted Felicity, who was in truth beginning to develop a splitting headache. "I haven't the least idea why Mr. Steed came here today. And I cannot imagine why he should come back again. You are, in short, making a great deal out of nothing. Now, if you don't mind, I think we should go in to dinner. Cook makes a dreadful fuss if her dinners are ruined because people cannot bother to sit down to table on time."

"Felicity—" Lethridge stopped her as she started toward the double doors that opened on to the dining room. Setting aside the half-empty glass, he turned her to face him. "You can trust me, you know.

Whatever I may have done in the past to make you doubt in me, you may believe I should always stand your friend in need. After all, I owe you my life. I should be a poor sort indeed if I left you in the lurch when you needed my help."

"But of course you would stand my friend, Will," exclaimed Felicity, suffering a pang of guilt at having caused him any uncertainty about himself. "And I do trust in you. I always have. It is only that there is nothing to tell you. I haven't the smallest notion why Mr. Steed was here."

She was lying. He knew it. There was, however, little that he could do about it. Not now, at least, he told himself as he led her into the dining room and seated her at the table. He could, however, keep his eyes and ears open. Sooner or later he was bound to discover what the elusive Miss Talbot was keeping from him. In the meantime, he must concentrate on regaining his strength.

He could feel that his excursion outdoors had already had a beneficial effect. While he was ruefully aware that he was a far cry from himself, his head had ceased to ache and his legs were a deal steadier than they had been before. He was on the mend. He had only to apply himself to building himself back up again, and to do that he must eat and force himself to walk. Henceforth, he would be a model patient, he vowed, agreeably surprised to discover that his appetite, at least, was well on its way to recovery as he sampled the first course, a concoction of chicken and leeks known familiarly as cock-a-leekie soup.

Lethridge, Felicity was soon to discover, despite the handicap of his impaired memory, could be as charming a dinner companion as she had often imagined he would be. Indeed, he was far more adept at leading her to talk about herself than she could have wished in the circumstances. Before she could stop herself, she was detailing any number of humorous incidents concerning her childhood, her older brothers, and their life at Breverton in her beloved Lake District.

Indeed, in between the buttered asparagus spears and the roast beef and Yorkshire pudding, she launched, without thinking, into an account of the one and only time she had ever managed to turn the tables on her brothers, who, in their youth, had freely indulged in boyhood pranks at her expense.

"It was dreadfully bad of me to lure Rutherford away from the house when I knew Miss Islington was due to call with her mama and papa. And then to lock him in the bull shed, leaving him no recourse but to crawl through the hay chute, was really outside of enough. He ruined his Jean de Bry coat with the padded shoulders that reached nearly to his ears and which he considered the height of sartorial splendor. The crowning glory, however, was that, arriving home to find Bertie basking in the smiles of the beautiful Miss Islington while he himself presented a wholly disreputable appearance, Rutherford did not hesitate to place the blame squarely on Bertie. I shall never forget the sight of Rutherford charging like an enraged bull after Bertie, with Miss Islington looking on with scandalous disapproval. It was sweet revenge for all the tricks they pulled on me. Best of all, I was never proven to be the culprit, which made it all the sweeter."

Felicity was about to add that, in the end, she had probably done both Rutherford and Bertie a favor, as Miss Islington, ever of a rather prim inclination, had become even more so in time. She had become, in fact, positively hidebound. The observation was frozen on Felicity's lips, however, as, glancing up, she was made aware of Lethridge staring at her with a peculiarly fixed expression.

"Will, what is it?" she exclaimed, laying her fork down on her plate. "You are looking at me in the strangest way."

"No, am I?" Lethridge, smoothly reaching for his glass of wine, smiled. "I beg your pardon. I was merely entranced by the charming picture you portray of Miss Talbot as a schoolroom miss. I have been wondering what you were like then. I could almost see you, as you talked. I daresay you were all arms and legs and had an enchanting scattering of freckles across your nose and cheeks."

"You would not think they were so enchanting if you had to submit to daily applications of cucumber lotions in the futile attempt to rid yourself of them," Felicity retorted, comically screwing her face up at him. "They were the bane of my existence."

"You have overcome it most delightfully," observed Lethridge, lifting his glass in tribute to her beauty and taking a sip. "Still, I think I am sorry I am unable to remember you as an impish schoolgirl. Did you find me very difficult? Did I tease you unmercifully in the manner of your brothers?"

No, Felicity answered wryly to herself. He had been kind and generous, treating her as an equal. More than that, he had stood her protector even then against her brothers' roasting, all of which was why she had fallen deeply and irrevocably in love with him. Aloud, she said, "No, my dearest Will. You were always my friend." Then, lightly, "Just as you are today. Nothing has really changed."

She was wrong, Will was to reflect no little time later as he stood in the rose garden indulging himself in the pleasure of one of Bertram Talbot's cigars. Whatever he had felt for her before he had awakened with his memory erased, it could not have been anything compared to what she inspired in him now. He was quite certain of it. Indeed, it occurred to him that, before a pistol ball had jolted his brains and robbed him of all that he was, he must have been utterly without the power of sight. He could not imagine, otherwise, how it was that he could have been near so vibrant and lovely a creature as Lady Felicity Talbot and still have failed to do his utmost to make her his wife.

A slow smile curved his lips at the thought. That, he told himself, was one mistake he had every intention of rectifying, even if it meant never recovering his memory.

Pleased with himself for having made that momentous decision, he flung away the cigar with the intention of returning into the house. Abruptly he froze at the distinct sound of the door to the house being pushed open.

"He are in a bad way, m'lady," drifted to Lethridge, who on some inexplicable impulse stepped deeper into the shadows. "He made me promise I'd bring yer. Said he'd cut me 'eart out if'n I didn't."

"Yes, well, I am here," came Felicity's response, low-pitched, "and I have every wish to see Captain Trent. Now, lead the way. And pray keep your voice down. You will awaken the entire household."

Neither Felicity nor the limping Huggins was aware, as they let themselves out of the garden, of the dark figure that, scant moments later, slipped through the gate after them.

Five

Felicity hardly knew what to expect as she approached the weathered fisherman's cottage which, long abandoned, stood lonely sentinel over the moonlit stretch of beach. Its black, gaping windows beneath a sagging roof were anything but inviting, she noted with a shiver. Nor did they give the least sign that anyone was inside anticipating her arrival.

She experienced a sinking sensation at the thought that Trent might have given up on her, indeed, might long since have made his departure. It was hardly her fault she was late. Before she could slip out to keep her rendezvous with the captain, she had had to wait until she was certain the household, and Lethridge most particularly, had retired for the night.

A plague on Trent, she thought. The hastily scrawled note he had sent her by means of Huggins was cryptic at best. After all, "Midnight. Fisherman's cottage. Bring the blunt," could hardly be construed as being overly informative. Felicity had not known if she should be encouraged to believe that Trent had found the object of his quest and was consequently demanding the payment due him or if, having squandered the not inconsiderable sum she had foolishly given him upon their previous meeting, he thought merely to squeeze more of the ready out of her.

If it were indeed the latter, Trent would soon discover she was not the consummate fool he thought her to be, Felicity vowed, squaring her shoulders before the yawning maw of darkness that was the doorway.

"Captain Trent?" she called, grateful that her voice sounded firm in the preternatural silence. "Are you within? Kindly come out so that I may see you."

"You can see me well enough inside. Dim the cursed lantern and come in," came gruffly back to her.

"I beg your pardon," retorted Felicity, hardly overjoyed at the prospect of entering the murky environs of the cottage. "I should be better pleased if you come out, Captain."

"I, however, would not be pleased at all," issued from the dark interior. "I've no wish to offer myself up as an easy target."

"Target!" Good God, thought Felicity, feeling the hairs rise at the nape of her neck. Resolutely, she refrained from giving in to the impulse to glance about her. "A target for whom, Captain? I believe I have the right to know who is after you."

"The saints alive, woman," snarled out of the interior. "Who the bloody hell do you think is after me?"

"One must presume you mean a certain gentleman who had the temerity to call on me at my home this very afternoon," Felicity retorted in censorious accents. "Faith, Captain Trent. What have you been up to since last we met?"

"Sticking my neck out, something in which I take little pleasure, ma'am. Are you coming in, or shall I leave you alone to contemplate my probable iniquities? I haven't all night."

"Beggin' your pardon, m'lady," Huggins whispered, showing the whites of his eyes. "Might be we should do as he says."

Grimly, Felicity agreed. "Indeed, Huggins, it would seem we are given little choice in the matter. Very well. Dim the lantern, if you please, and hand it to me. You will find cover and keep watch out here."

"Aye, m'lady. I'll be right outside in case yer needs me," Huggins hastened to assure her, and turned down the wick.

Seconds later, lifting her skirts with one hand and the lantern with the other, Felicity drew a deep breath and, suppressing a shudder of disgust at the distinct scutter of a rat somewhere in the vicinity of her feet, stepped gingerly over the threshold.

The interior of the cottage was every bit as unprepossessing as Felicity had expected it to be. Having long since given up to foragers whatever dubious household furnishings it had once possessed, the single room that made up what had been the living quarters was littered with debris, the detritus of its own slow disintegration, as was evidenced by moonlight filtering through holes in the roof. A loft, which had undoubtedly served as a crude sleeping chamber, had given way beneath its own weight and now leaned in a weary shambles against one wall. Nor did the decor of cobwebs and dust, not to mention the ambience of musty odors associated with long disuse, contribute in any way to a favorable impression. On the other hand, Felicity reflected wryly, the unwholesome environs would seem perfectly suited to a midnight rendezvous with a sea captain of dubious repute.

"Well, Captain?" she said, trying to pierce the gloom in search of the elusive Trent. "I am waiting."

"Heaven forbid that a member of the quality should be made to wait too long, eh, Lady Felicity

Talbot?" rasped through the unnerving quiet. A tall, dark shape detached itself from the shadows. "Never mind that Zachary Trent's been left to cool his heels in this wretched place for over an hour."

"A circumstance that could not be avoided. I do apologize, however, Captain," Felicity returned, nettled at the rogue's utter lack of civility. "I suggest you tell me why you summoned me here so that we might both remove as soon as possible to more pleasant surrounds. Have you news of Meggie?"

"Only in a manner of speaking," replied the captain most unsatisfactorily. "I've learned enough for me to believe she is alive and well, but not to determine where Steed is holding her."

"Really, Captain," Felicity offered impatiently. "Did you go to his house in Faversham? Annabel was sure Steed would take her there."

"Was she, now?" growled the captain with undisguised sarcasm. "And if you're so demmed certain that's where Meggie is, why don't the two of you just go and get her? Why bring me the bloody hell into it?"

"I should think that is obvious, Captain," Felicity said, struck by Trent's exceedingly odd behavior. At their first meeting, he had been impertinent, even rude, but he had hardly been surly. Something had worked a dramatic change in the devil-may-care sea captain. What in heaven's name had happened? she wondered, trying to make out his features in the gloom. "Annabel and I can hardly make inquiries on our own. To do so would be to reveal to Steed that Annabel is with me. However, if this assignment is not to your liking, I shall gladly relieve you of it. No doubt I can find someone to replace you. I daresay I could hire a Bow Street Runner for a deal less than I have offered you."

"Yes, but you won't," Trent odiously pointed out. "Rather than help you retrieve Meggie, a Runner would be more like to turn Annabel over to her husband. And that's what you're afraid of, isn't it, Miss Talbot?"

"Steed will never put his hands on Annabel again," Felicity stated without equivocation. "Not so long as there is breath in this body. Since you have obviously gone to some pains to discover who I am, you must realize I am not without influence, Captain."

"As it happens, I've known who you are from the beginning. Everyone in the vicinity knows Huggins serves the Duke of Breverton's daughter. Surely you're aware you're the talk of the countryside, Miss Talbot. Thanks to all your fine schemes to better the lot of women who've known nothing but wretchedness and a man's heavy hand. It doesn't make a whit of difference, unfortunately. You'll not find a soul who'd help *you* against Steed."

"Why?" demanded Felicity. "Because of the smugglers' creed, 'All and one'? I am well aware that the Gentlemen command whole communities to silence, Captain. It is a circumstance that any rational person must deplore. It is the sort of thing that breeds men like Josiah Steed."

"A practical man knows when it's best to hold his tongue," Trent countered with a shrug. "Things have a way of happening to anyone who meddles in Steed's affairs. A fellow could wake up to find his whole family dead. Even the daughter of a duke isn't safe from a man like him. If I were you, Miss Talbot, I'd think again before I took on the likes of Josiah Steed."

"I see," said Felicity, her eyes narrowing on the caped figure before her. "Is that what you have done, Trent? Have you had second thoughts?" Without warning, she caused the lantern to shine full on the captain's face.

The face that leaped into view bore little resemblance to the hard, young countenance she remembered. That other face had been strong-cut and undeniably handsome despite the signs of dissipation that had already begun to be evidenced in it. This, however, was a face that might have figured in one's nightmares.

"Merciful heavens," she breathed. Instinctively, her hand reached up as though to touch the battered features, only beginning to show signs of healing. She was stopped by the look in Trent's eyes. "Did Steed do this to you?"

"I've no doubt 'twas he who gave the orders." A smile, singularly devoid of warmth, flashed briefly across the captain's countenance. "Come now, Miss Talbot. Did you think to pity me? There's no need for it. The blighters who waylaid me have been made to see the light. You may be sure they'll not soon raise a hand against anyone else. I was fool enough to allow myself to be lured into a trap. But no matter. It changes nothing, save only that now Steed will die for what he's done."

"That was not part of our bargain, Captain," said Felicity, lowering the lantern out of deference to Trent's obvious discomfort. "You promised you would come to me with whatever you found out and that I should see to getting Meggie back."

"The terms have changed, Miss Talbot. You can choose to help me give Steed what's coming to him or not. It makes no difference to me. Either way, Annabel will have her Meggie back. A roll of the flimsies will only speed things along."

"I fail to see how, Captain," Felicity rejoined, vying for time while she considered these new complications. "I am not averse to supplying monetary support if it will help Meggie. I should, however, like to know how the funds are to be used."

"Like axle grease, Miss Talbot," Trent answered acerbically. "Only in this case, to grease some jaws. I could use my fists, but I'd prefer the more subtle means. It makes for fewer enemies."

"Yes, I daresay it would," Felicity agreed, suppressing a shudder at the implied violence behind his words. "I should be pleased, then, to provide the axle grease." Withdrawing a purse from the folds of her cloak, she held it out to him. "On one condition—that you keep me informed. I like to know how my investments are progressing—before you do anything we shall both come to regret. I must have your word, Captain."

She saw him hesitate, obviously torn between the temptation to consign her to the devil and the realization that she held in her hand the swift means to an end.

"The devil. You have it." Trent snatched the purse from her hand.

"Splendid," Felicity said dryly. Then, more gently, "You must see that Annabel and I will both do better if we are not left to stew in the dark."

Felicity was keen to note the strong, slender hand clench about the leather purse. "How does she go on, Miss Talbot?" came in muffled tones from the captain.

"She is clinging to the hope that you will discover some news of Meggie. Her resolve, however, is weakening. She is afraid she has brought us all to danger. It is my greatest fear that she will abandon all hope and fling herself in despair on Steed's mercy."

"Hell and the devil confound it. It is only the sort of nonsense I'd expect from her." The captain swung sharply around, his free hand closing like a vise on Felicity's arm. "You must keep her from it, if you have to lock her in the cellar. Do you understand? If she goes back to him, Steed will most assuredly kill her."

"Yes, Captain," Felicity answered, meeting the fierce glitter of his eyes with a steady look. "I believe I do understand. You love her, do you not."

It was a statement rather than a question. Felicity, after all, already knew the answer.

"Love her?" Releasing Felicity, Trent laughed harshly. "Love is a sentiment for women and fools. Do I strike you as a fool, Miss Talbot?"

"For loving a beautiful young woman with the sort of courage few men possess? I should think you a fool if you had not lost your heart to her."

"Then you know nothing about me, or Annabel Steed, for that matter. Ask her if there is any love between us. In the meantime, I suggest you take care to stay out of Steed's way. Farewell, Miss Talbot, until the next time."

Pocketing the purse, Trent strode swiftly to the door.

"Be sure that I shall ask her," Felicity flung after him. "And I suggest that *you*, Captain, have a care for yourself."

He did not bother to answer but stepped out into the night and was instantly swallowed up in the darkness.

With a thoughtful frown, Felicity followed after him. Poor Trent. It was obvious the young rogue was not quite so case-hardened as he would have liked the world to believe. Clearly, he was anything but daunted by the beating he had suffered at the hands of Steed's henchmen. If anything, he was more determined than ever to place himself at risk for a woman for whom he claimed not to have the smallest affection.

Rubbing a hand over her arm, which still tingled from the grip of powerful fingers, Felicity smiled humorously to herself. Trent was a dreadful liar. Certainly, his actions belied his words. The captain could not have more blatantly betrayed himself had he declared openly that he was head over heels in love with Annabel Steed. Furthermore, Felicity was almost positive that Annabel loved him in return. The pertinent question was, when had he first lost his heart to the girl? Before she belonged to Steed or after? He had said they went back a long way. Was it possible that he had loved her before Steed made her his wife? Could it be that Annabel had actually chosen Steed over the fiery young Trent?

Good God. Such a possibility loomed as utterly incredible to Felicity. She could not imagine any woman freely giving herself to a monster like Steed. Perhaps, then, Annabel had not been a willing party to so obvious a mésalliance. It was not unknown for a father to sell a daughter into marital bondage. It might have meant one less mouth to feed and money to provide for other, pressing needs. Female offspring might even be used in lieu of brass to discharge gambling debts. There might have been any number of explanations for how the girl found herself in her present predicament. Now, for the first time, it came to Felicity to wonder just how Annabel had come to marry Steed, especially if there had been someone else who was clearly a better candidate for her affections.

Sensing a tale of blighted love and tragedy, it did little good to tell herself that the how and why of the marriage was not really any of her affair. On the contrary, it occurred to her that resolving the mystery surrounding Trent and Annabel might very well provide the only solution to the young woman's unhappy situation. Indeed, Felicity could think of little else as, together with the groundskeeper, she turned to retrace her steps to Primrose.

Consequently, as she began to make her way up the grassy knoll rising from the beach, she failed utterly to detect a shadowy figure melt into the deeper shadows of a small coppice of trees at the top of the hill. Not even Huggins, who was wont to mumble to himself and cast wary glances over his shoulder, sensed that other, watching presence as he limped past within half a dozen feet of it. Indeed, neither witnessed the watcher sink heavily to the ground in the wake of their passing.

William Powell, however, was keenly aware of them.

It was no doubt fortunate that a full moon shone in a cloudless sky, Will reflected wryly as he ran a hand through his sweat-dampened hair, else he would most assuredly have lost sight of his quarry. Wryly, he cursed the weakness that dragged at his limbs in the wake of his recent exertions. He had been hard put to keep up, even with Huggins's labored gait, and had been compelled to stop any number of times to recoup his strength and catch his breath. Still, he had kept on with dogged determination, his curiosity piqued, not to mention his well-developed instincts, which warned him Lady Felicity was courting danger. Thanks to the light of the moon and the dim glow of the lantern Huggins carried, he had managed to keep track of the two in front of him.

Not that he had been able to draw close enough to witness what had actually transpired inside the hovel crouched at the foot of the hill. He had arrived too late to do more than watch with an infuriating sense of helplessness as Felicity stepped through the yawning maw.

Damn the girl! He would gladly throttle her if ever again she put him through the agony of waiting, his every sense strained in anticipation of the first signs that she had become the victim of any number of dire fates conjured up by his overactive imagination. Still, in spite of a particularly vivid image of Felicity struggling in the grasp of a murderous cutthroat intent on brutally robbing her of her virtue, he had, in the absence of actual evidence of foul play, grimly held his ground. He vastly preferred that the headstrong young beauty remain in ignorance of the fact that he had followed her to her midnight tryst with— whom? Who the devil was this Captain Trent?

He had known as well as Steed that Felicity was lying when she claimed she was unacquainted with Zachary Trent. The question had been not so much *why* she had lied as how there had come to be any sort of connection between Steed and Felicity Talbot, not to mention what part the mysterious Trent played in it. A pity that he, William, had been too far away to glimpse more than an obscure caped figure emerge from the hut. As it was, he knew no more now than he had known before he had given in to impulse to follow Miss Talbot to what suddenly gave every appearance of a lovers' tryst.

"Bloody hell!" he cursed, aware of a sharp wrench in the vicinity of his belly. He did not fool himself into believing it was anything other than a pang of jealousy. He was all too aware that he had fallen under the spell of the Duke of Breverton's only daughter the moment he had looked up into her cursed lovely eyes and realized he was not in the grips of a dream. Strange that he had not considered before the possibility that her heart might already be engaged by another. Nor was he prepared to accept that explanation for her exceedingly odd behavior. He had kissed her, after all, only that very afternoon.

A wry smile touched his lips at the memory of her charming response. In spite of her declaration to the contrary, he could not be mistaken in thinking not only that she had gained some fleeting pleasure from it, but that she had gone so far as to return his kiss in some small measure. Certainly, covered in confusion, she had colored most delightfully. At the very least, hers had not been the response of a woman whose heart was irrevocably committed to another. Indeed, if that were the case, why the devil had she stolen out to meet her mysterious lover in the dead of night and in the unprepossessing surrounds of a probably rat-infested hovel?

Even if this Trent were beneath her station, she maintained her own household separate from her father and brothers. Surely there was nothing to prevent her from receiving anyone she pleased in her own home, especially in the rustic environs of the country. It seemed even less logical to assume that he himself was the reason the two had chosen to meet in secret. Presumably in his present state of mind, she might have felt confident of presenting the captain to her houseguest in the light of an old acquaintance.

No, the notion that theirs had been a lovers' tryst was patently absurd, he told himself—unless, of course, it was Trent who was reluctant to be seen in her home or in her company. If the mysterious captain happened to be one of Steed's associates in the business of smuggling and pirating, he would naturally be reluctant to appear openly in the company

of the daughter of a duke. It would call a deal of
unwanted attention to him, not to mention ruin the
lady's reputation.

Egad! thought Will, a curious thundering in his
ears. *A brigand with the instincts of a gentleman.* That
would be a deadly combination in a rival for the lady's
affections. Indeed, he did not doubt that such a
rogue would prove most damnably irresistible to a
female of Felicity Talbot's fiery disposition. It would
also explain the "complicated situation" to which she
had referred and upon which she had based her ob-
jections to Will's ungentlemanly breach of conduct.

The devil, it would all seem to make sense. No
doubt it was little wonder that Lady Felicity Talbot
chose to rusticate in the relative isolation of the Kentish countryside instead of pursuing a life of gaiety
in London! Egad, it would certainly explain why Mrs.
Morseby would wish Will at Jericho. The housekeeper, fiercely protective of her mistress, would
hardly welcome an unexpected houseguest if Lady
Felicity were being courted by a bloody pirate! And
Steed, the devil take him. No doubt *he* had come with
the intention of warning the lady off. The last thing
the villain could wish, after all, would be to have the
powerful Duke of Breverton turn his attention to the
smuggling trade in Kent, and that would be precisely
what would happen were Breverton to learn that his
only daughter had developed a tendre for the captain
of a smuggling vessel.

Complicated? he thought. Hellsfire! It was beginning
to look as if he had blundered into a blasted quag-
mire. Indeed, the only gentlemanly, not to mention
rational, course of action would seem to be to politely
remove himself from the vicinity of Primrose Cottage
as soon as was possible.

That he subsequently did no such thing, indeed,

had, by the time he had made his way back to Primrose Cottage, determined on precisely the opposite course of action, he could no doubt attribute to some deep-seated perversity in his character. The fact of the matter was he could no more go away before having at least made certain the man who had won Felicity Talbot's heart was worthy of her than he could convince himself that the lady in question had not been at least in a measure receptive to his own, earlier advances. Indeed, so long as there was the smallest chance that Lady Felicity was not wholly enamored of her swashbuckling pirate with cursedly noble instincts, then he, William Powell, saw no reason to bow out gracefully.

Besides, he told himself, as he slipped through the French doors into the Blue Salon, there was still Josiah Steed with whom to contend. Will could hardly leave Lady Felicity now, when there was every evidence she was being stalked by a man of Steed's ilk. Even had he not owed her the immeasurable debt of having saved his life, he would have been duty-bound to protect her.

It came to him as he made his way silently up the stairs that, at the very least, he could hardly leave before he had seen Felicity's paragon of virtue for himself. If Trent measured up, Will would be honor-bound to step aside. On the other hand, he was damned if he would do so before he had made certain that Felicity was out of harm's way. The devil of it was he would be in little better case if the captain turned out to be something other than the lady believed him to be. Rather than see Felicity harmed, Will would be compelled to take steps to bring the affair to an end. Egad, he could not conceive of a course more certain to condemn him in the lady's eyes.

In his room, his glance fell on the walnut case that
resided on the dressing table. His lips thinned to a
grim line. Curious, he mused, that he had thought
to bring his dueling pistols along.

At last, flinging himself fully dressed across the
bed, he closed his eyes and fell almost instantly into
exhausted slumber.

Not so Felicity, who, having long since dismissed
her abigail, remained awake, pacing. No doubt she
could attribute her insomnia to the pistachio cream
in which she had indulged at dinner, she told herself
irritably, and not to the nagging awareness of a certain nobleman in residence a mere two doors down
from her own.

The truth was, however, that she could no more
dismiss Will Powell from her mind than she could
still the nagging voice that insisted she might entrust
Lethridge with the truth about Annabel and Josiah
Steed; indeed, that she could do no better than to
enlist his aid in finding Meggie. He had already
guessed that she was in trouble and that Steed was a
threat to her, she ruefully reminded herself. She
could not forget that he, without knowing the whole
of it, had not hesitated to offer his help. She had only
to confide in him the toil she had got herself in, whispered that traitorous voice, and she need no longer
stand alone against Steed.

The idea was out of the question, she told herself,
flopping down on the window seat and immediately
jumping to her feet again. The very last thing she
could wish was to involve Will in her problems. She
might as well go to her father, the duke, or to either
of her brothers and admit she was ill prepared to
govern her own life. Sternly, she reminded herself

that at three and twenty she was perfectly capable of working things out for herself, only immediately to have the image of Zachary Trent's battered features rear up to haunt her.

Good God, what a fool she had been, she told herself as an unwonted feeling of panic gripped her. It was bitter gall to realize she was in no case to defend herself, let alone Annabel, should Steed decide to resort to forceful means of retrieving his wife. Trent was all too much in the right of it when he said there was no one who would help her—*no one but Lethridge,* whispered the cursed voice of reason. Even without his memory, William Powell would be a powerful force on her side.

Hardly had that compelling argument sounded in her brain than she clapped her hands over her ears in dismay.

"Stop it, Felicity Talbot," she said to her image in the looking glass. "Enough is enough. You will not listen to the voice of temptation. If William Powell had not shown up on your doorstep, you would not now be having this conversation with yourself. You would be devising a way to resolve the coil you have wrought for yourself. Everything else is only a rationale to persuade you to give into your heart's desire. You will not do it. Do you hear me? Will loves Zenoria, not you, a pertinent fact that will come back to him any day now."

Perhaps, agreed the voice with infuriating persistence, but in the meantime, Felicity Talbot had the distinction of being the only woman he had ever known. Why did she not simply grasp this fleeting chance at happiness and enjoy it while she may? Had their places been reversed, Felicity could be sure that Zenoria would not hesitate to take advantage of the opportunity offered her.

No, she would not listen, she thought, out of all patience with herself. She was not Zenoria. She was Felicity Talbot, and she would not stoop to entrapping the man she loved, certainly not under false pretenses, no matter how much she might wish to have done.

That return of resolve, no matter how bolstering to her sense of dignity, was hardly conducive to her comfort. Indeed, it was with a sense of longing that she recalled the peaceful tenor of her life before Lethridge had appeared, unbidden, on her doorstep. Then, she had had only the as yet unrealized threat of cutthroats and thieves to cut up her existence. How much simpler the dark plot surrounding Annabel now seemed in comparison to the unruly yearnings of her own traitorous heart! Surely her life could not become more complicated.

Hardly had that thought formulated itself in her mind than the silence was shattered by the clatter of hoofbeats on the cobblestoned drive that led up to the front of the house.

Goliath in accompaniment with the two stable hounds set up a din of alarm.

Good God—Bertie, she thought. Immediately, she suffered a sinking sensation as it came to her that he would not be pushing his mount with such urgency unless the tidings were less than felicitous. Faith, the unthinkable had happened. Shelby had cut his stick, and now Lethridge must in all haste flee the country!

Snatching up her dressing robe, Felicity flung open her door—and was met with the sight of Lethridge, fully dressed and wearing a singularly forbidding aspect.

"Will, what—?"

She was not allowed to finish.

Lethridge, enjoining her to silence with a gesture,

caught her arm. "Softly, my girl," he murmured, thrusting her backwards into her room and closing the door behind them. "I suggest you prepare yourself. We are about to have callers."

"I know." Felicity rushed on, "Will, it is very likely Bertie, and I should warn you he might have disturbing news to impart. No, please not yet," she said, lifting a hand when it became clear he was about to interrupt. "Let me say what I have to say first." Then, twisting her hands in the folds of her dressing robe, which in her confusion she had utterly forgotten to put on, she said, "Dear, I cannot think how to tell you . . . I mean, it is all so very sudden. Well, actually not sudden, precisely. I have been expecting him, of course, but hardly tonight. Or at least not in the middle of the night, though I knew it might come to this when he . . ."

Abruptly she broke off, quite unable to find the words to break the unhappy tidings, not to mention to reveal the fact that she had deliberately concocted an elaborate scheme of lies to keep Will at Primrose Cottage. Indeed, the task, now that she was faced with it, loomed a deal more dreadful than she had anticipated. Suddenly flinging up her hands along with the dressing robe, she wheeled away from Lethridge. "Oh, how very like Bertie to—to—well, to arrive in such a manner without the least regard for—for—"

She was interrupted by an imperative assault on the front door, which quite set the gimcracks to rattling with the force of it.

"Good heavens!" Felicity exclaimed, her eyes flying in consternation to Lethridge, who was regarding her with sardonic appreciation. "What—? I mean, who—?"

"Rest assured," William replied in exceedingly dry accents, "it is not your brother Bertie."

"But of course it is not. He would never assault my door in such a manner. But then who—?"

The answer came couched in an imperious shout. "Open up, I command you in the name of His Britannic Majesty!"

"Good God," said Felicity, wondering if she had lost all sense of reason. "Soldiers!"

"Excisemen, to be more precise," replied Lethridge, gently but firmly taking the dressing robe from her hands and holding it up to help her into it. "It is what I have been trying to tell you. No doubt you will pardon my curiosity. You are not, after all, in the business of smuggling, are you, Cousin?"

Six

Felicity, made suddenly to realize that she had been standing before Lethridge for all of five minutes dressed only in her white cotton nightdress, her bare feet clearly visible below the hem, felt her cheeks go a dusky red. "For heaven's sakes, you know very well I am not a smuggler," she exclaimed, thrusting her arms through the sleeves of her dressing robe and her feet into her red velvet slippers. "Faith, it needed only this. If you ever breathe a word that you saw me in my nightdress, William Powell, I shall—"

"You may be sure I am about to come down with an acute case of amnesia," prophesied Lethridge with a wry glint in the look he bent upon her. "On the other hand, I confess I have never seen you look more charming."

"Devil," choked Felicity, hard put not to give in to a burble of laughter. How dared he make her laugh when excisemen were below threatening to batter down her front door! "You already have an acute case of amnesia," she reminded him.

"No, do I?" murmured William, quizzically arching aristocratic eyebrows. "I'm afraid I had forgot. It would seem, however, that the gentlemen below are growing impatient. No doubt you will pardon me if I confess to a certain curiosity. Have you anything that might perchance be of interest to them? You are not, are you, concealing French brandy in the cellars, or any captains of smuggling vessels?"

"Captains of smuggling vessels," repeated Felicity in tones of incredulity, though, inside, her heart had given a wholly unsettling leap. "I wish you will not be absurd. What the devil should I be doing with either in my cellars?"

"I should never dream to presume what you might do with what would seem to comprise all the elements for an impromptu evening of entertainment—a little wine, a dashing sea captain or two—a company of excisemen. I only ask because at any moment your importunate callers below are going to gain admittance. And then, Felicity, my dove, they are the ones who will be doing the asking. I suggest you tell me now if there is anything for which I need be concerned."

It was on Felicity's tongue to retort scathingly in the negative when the one thing she would wish to keep hidden from the excisemen came to her. "Good God—Annabel," she exclaimed, a hand going involuntarily to Lethridge's sleeve. "No one must know she is here. It is imperative to keep her hidden."

"*Annabel!*" Lethridge's eyebrows fairly snapped together. It was hardly the answer he had expected. And yet, he thought, perhaps it did make some sort of strange sense. Certainly it would bear cogitation at some later date. For now, however, there were clearly more pressing concerns. "I suggest," he said, a hand on either of Felicity's shoulders, "that you go below and make your visitors welcome. Offer them tea, show them the cellars if you must, anything to keep them occupied until I am able to join you downstairs. If you can, contrive to have Mrs. Morseby come up."

"Yes, yes, but what do you intend to do? There is no place to hide Annabel that they cannot easily discover."

"Then we shall not hide her."

"Not hide her? But—"

"*Trust* me, Felicity," Lethridge urged, impelling her toward the door. "Go now. This is hardly the time for explanations."

He was right, of course, Felicity realized. From the din issuing below, it was clear that Mrs. Morseby had granted the king's agents admission and now was sorely pressed to keep them from barging up the stairs.

Gathering her wits about her, Felicity made her way down the hallway.

There was no question that the blood of dukes ran in the veins of the woman who descended with regal poise into the midst of chaos. Indeed, Felicity did not doubt that her mama would have been exceedingly proud of her daughter's entrance upon the scene of five armed men confronting a highly incensed Mrs. Morseby, not to mention Cook, the scullery maids, the upstairs and downstairs maids, and Freddie the footman, all of whom were crowded in and about the foyer in various attitudes of alarm.

"Do you know whose house this is?" demanded the housekeeper, clad in cap, nightdress, and wrapper. "Lady Felicity Talbot is not the sort to harbor brigands in her house. My mistress, I'll have you know, is the daughter of the Duke of Breverton."

"She might be the daughter of a prince and 'twould make no difference," spoke up a very young officer wearing the insignia of a leftenant in the king's navy. "I should still have to search the house—

for the lady's own protection. We have received word Zachary Trent, who is well known for his smuggling activities, was seen skulking about the premises."

"These premises. Indeed?" pronounced Felicity from the curve in the stairway. "You must be mistaken, Leftenant. You may be certain I should know if there were a smuggler in my house."

That declaration couched in tones of composed assurance served as nothing else had done to bring order to the scene of chaos. The excisemen went instantly rigid, their eyes fixed on the vision of loveliness gazing down at them from on high.

"Well, sir?" queried Felicity, when no response seemed to be forthcoming.

It remained to the young leftenant to break what was fast becoming a telling silence.

"Ahem!" he pontificated on an explosive breath.

"Quite so, Leftenant," Felicity concurred.

A distinct tinge of color suffused the officer's cleanshaven cheeks. Manfully he straightened to attention, chest thrust out and chin high. "I beg your pardon, ma'am, for this intrusion. As it happens, we were not made aware who resided in this house. Our informant, as a matter of fact, intimated we should discover a smugglers' den on the premises."

"A smugglers' den? Really, Leftenant," Felicity crooned indulgently as she descended the rest of the way into the foyer. "I fear, sir, you have been made the victim of a jest. Do I appear to you to be the head of a smuggling ring? Can you think little Daisy, here," she added, indicating the twelve-year-old scullery maid, "one of my desperate band?"

"N-no, ma'am, indeed not," blustered the leftenant. "Still, these smugglers are bold. One never knows what they might try next. And this Trent is a bad 'un out of a bad lot. Duty alone demands that we search the house. For your own protection, ma'am."

"For my protection?" exclaimed Felicity. A slender hand fluttered to her breast. "Dear me, you actually think one of these villains has taken up refuge in my house while, unknowing, I lay in my bed? Faith, Leftenant, the very thought makes my head reel. Indeed, Hannah, dear, I think I must have my smelling salts."

"Smelling salts?" echoed Hannah Morseby with an air of incredulity. "And where, m'lady, would you suggest I find them?"

"Why, you know very well where," replied Felicity in fading accents. The back of a hand to her brow, she flashed the housekeeper a pointed look. "Upstairs. Pray do not tarry. I feel—I feel—queer."

The leftenant, feeling the lady sag heavily on his arm, gave every evidence of one on the verge of a panic.

"Yes, yes, hurry, woman! Can you not see your mistress is in a faint? You, there. Brinknel. Help me carry her to a sofa."

"Smelling salts indeed," muttered Hannah Morseby, plodding up the stairs, one hand heavy on the rail, while behind her her mistress who had never been known to faint a day in her life, was borne with great tenderness to the withdrawing room, where she was carefully deposited upon the sofa.

"There, there, ma'am," the leftenant said soothingly, awkwardly patting Felicity's hand no doubt in the hopes that by that he might revive one who gave every evidence of being as delicate as she was divinely beautiful. "I have no doubt you will be better soon."

"Indeed, Leftenant," sighed Felicity, favoring the officer with a smile calculated to bedazzle a harder heart than his, "you are all kindness. I cannot think what came over me. I fear I am unused to men bearing arms in my foyer. I daresay I should do better with a dish of tea. I wonder, would you be so good as to summon the maid? No doubt you and your men will join me. Really, Leftenant, I insist."

It was to occur to the leftenant no little time later that he had never before met a more charming hostess than Lady Felicity Talbot, who, sending her servants to their beds, herself ushered her unexpected guests down to the kitchens, where, with their ready help, she built up the fire and set the pot to boiling. Not satisfied with serving tea and biscuits, what must she do but set out a cold collation of thinly sliced ham and roast, hearty slices of saffron bread spread thick with butter, various offerings of cheeses, and leftover pistachio cream the likes of which he had not tasted since he was a boy in his home county of Sussex. Certain it was that his men had never known the likes of the feast that was spread before them, or of a duke's daughter, for that matter, who treated them with such fine condescension. Indeed, it was doubtful that amid the merriment of partaking of good food in congenial surrounds it would have occurred to any of the king's excisemen to remember their original purpose in coming to Primrose Cottage had not the leftenant been a man of singular dedication to duty and had not the lady's cousin, arriving on the scene just as the platter, so to speak, was swept clean, served to remind them of it.

"I say, Cousin," drawled the gentleman, observing the assembled company through a quizzing glass suspended about his neck on a black riband—one of Bertie's affectations, Felicity noted in startled amusement. "I was not aware that we were entertaining tonight. Friends of yours?"

"William," pronounced Felicity, perched on a stool. Her eyes searched his. Lethridge, however, presented a maddeningly unreadable front. "Allow me to present Leftenant Wilkers and his men. Gentlemen, my cousin, Viscount Lethridge."

"Gentlemen. What, may I ask, brings you out in the wee hours before dawn? I'm afraid I cannot say much for your protocol. Pounding on people's doors in the dead of night is hardly likely to endear you to the local populace."

"The local populace has made it clear that they do not care either for us or our mission, my lord," stiffly observed Leftenant Wilkers, who had, followed in a disorderly din of scraping chairs and shuffling boots by his men, shot to his feet at his lordship's entrance. "I fear they cannot be made to understand that we are here to rid them of the murderous element among them, to wit, the bands of pirates, smugglers, and thieves who ply their illicit trade along these coasts. As it happens, we came tonight in pursuit of one of them."

"Have you indeed?" queried Lethridge, amused at the leftenant's youthful fervor, not to mention the studiously blank aspects of his subordinates, some yet masticating the repast that had so graciously been provided them. "And who might that be?"

"Captain Zachary Trent of the *Annabel*, a schooner out of Ramsgate, my lord. We received word he was seen tonight hereabouts."

"And you came directly to Miss Talbot's house? Curious. Surely you cannot think my cousin in league with the devil."

"No, indeed not, sir," vehemently denied the officer. "Lady Felicity—Miss Talbot, that is, is—is the finest, most generous lady one could ever hope to meet. At it happens, we had no notion to whom the cottage belonged. Mr. Steed said only that Captain Trent was to be found here in the company of his har—" His lordship's eyebrow shot up. Leftenant Wilkers abruptly broke off. "Er—his lady friend, that is," he amended, visibly reddening.

"His lady friend?" Felicity echoed, her gaze going quizzically to Lethridge.

Lethridge eloquently shrugged. "It would seem, my dear," he said acerbically, "that the plot thickens."

"It would indeed," agreed Miss Talbot, to the young officer's obvious discomfort. "And who, Leftenant, might this woman be?"

Leftenant Wilkers gave every impression of a man who has blundered through no fault of his own into a bed of thorns. "A Mrs. Annabel Steed, ma'am," he answered, manfully standing his ground, "who, I believe, is presently residing beneath this roof."

"No, do you?" murmured Felicity, her eyebrows lifting. "And, truly, how should you not, if this person Steed has said it is so. I daresay it would not do for me to simply tell you you will find no one other than my cousin, myself, and the members of my household under this roof. No, no, Leftenant," she added imperiously when the young officer made as if to protest, "you have made your duty clear. Search the house and be done. Doubtless I shall be pleased to accept your apology when you have finished what you came here to do."

"You have it now, ma'am," Wilkers declared gallantly. "Men, take up your weapons. Brinknel, you and Hollingworth search the cellars and servants' quarters. Bledsoe and Fitzpatrick, come with me. With your permission, ma'am, we shall proceed upstairs."

"By all means, Leftenant," said Felicity, grateful

that her voice sounded calm when, inside, she had an overpowering urge to scream. "Allow me to show you the way."

There was something exceedingly demeaning about conducting strangers through one's house for the express purpose of allowing them to search it against one's wishes. The young leftenant might choose to give his actions the facade of civility by asking Felicity's permission, but she knew as well as he that she had had no recourse but to give him leave to invade her privacy. Worst of all, it was being done on the word of an infamous felon.

Josiah Steed, it would seem, was not above anything, not even enlisting the services of excisemen to flush out his errant wife. There was a crude sort of irony to that that Felicity found particularly galling. No doubt it had been meant as a particularly pointed message as well: No one, not even the daughter of a duke, was beyond the reach of one of the Gentlemen. Next time it would not be the mere inconvenience of excisemen battering at her door, but something far more sinister.

Only, this time Mr. Steed would discover he had not a leg to stand on, she told herself firmly. Nevertheless, she glanced sideways at Lethridge as if for reassurance that somehow Wilkers was not about to find Annabel Steed in the attic room they were even now approaching.

It was hardly reassurance, however, that she received from the nobleman, who, stepping without warning in front of the leftenant and his two subordinates, planted a forbidding hand on the closed door. Nor did his words to the startled excisemen seem meant to be in the least propitious.

"I suggest, Leftenant," he said, maddeningly cool, "that neither you nor your men step inside this room.

For your own protection, as it were. I assure you there is nothing beyond this door to interest you."

All in an instant, tension ran rife among those crowded in the narrow corridor. Good God, thought Felicity, wondering if Lethridge had in truth lost his mind. She fully anticipated utter mayhem to break loose at any moment. And poor Annabel. What was to become of her? Felicity had little doubt that Leftenant Wilkers had orders to take Captain Trent's alleged lady friend into custody, not only as some sort of accomplice to smugglers, but as a runaway wife!

"Are you denying us entrance, my lord?" demanded Wilkers, who could not but be keenly aware that he and his men were at a distinct disadvantage in their present crowded conditions, which rendered their long-barreled muskets wholly useless.

"Not at all, Leftenant." Smiling in a conciliatory manner, Lethridge lifted his hand from the barrier. "I shouldn't dream of it. I thought merely to warn you. Naturally, you and your men may be perfectly safe to enter. On the other hand, I thought you should be made aware . . ." Reaching to turn the handle, he pushed the door open—and was greeted by what sounded distinctly like a low groan of anguish. "It would seem my tiger has contracted an acute case of the mumps. Both sides, as it were, poor lad."

The excisemen leaned in concert to peer into the room lit by a single flickering candle. Face swathed in a bandage that ran about the top of the head and under the chin, the "poor lad" lay, pitifully moaning, in bed.

Stepping aside, Lethridge gestured invitingly toward the scene of suffering. "Feel free, Leftenant, to conduct your search."

Bledsoe and Fitzpatrick, who undoubtedly would

never have hesitated to take on the burliest of smugglers or even a handful at once, visibly wavered in the face of the mumps. Certainly, Leftenant Wilkers demonstrated no pressing desire to follow duty through that door into uncertain territory.

"I see no need to disturb the lad in his suffering," Wilkers offered magnanimously. "It appears that Mr. Steed has led us on a wild-goose chase, a circumstance for which I humbly beg your pardon, Miss Talbot."

"I shall, of course, accept your apology, Leftenant," said Felicity, "though I shall not soon forgive your invasion of my privacy. You may be certain my father will hear of this. Furthermore, I suggest you consider the distinct possibility that, if Mr. Steed gave you misinformation this time, very likely his word is not to be trusted. It is quite possible this Captain Trent is not at all what he has been painted to be. Perhaps you should even be asking yourself what your Mr. Steed hoped to achieve by sending you on this bootless errand. Perhaps it suited him very well to have you and your men occupied here when you might otherwise have been somewhere else."

It was no doubt to the leftenant's credit that he appeared to be much struck by Miss Talbot's final suggestion and not a little chagrined at the manner in which he had repaid her hospitality. Certainly, it seemed that Wilkers would not soon forget that evening's fiasco or the part that Josiah Steed had played in it.

"Thank heavens, that is over," breathed Felicity, when at last the door closed behind the excisemen. She turned shining eyes on Lethridge. "Faith, but that was brilliantly done. Whatever made you think of the mumps?"

"Have you ever seen a grown man stricken down

by that particular malady?" Lethridge answered with
a bemused smile. Egad, he reflected, if he had not
already fallen head over ears to his angel's spell, that
look in her eyes would most certainly have done him
in. "Believe me, it is no laughing matter. Not only is
it a singularly painful experience, but it can be devastating to a man's hopes for future progeny."

"It certainly gave the leftenant and his men pause
for thought, and little wonder." Felicity sobered as it
came home to her that they had just willfully ob-
structed king's agents in the pursuit of justice. "Still,"
she added, suffering an unwitting pang of conscience, "I could almost feel sorry for poor Wilkers.
He was, after all, only doing his duty, and he is in the
right of it. These smugglers and pirates must be
stopped."

"Are you quite sure you share his sentiments?"
queried Lethridge as Felicity reached down to douse
the lamp on the occasional table beside the withdrawing room sofa. "Your defense of this Captain Trent
was, if nothing else, eloquent. One might suppose
you were personally acquainted with the man."

Felicity's hand froze for the barest instant. Then,
turning down the wick, she straightened. "As it happens, I have had occasion to meet the captain on two
separate occasions—on Annabel's behalf. I have
good reason to believe they are quite fond of one
another. Unfortunately, as you heard, she has the misfortune to be married to Josiah Steed."

"And he, one must presume, wants her back,"
speculated Lethridge, a great deal about "Miss Annabel Jones" made suddenly and abundantly clear.
"Which is why it was imperative to keep her hidden
from Leftenant Wilkers and his men." It would also
explain why Steed had shown up on Felicity's door-

step and why Felicity had kept a midnight tryst with Captain Trent.

Wryly, he was aware that a great weight seemed to have been lifted from him.

"Yes, he wants her back," Felicity admitted bitterly. "I, however, have seen what he is capable of doing. When she came to me, she had been beaten savagely, almost to death by her loving husband. I will not let her fall into his hands again. I care not what I have to do to prevent it. At least, thanks to you, we have bought some time. I daresay Mr. Steed will be somewhat uncertain how to proceed, now that it has been demonstrated his wife is not to be found on these premises."

"Perhaps," Lethridge temporized, far from being convinced. "On the other hand, it may not be so easy to pull the wool over Steed's eyes. He may surmise that our ailing tiger might very well be a female in disguise. No doubt you will pardon my curiosity if I confess to wondering why you have not simply taken steps to remove Mrs. Steed from the vicinity. I daresay she would be safe enough at Breverton or any other of your father's several estates."

"You do not know Steed," replied Felicity, who had been dreading that particular question. There had been little choice but to tell Will the truth about Annabel's circumstances. Wilkers had made it pointless to do anything else. She hesitated, however, to tell him the whole of it. If he knew about Meggie, he would undoubtedly insist on involving himself further in the coil in which she found herself, and she had no right to ask that of him. A half-truth would have to do for the time being, she decided, saying, "He has spies everywhere. As soon as ever we tried to move her, he would know of it and come after us.

No, she will do better here for the time being, until I can devise a means of insuring her safety."

"Oh, indubitably," agreed his lordship without so much as the blink of an eyelash. Egad, he thought, how the deuce did she propose to do any such thing against murderous pirates and smugglers? She might just as soon expect pigs to fly. "And for that you are relying on the help of this Captain Trent, is that it?"

"As it happens, I have engaged the captain's services on Annabel's behalf," Felicity admitted, her chin lifting ever so slightly in unconscious defiance. "Trent has the singular advantage of being well acquainted with the seamier elements along the Swale."

"No, does he?" queried Lethridge with perfect gravity. "He sounds a capital fellow. Am I to assume, then, he is also the smuggler and pirate that Wilkers believes him to be?"

"Now you are being unfair," Felicity accused him, though that was precisely what she herself had suspected of the captain. "I have no evidence that he is either. As it happens, I was given a very favorable impression of Captain Trent. I depend upon him to discover a means of persuading Steed to grant his wife's release."

"The devil you do." In spite of himself, Lethridge experienced a fresh stab of jealousy. She might not be in love with the sea captain, but it was cursedly obvious she would rather depend on a brigand than on himself to extricate her from her present difficulties. Did she consider William Powell so damnably untrustworthy?

"You disapprove, my lord?" queried Felicity in tones meant to cut him to the quick. How dared he, after all, presume to judge her! She had not asked him to meddle in her affairs. Indeed, she would vastly prefer that he not, she told herself firmly.

"No. How should I?" Lethridge gave a shrug of indifference. "No doubt it is perfectly logical to place one's trust in a man who may or may not be one of the Gentlemen, but who, at the very least, is on intimate terms with the cutthroats. I cannot but wonder, however, what this Trent hopes to find that could possibly persuade Steed to give up all claims on his wife—especially as Steed seems particularly set on doing precisely the opposite."

"Well, how should I know?" demanded Felicity, in no mood for a Spanish Inquisition, especially now when she was out of all sorts with William Powell, not to mention with herself. "Perhaps it will be something as simple as a sum of money. I should willingly pay him off if it meant Annabel were to be free of him at last."

"Unfortunately, with a man like Steed, one could never be sure of any such thing," Lethridge was odiously quick to point out. "I, for one, should be loath to trust the word of a pirate. I suggest, my girl, that this Trent would do far better to set a trap for Steed and let Jack Ketch have the honor of permanently removing him. It would seem the ideal solution."

It would, in fact, seem the *only* solution, thought Felicity, wondering why it had never occurred to her. But then, it would hardly be a simple matter to set a trap for a pirate. Indeed, she did not see how she should go about it. Nor was it the sort of thing that she could see herself looking to Trent to do for her, she reflected, thinking of the sea captain's propensity for hot-blooded action, when what was needed was one noted for having a level head in a crisis.

Inevitably, an image of Lethridge coolly setting his trap for Shelby came to mind. In spite of her horror and dismay at the reasons for what Will had done, not to mention the eventual outcome, she could not but thrill to her brother's account of the Viscount's carefully contrived scheme to force Shelby into a duel without bringing Lady Zenoria's name into it. It was just the sort of thing she might have expected of William Powell, who had ever, save in the case of his infatuation for her cousin, been a man of infallible logic. "Just what sort of trap did you have in mind?" she felt compelled to ask in spite of her resolve to involve him no further in the matter of Annabel Steed and her sinister husband.

"The sort that places Steed in the unenviable position of being caught with the goods, so to speak," replied Lethridge. "The key elements would involve some sort of bait to draw him out, and our new friends, Leftenant Wilkers and his excisemen, to spring the trap. Naturally, it would be advisable that neither party realize they have been manipulated."

"Faith, and I thought you were proposing something difficult to achieve," Felicity said acerbically. "All we have to do is persuade some ship's captain to offer up his cargo for the taking, then find some way to dangle it before Steed without his knowing who is doing the dangling, not to mention maneuver Wilkers aboard in time to nab Steed in the act of cutting the ship's anchor. I wonder that I did not think of it."

"Sarcasm, my dear," drawled Lethridge, insufferably smiling, "does not do you credit. What you have failed to take into consideration is that we have the advantage of an ace up our sleeve. Your Captain Trent, if he is willing, may serve as both the hound and the hare."

"Your profusion of mixed metaphors notwithstanding, I'm afraid I haven't the least notion what you are proposing," Felicity retorted, failing to take note of his use of the inclusive "we" in his proposal, a circumstance that could no doubt be attributed to her sudden and acute awareness that she was standing alone in the dark with Will Powell and that the entire household was abed and fast asleep. She swallowed dryly and, turning sharply, made for the foyer and the candelabra left burning on the oak side table. "Surely you cannot mean to persuade Trent to offer up his schooner as the bait," she said over her shoulder. "I daresay Steed would see immediately through such a ruse."

"He would, indubitably," agreed Lethridge, who, having followed his hostess into the foyer, could not but note the manner in which the candlelight seemed to draw sparks of gold from Felicity's hair. "On the other hand, as the cohort of pirates, Trent would do admirably as the means of leading Steed to the mark. And as a wanted fugitive, Trent would be equally effective at drawing our local excisemen to the scene in the nick of time to perform a rescue. I should be greatly surprised if your enterprising Trent could not even name some ship's captain who, for a price, would be willing to play the part of the decoy. Certainly it would be worth the trouble of asking him."

It would indeed, Felicity was forced to agree, silently to herself, but only if Meggie could be found and rescued before the trap was sprung. Otherwise, with Steed either dead or in the custody of excisemen—or, worse, on the loose and fleeing capture—the girl might be lost forever. No, until Trent returned with word of Meggie, there was nothing to be done but wait and hope to keep Annabel's presence at Primrose Cottage a secret.

This was not something she wished to divulge to

William, however. Any day now, Bertie would be arriving with word of the outcome of the duel with Shelby. When her brother did come, Will must be free either to flee into exile or to return to the woman he loved. Either way, he must not be entangled in a dangerous plot which he would feel honorbound to see through to the end for a female for whom he felt only a brotherly affection. It simply was not to be thought of. Indeed, it would be far too humiliating.

"You may be sure I shall ask Trent," she said, reaching for the candelabra, "should I happen to hear from him again."

"Surely there is little doubt that you will hear from him," Will pointed out. "You did say, did you not, that you had engaged his services? I assume from that that you have paid him something for his trouble."

"Yes, I have paid him," Felicity admitted, heartily wishing this interview at an end. The last thing she wished to discuss was her admittedly loose arrangements with Captain Zachary Trent.

"Well, then," Will odiously persisted. "He must have given some indication when he would contact you."

"His final words to me were 'until the next time.' Does that tell you something?"

"It tells me that your Captain Trent is a loose cannon. Hardly the sort to stack up against a man like Steed."

"It tells me, on the other hand, that Trent is something of a law unto himself, one who comes and goes as he pleases. Certainly he is not the sort to be summoned, especially now that the excisemen are in pursuit of him. He did give me his word, however, and I cling to the hope that, for Annabel's sake, he will be true to it."

"Because he has a *tendre* for her."

"Because I believe he loves her."

"Then you would both be wrong, m'lady," pronounced a voice from the stairway.

Felicity and Will turned in unison to see Annabel, gazing down at them with huge, shadowed eyes from the head of the stairs.

"He did l-love me once," said the girl, gripping the banister with both hands as if that were all that held her upright. "A long time ago. Before—Steed. Now, he must surely despise me. He ruint himself for me, and I—I turned my back on him. I sold m'self to Steed. I sold my soul to the devil, and now I can never get it back again!"

Seven

Felicity watched in horror as Annabel's knees appeared to buckle beneath her. Will, however, after a single glance up at the young woman, was already on the move. Bounding up the stairs two at a time, he was in time to reach Annabel as, still gripping the rail, she sagged to her knees.

"Here now, my girl," he said, kneeling beside her. "We cannot have you toppling down the stairs, now, can we? Especially after your game performance before Leftenant Wilkers and his men."

"I beg yer pardon, m'lord," Annabel smiled wanly. "I fear I'm not m'self yet. I was never used to wilt like a pansy."

"It is little wonder if you are a trifle downpin, Annabel, dear," said Felicity, who had wasted little time in following Will up the stairs. "I feel a bit shaken myself. It is not every day that we have excisemen battering at our door."

"It wasn't that so much, m'lady. Though 'tis true I feared they would find me out," declared Annabel all in a rush. " 'Twas what you said about Zachary Trent and m'self. It brought it all crowdin' back again, how it was my fault his papa threw him out and disowned him on account of Zachary swore he loved me and would have me for his wife—me, Annabel Jones, that his mama took in to be a scullery maid when me mum passed on."

"Hush, my child. There is no need to explain to us," Felicity gently interrupted. "Whatever lies between you and Zachary Trent is your own affair."

Annabel lifted her eyes earnestly to Felicity. "But I want to tell you. You've been kind to me. I'd feel better if you knew the truth about Zachary Trent."

"Then tell your story, if you will," said Lethridge, "but not here. It will hold till we have got you to your room."

"His lordship is right, Annabel," Felicity was quick to add in Will's support. "You are like to catch a chill out here, as are we all. Here, let us help you."

With Lethridge and Felicity on either side to steady her, Annabel was soon established in her room, not in the attic but at the end of the hall a few doors down from Felicity's.

"You mustn't think bad of Zachary," Annabel said anxiously as Felicity tucked a quilt about her in the chair before the fireplace. "He'll keep his word. He's a good man and honest. An' if there are folks that talk bad on 'im, it's because he was used to be some 'un. His papa's Elias Trent, that owns the second largest brewery in Faversham."

"Elias Trent! Faith, I've heard of him," Felicity exclaimed softly, her glance meeting William's across Annabel. "He is a prosperous merchant, a man of some influence in the town of Faversham. I knew the boy came of a good family. I simply never thought to put the two together."

"Zachary's his only son," Annabel offered for their elucidation. "Or he was, till Mr. Trent cut 'im off without a farthing. Disowned him because his only son was never meant for the likes of Annabel Jones, a penniless orphan that never knew her father. And he was in the right of it. I was never good enough for Zachary Trent, nor never will be."

It was true enough, Felicity reflected practically. It would hardly be considered acceptable for the son of a well-to-do family, no matter how common its ancestry, to marry a scullery maid. Indeed, it was not, in the norm, to be thought of. These, however, were hardly normal circumstances. Zachary Trent, it seemed clear, had ruined himself for love of Annabel Steed.

"I cannot think that Captain Trent would agree with you," Felicity gently pointed out. "Is that why you settled for a man you could not possibly hold in affection? Certainly you deserve better than Josiah Steed, no matter what reasons you might have thought you had for marrying him."

"I *hate* Steed," declared Annabel, lifting her head with an unconscious air of defiance, which gave some hint of the fiery creature she had been before she had the misfortune to be wed to a man who had taken pleasure in breaking her spirit. "You're a kind lady, and fine. But you don't know the terrible thing I've done."

"Then suppose you tell me, and let me be the judge," said Felicity, squeezing the younger woman's hand. "You said Mrs. Trent took you into her household upon the death of your mother. How old were you, Annabel?"

"I was but nine when Mrs. Trent put me to work in the kitchens scrubbing the pots and the pans."

It had been an act of charity. It had, in fact, kept the child from a far worse existence in an orphanage for nameless waifs. Had the brewer's wife known then that Annabel would grow into a beauty to outshine the two daughters of the house, she would undoubtedly have banished the child to a workhouse long before Annabel caught the eye of young Zachary. As it was, Mrs. Trent had taken pity on the child. At twelve, Annabel was made an apprentice of sorts to Mrs. Trent's own abigail, with the intention of preparing her for the position of lady's maid when she was come of age.

Annabel had never dreamed to reach so high a position. Certainly she had never once given thought to attracting the notice of so grand a personage as the mistress's son.

Annabel was only thirteen when Zachary, two years older, was sent down from school for having drawn the cork of a Lord Fontesquieu in a bout of fisticuffs. It was to be said in defense of the merchant's son that, while Fontesquieu might have been his social better, the young peer was hardly his superior. Fontesquieu, seventeen and with a good thirty-pound advantage over the wiry upstart, had been engaged in the brutal intimidation of a younger boy from the lower forms. Not only had Zachary bloodied the lordling's nose, but he had done so with telling efficiency, which had earned him the sobriquet of "Dragon Slayer."

It was soon to prove apparent that the incident that had disgraced him at school was not an aberration of behavior but a distinct aspect of his character. Hardly had he arrived at home than Annabel, sent to the brewery on an errand for her mistress, was set upon by a pair of young ruffians intent on forcing their attentions on her. Zachary had descended on them seemingly from out of nowhere, his handy pair of fives up to defend the honor of a young, defenseless girl obviously of the lower orders.

"He didn't even know who I was," confessed Annabel, filled with wonder. "He just lit into them because I couldn't defend m'self. Only they were too much for him. While he was busy fighting off the one, the other came at him from behind with a knife. I didn't even think. How could I? He was the master's son, and I couldn't stand by and do nothing."

"No, I daresay you could not," agreed Lethridge, regarding Annabel with impenetrable eyes. "Instead, you grabbed the knife."

Annabel gave vent to a startled gasp. "How could you've known that, m'lord?"

Smiling gravely, Lethridge took Annabel's hands and turned them up. "I could not help but notice," he murmured, indicating the thin line of a scar across each palm. "It was bravely done, child, but rather foolhardy. You might have been seriously damaged."

"I wish the brute had cut me stick for me," declared Annabel, closing her hands into fists over the scars.

"Hush, child," Felicity scolded. "You do not mean that."

"But I do. It would have saved everyone a parcel of trouble. The blighters ran, and the next thing I knew, Zachary Trent was kneeling beside me, trying to stop the blood." She lifted tormented eyes to Felicity. " 'Twas the first time he ever really looked at me. Afterwards, he always made a point to speak kindly to me. I thought it was because of that day, because he felt obliged to me for doing what anybody would've done. I never dared to think it could ever be anything more. How could I? He was far above me touch. Mrs. Trent would've sent me away if she'd a glimmering what he was thinking—that one day I'd be his wife." Annabel's eyes clouded with anguish. "I wish she had known!" she cried. "I wish she had sent me away before ever he opened me eyes and me heart to what might have been. Before he flung all away for naught."

"But why for naught?" Felicity demanded, sensing some terrible truth as yet beyond her grasp. "If he loved you, then why—?"

She was silenced by Will's hand coming to rest on her shoulder.

Annabel's fingers twisted in the coverlet. "I was with child," she said. "Steed's child. There was never any other choice for me. Mr. Trent paid Steed to make an honest woman of me."

"Woman!" Felicity exclaimed to Will several minutes later in the hallway. "She could not have been above fifteen. Steed took advantage of her. There can be no other explanation for it. And Elias Trent paid to make certain she could never marry Zachary."

"You can hardly blame Trent," observed Will. "Just or not, you will admit it is the way of the world. To Trent's credit, he did insure Annabel's child would not be a nameless bastard."

"Better a nameless bastard than the acknowledged offspring of a man who would sell his own flesh and blood into slavery," Felicity declared passionately. "That is the threat that Steed held over Annabel's head whenever she threatened to . . ."

"Leave him?" supplied Will when Felicity suddenly broke off with the realization of what she had blurted. "Is that why she is grieving? The devil, Felicity. Why did you think it necessary to keep that pertinent piece of the puzzle from me? Steed has Annabel's child, and neither of you knows where he is keeping it, or even if it is still alive and well."

"She is not an 'it,' " Felicity snapped, furious with herself and her unruly tongue. "Her name is Meggie, and she is only four years old. And yes, Steed has her,

if he has not sold her in London as he has sworn he
will do."

"If he has, we will find her and bring her back,"
Will promised in a voice that sent shivers down Felicity's back. "In the meantime, I suggest we see what
we can do to locate Captain Trent. The sooner we
lay our trap for Mr. Steed, the better."

"But that is the last thing we must do," Felicity
exclaimed in sudden alarm. "Until we have Meggie
safe, we dare not antagonize Steed further. There is
no telling what Steed might do to Meggie. Surely you
must see that. Trent is searching for the child. He
will find her, I am sure of it. And then we shall deal
with Mr. Steed. Promise me you will do nothing until
then, Will."

Lethridge, far from convinced of the advisability
of putting the matter off indefinitely, especially in the
wake of their unexpected visit by excisemen,
schooled his features to reveal nothing of his doubts.
"You have my word I shall be ruled by you in this so
long as you swear you are keeping nothing else from
me, Felicity. I should like to believe that you trust me
enough not to hide the truth from me."

Hide the truth from him, egad! thought Felicity,
hard put not to give into a groan. Practically everything she had told him from the moment he had
regained consciousness had been designed to keep
the truth from him. Nor dared she rectify that regret-
table set of circumstances now, before he had got his
memory back. Until he was himself again, he was
hardly in any case to deal with the repercussions of
his duel with Shelby, she firmly reminded herself,
though somehow it had a hollow ring to it. The truth,
were she to be honest with herself, was she had not
the courage to betray herself to him, not now, when
he was looking at her with those penetrating blue

eyes that had the disconcerting power to utterly disrupt her normally quite lucid thought processes. She simply *could* not bear the thought of seeing those eyes grow suddenly cold and opaque with contempt. Especially not now, when her nerves were positively frayed in the wake of one of the most trying days of her life. Really, it would be too much to ask of her.

"Pray do not be ridiculous, Will," she said instead, not quite able to bring herself to meet his gaze as she prepared to add to her list of falsehoods. "You know everything there is to know about Annabel's unfortunate situation. What could I possibly be keeping from you?"

Will smiled wryly, keenly aware that she was evading the subject. "I daresay you would be in a better position than I to answer that particular question, Cousin."

Felicity perceptibly flinched at his use of the term of kinship. Faith, if she did not know better, she might think Lethridge was deliberately baiting her. But that was absurd. There really was nothing in what he had said to lend credence to such a suspicion. No doubt it was only that she was weary to distraction. "Then no doubt I give you my promise," she said lightly, and turned away that he might not read the deceit that she knew must be writ plain on her face. "And now, if you don't mind, I believe I should like nothing more than to go to bed. And little wonder. If I am not mistaken, that is the sun coming up."

It was true, Will realized. The gloom of the hallway had indeed lightened perceptibly, giving unmistakable evidence that he had spent nearly the entire night in the company of Felicity Talbot. A pity it had had to be wasted on excisemen and an intrigue that promised in future to be an unavoidable distraction from the more pertinent business of overcoming Felicity's distrust of him, he reflected. He smiled sardonically to himself, all too cognizant of the fact that she had been deliberately vague in her "promise" to him. Not that it signified. It had been a promise of sorts, and he meant to hold her to it.

"You are right, of course," he said, reaching to open the door to her rooms for her. "You get some sleep. There will be time enough to deal with Steed."

"Yes, I am sure of it." Turning, Felicity made as if to enter her room. "Will," she said, suddenly coming about again. "I . . ."

She stopped, hardly knowing what she had been about to say. He appeared suddenly so comfortingly tall and broad-shouldered, standing there before her. She was overcome with a most unsettling urge to lay her cheek against his chest and feel his arms close around her. But that was absurd. To do any such thing would be quite utterly disastrous, not only to her resolve not to take advantage of his memory loss, but to her future well-being as well. If ever he were to take her in his arms, she was quite certain she would never be able to bear to lose him. Every instinct of self-preservation cried out against such a notion.

"Felicity?" William gently prodded. "What is it?"

"N-nothing," answered Felicity, shaking her head. "I wish only to thank you again for what you did tonight for—for Annabel. You did not have to, you know."

"Gammon," William unequivocally retorted. "Now you are talking flummery, my girl."

"I am not, Will, and you know it," Felicity protested. "Had you been in the least sensible, you would not have set yourself up against men who were only doing their duty. You could have gotten into a

We'd Like to Invite You to Subscribe to Zebra's Regency Romance Book Club an Give You a Gift of 4 Free Books as Your Introduction! (Worth $19.96!)

If you're a Regency lover, imagine the joy of getting **4 FREI Zebra Regency Romances** and then the chance to have th lovely stories delivered to your home each month at the lowest prices available! Well, that's our offer to you and here's how you benefit by becoming a Regency Romance subscriber:

- **4 FREE** Introductory Regency Romances are delivered to your doors

- **4 BRAND NEW** Regencies are then delivered each month (usually befc they're available in bookstores)

- Subscribers save almost $4.00 every month

- Home delivery is always **FREE**

- You also receive a **FREE** monthly newsletter, which features author profiles, discounts, subscriber benefits, book previews and more

- No risks or obligations...in other words, you can cancel whenever yc wish with no questions asked

Join the thousands of readers who enjoy the savings and convenience offered to Regency Romance subscribers. After your initial introductory shipment, you receive 4 brand-new Zebra Regency Romances each month to examine for 10 days Then, if you decide to keep the books, you'll pay the preferrec subscriber's price of just $4.00 per title. That's only $16.00 for all 4 books and there's never an extra charge for shipping and handling.

It's a no-lose proposition, so return the FREE BOOK CERTIFICATE today!

Say Yes to 4 Free Books!

Complete and return the order card to receive this $19.96 value, ABSOLUTELY FREE!

If the certificate is missing below, write to:
Zebra Home Subscription Service, Inc.,
P.O. Box 5214, Clifton, New Jersey 07015-5214
or call TOLL-FREE 1-888-345-BOOK
Visit our website at www.kensingtonbooks.com.

FREE BOOK CERTIFICATE

YES! Please rush me 4 Zebra Regency Romances without cost or obligation. I understand that each month thereafter I will be able to preview 4 brand-new Regency Romances FREE for 10 days. Then, if I should decide to keep them, I will pay the money-saving preferred subscriber's price of just $16.00 for all 4...that's a savings of almost $4 off the publisher's price with no additional charge for shipping and handling. I may return any shipment within 10 days and owe nothing, and I may cancel this subscription at any time. My 4 FREE books will be mine to keep in any case.

Name _____

Address _____ Apt. _____

City _____ State _____ Zip _____

Telephone ( ) _____

Signature _____
(If under 18, parent or guardian must sign.)   RN070A

Terms and prices subject to change. Orders subject to acceptance by Zebra Home Subscription Service, Inc. Offer valid in U.S. only.

REGENCY ROMANCE BOOK CLUB
Zebra Home Subscription Service, Inc.
P.O. Box 5214
Clifton NJ 07015-5214

PLACE
STAMP
HERE

deal of trouble for what you did, and it would have
been all my fault."

"It would have been no such thing, Felicity. You
are clearly befuddled from lack of sleep if you think
I should stand by and do nothing. And even more
so if you think for one moment I should have done
it for Annabel."

To her dismay, Felicity flushed to the roots of her
hair at the unmistakable implications of that telling
speech.

"Quite so, my dear," murmured William, an almost
undetectable twitch at the corner of his lips. "And
now, enough said on the subject. Off to bed with you,
Miss Talbot. I shall instruct the servants you are not
to be disturbed until well after noon."

Gently he impelled Felicity into the room and
firmly closed the door behind her. Then turning on
his heel, he strode purposefully down the hall to his
own quarters.

He had a great deal to do before his angel awakened from her much-needed rest, and little time in
which to accomplish it.

In the days that followed Steed's unsuccessful attempt to flush his errant wife out of her haven of
safety, Felicity could not but be pleased to see
Lethridge demonstrate a remarkable physical recovery. Despite his continued inability to recall his past,
he gained dramatically in strength until he was to all
outward appearances the William Powell of old.

There was one dramatic difference, however, that
could not but have a disquieting effect on Felicity's
state of mind. Where before Lethridge's adverse encounter with a pistol ball, he had demonstrated a
careless affection toward her that had been singularly

lacking in anything that might remotely have been construed as an amorous attraction, he now manifested every sign of a man on the hunt.

It was not that he was conspicuous in his pursuit of her. Showering her with flowers or composing poetic lines ascribing her a position as the goddess of his affections was hardly in his style. Nor was it his practice to assail her with flattery, to impose his constant presence on her, or to in any overt fashion seek to impress her as a viable candidate for her affections. He was far too astute not to have known that, had he attempted anything of so blatant a nature, she would not have hesitated immediately to call him to task for it.

No, his was a far more subtle campaign, Felicity reflected ruefully one morning as she stared out the withdrawing room window over the cherry orchard. His was a campaign that seemed calculated to overwhelm her defenses with innumerable small acts of thoughtfulness.

The breakfast tray bearing a small posy of lilacs that she had found waiting for her when she awakened the afternoon following the event of Leftenant Wilkers's unheralded visit had been merely a foreshadowing of what was to come, she mused, smiling wryly to herself. After that, and more importantly, there had been the gift of William's silence on the matter of Annabel and Steed, something that had taken her quite unawares. Indeed, she had been dreading going downstairs to what she had fully considered an inevitable interrogation on the subject, not to mention an anticipated masculine disapprobation for what her father and brothers would have called her woman's naiveté in worldly matters. *They* would never have countenanced her work to better the existence of destitute women. How much less must they have approved of her effort on behalf of Annabel Steed, especially in light of the complications that had accrued from it! While she had fully expected just such a male reaction from Lethridge, who might have been, because of his own unwitting involvement, somewhat justified in questioning her actions, she had been met with a constraint that could only win her everlasting gratitude.

Nor had that been all to batter at the barriers she had erected about her all too vulnerable heart. Perhaps most devastating of all had been the event of three days ago. She had been called out to see a Mrs. Gosset, a widow with four children, whom Felicity had helped to establish as a seamstress for the wives of the local gentry. Electing to walk the half mile to the woman's cottage in order to enjoy some time to herself, she had, upon her return, been caught in a sudden downpour. She had been drenched to the bone, and, worse, the road had been transformed almost instantly into a hasty pudding. It was little wonder that she had been overjoyed to behold the approach of the carriage. She had also been more than a little surprised at the skill with which Huggins appeared to be handling the ribbons in what could only be described as adverse conditions. But then, Huggins, whom she retained out of sympathy for the sacrifices that had been demanded of him in the recent wars against the French tyrant, had not been driving.

Felicity could only be amazed at her failure to guess at once who was at the reins. It could, after all, only have been a top-of-the-trees sawyer, a man noted for his ability to drive complete to a shade even in the most extreme circumstances, a man who had once taken a wager to race his prize bays from Thirsk to Newcastle in under two and a half hours and had handily won.

For once, she could only be grateful to find herself looking up into William Powell's stern features and to thrill to the strength of his hand closing about her own small member as wordlessly he pulled her into the hooded shelter of the carriage. The enveloping warmth of the fur lap rug he flung over her had afforded exquisite relief even in her sodden state. Before turning the horse with consummate skill, he had thrust a flask of brandy into her hand.

"Drink," he ordered curtly. "You are shivering from cold."

Somehow a single glance up into eyes that shone with a sardonic glint was enough to still the instinctive protest that leaped to her lips. The devil, she fumed. It was obvious he fully expected an argument and was no doubt bored at the prospect of pointing out the benefits to be accrued from the stimulant, especially as a lengthy debate was clearly inadvisable with the carriage horse standing in the rain. It was time he was made to realize that, far from being a featherheaded female, she was of a wholly practical disposition. Rebelliously, she threw back her head and tipped the flask.

It was all she could do not to choke as she unwittingly downed a hefty swallow of the fiery liquid, which had the effect of flushing her face a livid red and leaving her gasping for air. Still, she could only be grateful a moment later to feel the heat of the brandy explore her belly. The soporific effect was immediate and wholly irresistible. Indeed, she was not in the least aware how she came suddenly to be resting with her head against Lethridge's shoulder, or how it was that, once she did realize it, she could not summon the smallest inclination to alter her position. Worse, she had been keenly aware of a feeling of disappointment when the carriage had pulled up before the house, signaling the end of her adventure!

Only it had not been the end. Hardly had Huggins appeared to drive the carriage to the stables than she had found herself lifted from her seat and borne in William's arms into the house. Nor had he been satisfied merely to have delivered her safely home. Ignoring her protestations that she was perfectly capable of taking herself to her room, he had crossed the foyer with long, purposeful strides and proceeded to carry her up the stairs. No doubt Sutton, her abigail, had been more than a little startled to see Viscount Lethridge burst into her mistress's chambers with Lady Felicity clasped in his arms. Certainly, the rest of the household had demonstrated a tendency to gaping jaws at the sight, a condition that had instantly given way before the viscount's terse command to cease standing idly about and to fetch Lady Felicity a bath and a tray of hot soup at once. The alacrity with which his orders were carried out Felicity could only attribute to her clearly disreputable appearance.

Her smart sealskin hat was a sodden mass, and her sleeveless olive green habit shirt, trimmed in swansdown and worn over a white muslin walking dress, made quite transparent by the wetting, was all that prevented her from being rendered totally indecent in their eyes. William Powell, however, appeared not even to look as he set Felicity on her feet before the fire.

"See to your mistress, girl," commanded her rescuer, spinning on his heel and making a discreet withdrawal. "I shall not expect to see you before breakfast, Felicity," trailed over one indecently broad shoulder; and then he was gone before she could do so much as thank him for all his trouble.

The incident still fresh in her mind, Felicity blushed. Faith, she had been ever so mortified at the thought of having to face him the next day with the knowledge that he had seen far more of her than was in any way acceptable, or that, far worse, she had derived no little pleasure, no matter how unwittingly, from being carried in his arms. She had not taken into account, however, William Powell.

Upon awakening to the memory of what awaited her, she had been sorely tempted to fling the covers over her head and keep to her bed. Only the knowledge that nothing would be served by playing the coward had at last shamed her into rising and calling her abigail to dress her. Still, her descent to the breakfast room had been accomplished with a deal of dread. In spite of the cheerful mask she had donned for the occasion, she was heartily wishing her rescuer, if not precisely to the devil, then at least somewhere removed from the immediate vicinity of the breakfast nook.

She might have saved herself a deal of worry over nothing. At her entrance, Lethridge, glancing up from reading the weekly paper, which Felicity had delivered to the cottage from Faversham, rose unaffectedly to his feet.

"My dear Felicity, good morning. How charming you look. Shall I fill a plate for you? I do not hesitate to recommend the turbot. Or perhaps you would prefer the scrambled eggs?"

"No, thank you," Felicity replied hastily, and stemmed a shudder at the very notion of fish or eggs for breakfast that morning. "Pray go on with your reading. I am perfectly capable of serving myself."

"But of course you are," agreed William, smiling easily. "Perhaps you would care for a section of the paper. You might find it interesting to note the

American steam vessel *Savannah* is to attempt a crossing of the Atlantic from New York to Liverpool. The
Americans claim she will manage it in less than a
month. I wonder, have I ever been involved in sailing?
Somehow the Americans' boast strikes me as rather
overconfident."

"As a matter of fact, I believe you have never sailed,
William." Felicity, sitting down with her meager
breakfast of coffee and buttered toast, accepted a section of the newspaper detailing the proposed voyage
of the *Savannah*. "On the other hand, you very likely
have not forgot your lessons in geography. The un-
dertaking would be a very notable achievement if the
Americans can pull it off. The Atlantic is a vast ocean,
after all."

The rest of the meal had been passed in a discussion of incidents of steam navigation, which had in-
cluded the five steam vessels plying Scottish waters
and John Dodd's introduction of a steamboat to the
Thames some three years previously. This had in turn
led to a discourse on the manner in which William
was wont to spend his time in running his papa's
estates and breeding and racing prime bits of cattle.
It was not until the hall clock chimed the hour of ten
that Felicity was made aware that she had been con-
versing with William quite comfortably for all of an
hour and ten minutes without a single mention having been made of the previous afternoon's embar-
rassing, not to mention compromising, events. But
then, she did not doubt that was just as William had
intended.

How very thoughtful he was, to be sure. And kind
and generous, not to mention patient and forbearing. Indeed, *infuriatingly* patient and forbearing, she
thought, flinging herself away from the window. And
noble-hearted and obstinate, too. One should not

forget *those* aspects of his character, especially where Zenoria was concerned. Certainly, he had been patient, forbearing, noble-hearted, *and* obstinate in his pursuit of the feckless blond beauty, who thus far had led him a merry chase. Felicity had known since the age of ten that William Powell was everything she herself had ever wanted in a man. He, however, had had to have a pistol ball crease his skull to even realize she was a woman, a woman, moreover, who was not all that bad to look upon. And now what must he do but display every manifestation of a man intent upon breaking down her reserve through kindness.

Really it was too much. Indeed, she did not see how she could find the will to resist this new turn of events. The previous day she had resorted to one pretext after another, from begging off from their morning walk in order to go over the week's menus with Cook to pleading a headache at dinner and having a tray sent up to her room, to avoid being alone with him. Obviously, she could not avoid him forever. If she had the least sense of self-preservation, she would tell him everything and bring the farce to an end.

Suddenly she straightened, her eyes glinting gold sparks of determination. But that was precisely what she *would* do. She would tell him the whole miserable truth and be done with it. Furthermore, she would do it today, this very morning. After all, he had his strength back. He was perfectly capable of taking care of himself. There really was no reason to prolong the charade for so much as a day or even an hour. Indeed, it came to her with telling clarity that to do so would serve only to make her deceit all the more inexcusable.

The light, thrilling step in the hall brought Felicity suddenly around, her heart behaving in a most reprehensible manner beneath her breast. Indeed, it was all she could do not to press a hand over that all too revealing organ as Lethridge's tall figure loomed in the doorway.

"Good, you are here," pronounced that worthy, seeming to fill the room with his presence. "I was hoping you would be."

"Were you?" Felicity answered, summoning a smile that felt tight against her teeth. "What a coincidence. As it happens, I have been hoping to see you this morning, too."

Though a glint flickered beneath the heavily drooping eyelids, the handsome features did not betray by so much as the leap of a muscle that Lethridge had come sharply to attention at that unexpected announcement. "You cannot know how happy I am to hear it," he answered smoothly. "I had begun to think of late you were grown weary of my company."

"Pray don't be absurd, Will Powell," exclaimed Felicity, rather more sharply than she had intended. "You know very well I should never grow tired of your company."

"No doubt you relieve my mind," William observed dryly, noting the sparks in her eyes. "You had something else in mind then, one must presume. You have not, I trust, had word from the elusive Captain Trent, have you?"

"Trent?" Felicity, who had been occupied with trying to formulate in her mind the words to tell Lethridge the truth about how he came to be at Primrose Cottage, impatiently shook her head at that irrelevance. "No, no. Nothing. No doubt Trent has taken himself off to some dark, dreadful place in pursuit of knowledge of Mr. Steed's loathsome deeds."

"I see," murmured Will, closely studying his companion's air of distraction. "It is not Trent, then, whom I must thank for this intriguing dialogue." It

was all Felicity could do to hold her ground as
Lethridge loomed suddenly over her. Indeed, she
had the curious sensation of having been rendered
quite powerless to move as the side of his index finger
came under her chin and gently tilted her head back
so that she must look at him. A frown etched itself
between his eyebrows. "Something, however, is troubling you. Annabel has not taken it into her head to
do something foolish, has she?"

Felicity, quite distracted by his nearness, not to
mention the feather-light brush of his thumb over
her cheek, felt the foundations of her resolve sustain
a distinct crack. Really it was too much to expect her
to unveil the truth about her lies and manipulations,
when she was being assailed by the mingled masculine scents of shaving soap, clean linen, and tobacco.

"No. Annabel is quite safe in her room," she managed, keenly aware that the sensible thing to do was
to put some distance between herself and William
before she was quite lost to all sense of rationality.
Unfortunately, she was held in the sway of emotions
that were far stronger than that fading voice of reason.

"Excellent. No doubt I am glad to hear it," observed William with only a hint of dryness. "However,
if this is to be a guessing game, I fear I shall soon
run out of possibilities. You are not coming down
with something, are you?"

Before Felicity could find the wit to assure him
that, far from taking a cold or the ague or anything
else, she had never been sick a day in her life, she
was subjected to the disturbing sensation of a masculine palm pressed gently against her cheek and then
her forehead. "Your cheeks are quite flushed, and I
should say your pulse is somewhat elevated, but your
skin is cool to the touch."

Egad, thought Felicity, who did indeed feel peculiarly as if she were suffering all the symptoms of one on the verge of a sharp decline. The impossible man had not the smallest notion of what he was doing to her! "I assure you I am quite well, thank you," she submitted in a voice that came out sounding, absurdly, like a croak.

William's eyebrows shot up in patent disbelief.

Felicity felt herself blush even redder than before, if that were possible. "Pray do not look at me like that," she blurted in mounting exasperation. "You need not concern yourself with my health. I am fine." At last, through sheer desperation she made as if to pull away. "At any rate, you may be certain that is not what I wished to discuss with you."

"No, I did not suppose that it was," conceded William, who could not but think his impossible angel was positively adorable whenever she was in the least flustered. No doubt it was irresistible impulse—or the overpowering suspicion that she was not so averse to his attentions as she pretended—that compelled him to move after her. "You are far too independent, stubborn, and proud ever to admit you are not feeling quite the thing."

"But I am *not*—" Felicity blurted, backing another step in alarm at suddenly and correctly interpreting his intentions.

Whatever it was that she was not, however, she was not allowed to say.

William, pulling her without warning into his arms, bent his head and covered her mouth with his.

Unlike his first kiss, this was no fleeting brush of the lips. No doubt the fact that he kissed her fully and unrestrainedly could be attributed to his having been forced for the past several days to keep just such inclinations under a tight rein. Having been given, only three days before, to glimpse his darling Felicity in what could only be described as Revealing Circumstances had not but had a debilitating effect on his normally iron resolve. But then, to find her apparently anxiously awaiting his appearance in the withdrawing room in what his every instinct warned was her intent to inform him that, as he had regained his strength, it was prudent to send him on his way, he had found himself in somewhat desperate straits. The last thing he could wish at this time was to be separated from the woman who was not only entangled in a sinister coil, but who was, he had not a doubt, the key to his future happiness.

To avert that undesired end, he had flung caution to the wind with what gave every evidence of being most rewarding results.

Felicity, stiffening in protest one moment, had the next found her arms stealing up around William's neck as if they had a will of their own. Indeed, it seemed that more than her arms demonstrated a total disregard for the voice that cried out against this renewed assault on her already beleaguered sensibilities. Not only did her knees threaten to buckle beneath her, but she was given to experience in the pit of her stomach a peculiar melting sensation that spread rapidly outward to her extremities. In addition, her head was set to reeling, scattering her thoughts and leaving her prey to emotions over which she seemed to have lost all control.

When William at last released her, she felt dazed and disoriented. Indeed, she could not for the life of her recall what had precipitated this unexpected turn of circumstances. She felt only a delicious sort of languor and a deep reluctance to remove herself from the warmth of William's arms.

With a feeling of bemused wonder, she watched the corner of William's lips curve slowly upward.

"When you smile like that," she said in a whimsical voice, "you look just as you did at seventeen, the first time you came home with Bertie. I thought you were the handsomest creature I had ever seen."

"No, did you?" Gently Will brushed a stray lock of hair from her forehead.

"You know very well I did. I followed you around like a hopelessly lost puppy. Which is just how you have treated me ever since."

"As it happens, I am quite fond of puppies. On the other hand, I do not make it a habit to kiss them. In case you have failed to realize it, my darling girl, I do not see you in the light of a puppy, hopelessly lost or otherwise."

"Oh, but you will," said Felicity, the spell abruptly and irrevocably broken. "I daresay you will see me in a far worse light when I tell you—"

"Enough, Mrs. Morseby! Pray do not *tell* me my cousin is not home to callers. I know she is here somewhere, and I *will* see her. How *dare* you stand in my way!"

The sudden shrill commotion outside in the foyer served quite effectively to cut Felicity off from what she had been about to say. Indeed, having instantly recognized the voice of impending doom, she forgot everything but the engulfing queasy sensation in the pit of her stomach.

"Good God!" she exclaimed, her face going pale. "Zenoria!"

Eight

Felicity, wishing her uninvited caller without remorse to the devil, carefully closed the withdrawing room door behind her. She could only hope William would be ruled by her hastily uttered plea to trust her in a matter that was not only delicate but must be fraught with dire consequences were Lady Zenoria Eppington, her cousin, to discover her in Viscount Lethridge's presence.

"I shall explain everything to you when I have seen her on her way," Felicity had promised, her eyes pleading with him to leave unvoiced the myriad questions writ plain on his face. "I beg you will remain unseen until I have dealt with this, Will. I promise I shall never ask anything else of you again."

Without waiting for an answer, she had fled the room. She hardly dared to believe she had cleared that first hurtle so easily. Indeed, she was still half expecting Will to come bolting out the door after her—or into the beautiful Zenoria's arms, perhaps, she amended ironically to herself. There was, after all, every chance that the sudden appearance of Lady Zenoria at Primrose Cottage would be the very thing to jar Will's memory. If, on the other hand, even the shock of hearing the name and the voice of the woman he had loved enough to risk his life and reputation for did not bring his memory back, Felicity had no intention of allowing her kinswoman the opportunity to manipulate his infirmity to her own ends. It was one thing to stand by and witness Viscount Lethridge make a fool of himself when he had all his faculties about him. It was quite another to willingly turn an amnesiac William Powell over to the tender ministrations of an unscrupulous female. Indeed, Felicity shuddered at the dire possibilities inherent in such an issue.

At last, drawing a deep, steadying breath, she strode purposefully forward to greet her cousin, who was at that moment threatening Mrs. Morseby with summary dismissal for the housekeeper's refusal to step aside and let Lady Zenoria search the premises at once.

"It is all right, Hannah," Felicity announced, noting that the blond beauty trying to force her way past an immovable Hannah presented, despite her beehive bonnet with the draping plume, her green Spanish pelisse of shot sarcenet trimmed with white Egyptian crepe and antique cuffs, and her green kid gloves and matching slippers, something less than her usual immaculate appearance. There was about the fashion plate a distinct air of a woman at the thin edge of her control, which could not but pique Felicity's curiosity more than a little. "You may admit Lady Zenoria, Hannah. Kindly see that Miss Hennesey is given some refreshment. My cousin and I shall have tea in the solarium. I daresay Lady Zenoria is famished after her journey."

"Gracious, as always, Cousin Felicity," observed Lady Zenoria, flinging contemptuously past the dourfaced housekeeper, Miss Hennesey, her lady's maid and companion, following respectfully in her mistress's wake. "A pity one cannot say the same for the help you keep," she added, removing her gloves and pelisse and thrusting them at Mrs. Morseby, who accepted them with all the aplomb of a trusted retainer of long standing.

"I left instructions I was not to be disturbed," replied Felicity, dismissing the housekeeper with a nod. "Hannah was only doing precisely as she had ought. No doubt you will pardon my curiosity, Zenoria. I cannot help but wonder what should have brought you all the way to Kent in the middle of the Season. Somehow I cannot think it was due to a sudden fondness for my company."

"And why should it not, dearest cousin?" Zenoria, flinging a cursory glance around at her tasteful, if unpretentious, environs, gave vent to a distinct sniff. "Faith, Felicity, how can you bury yourself in the country—and in such primitive surrounds—when you could be in residence at Brierly Lodge in Notting Hill Square?"

"As it happens, I prefer the country." Felicity, leading the way into the solarium, crossed directly to the table where earlier she had been involved in repotting geraniums. "The peace and serenity," she added, slipping on her work gloves and taking up where she had left off, "suit my temperament."

"Faith, what a hubble-bubble," declared Zenoria, wholly immune to the colorful profusion of tulips, lilies, purple asters, yellow primroses, Queen Anne's lace, and blushing poppies that transformed the solarium into a perfumed garden of visual delight. "Only *you* would choose Primrose Cottage in Kent over The Dukeries in Kensington, especially with the duke and duchess away. Or perhaps you are unaware they have taken themselves off on a walking tour of Scotland."

"Mama wrote to say they might do some such

thing. It is something the duke has wished to do for some time."

"You knew, and you did not come down for the Season? Faith, Felicity, were I you, I should not be wasting away in the barren fastness of Kent, when I could be the envy of the *ton* hosting gala events in Brierly Lodge."

"Really, Zenoria, I wish you will not be absurd. I should cut a pretty figure, entertaining in my father's house with my parents away. Were I to do anything so patently improper, I should not be the envy of the *ton*, but the talk of the Town."

"I daresay even that would be better than being a nobody in Kent," declared Zenoria, flinging herself down on a rattan settee, only to spring immediately up again as if she could not contain the nervous store of energy that appeared to be driving her. "The trouble with you, Felicity, is that you have no sense of adventure. Where should I be had I done the proper thing? I should be Viscountess Lethridge now, very likely with one brat mewling at my knee and another on the way. That is, you will admit, the predominant feature of the Powell clan. They are all prodigious breeders."

"They are, I hope you will agree, a deal more than that," Felicity observed, digging the trowel into the potting soil with a sudden vengeance. "The Powell sisters, after all, are married to four of the most influential men in England. Furthermore, I daresay there are not three more respected gentlemen to be found anywhere in the country than the Powell brothers. Being married to Bancroft's heir apparent is hardly something to sneeze at."

"No, but it would be prodigiously dull. Do you know that Lethridge actually supposed I should *relish* living in the North Yorks with his mama and papa? Can you imagine that?"

"I daresay in your case I cannot," agreed Felicity, who obviously knew her cousin a deal better than Lethridge ever had and who, further, could imagine nothing she would like better for herself than to reside at Greensward as daughter-in-law to the earl and his countess. "Did you tell him that?"

"Heavens, no. What do you take me for?" demanded Zenoria with a tinkling laugh that had the unfortunate quality of grating on Felicity's nerves. "When will you ever learn, Cousin, that a lady does not tell a gentleman the plain truth? Why, it is little wonder you have a noticeable lack of admirers if that is the way you conduct yourself with gentlemen."

"Dare I to correct a misconception, Cousin?" retorted Felicity, coming near to driving the trowel through the bottom of the ceramic pot in her fervor. "I have had the honor to receive four advantageous offers of marriage."

"And I have turned down so many, I no longer can keep count. What has that to say to the matter?"

"Nothing, it would seem," conceded Felicity, who was mentally kicking herself for having sunk so low as to boast about her marriage offers. Egad, it was outside of enough!

"Precisely," Zenoria preened. "It is easy enough to bring a gentleman up to scratch. The trick is to turn him down in such a manner as to keep him interested."

"Keep him dangling, you mean," Felicity flatly amended. Slamming the trowel down on the table top, she fairly snatched up the innocent geranium waiting to be transplanted.

"Well, of course, though I should never put it so crudely. A woman never knows, after all, when a man might be useful." Felicity sardonically noted that Zenoria, glancing down at the manicured fingernails of one slender white hand, appeared at last to be homing in on her purpose in coming. "I suppose you have heard the latest *on dit* from Town about Lethridge."

Felicity only just managed not to rip the poor, inoffensive plant from its depleted soil. "No," she replied, amazed that she could sound so indifferent when in reality she was fairly seething inside with resentment. "How should I? I haven't been to Town for months."

"No, of course you have not. Silly of me to suppose you had. You have not, then, heard from Bertram."

"I believe I said I have not." Settling the roots in the new pot, Felicity pressed the soil down around them with her gloved fingers. "Faith, do not tell me Bertie has engaged in some insane new wager with Lethridge. If he has undertaken to put his grays up against Lethridge's bays, His Grace will most assuredly withhold his allowance for the entire next quarter."

"No, no, it is nothing like that." Zenoria gave an impatient wave of the hand. "As it happens, Lethridge has engaged in a duel, with Bertram as one of his seconds."

"A duel. Good God, with whom?"

"With the Marquess of Shelby. Silly, is it not?" Zenoria cast Felicity a sidelong glance that was plainly assessing. "I should never have expected anything so devilishly rash from Lethridge. It is said Shelby is lingering close to death's door."

"And Lethridge?" Felicity turned deliberately to face her cousin. "How does *he* fare?"

Zenoria flung up her hands in what seemed the first indication of real feeling. "That is just it. No one knows. I have heard the Duchess of Lathrop is asking about him everywhere. I have it from Mr. Grantham that Lethridge was most certainly wounded, but not even he could tell me how seriously. I was hoping you might have heard something. The devil, Felicity. You *must* know something! I have been frantic with worry."

"No, *have* you?" queried Felicity, greatly taken aback at her cousin's obvious distress. Indeed, she was given to suffer a pang of guilt at the possibility that she might have gravely misjudged Lady Zenoria. It was to be a short-lived emotion. "Strange, all these years Lethridge has pursued you, I had not thought you cared a whit for him."

"Care for him!" Zenoria flung out in a magnificent pique. "A pox on Lethridge! This is all his doing. If Shelby by some miracle should live, I shall be ruined."

Faith, thought Felicity, clenching her hands into fists at her sides. She might have known Zenoria was thinking only of herself. "Ruined? How?" she demanded, mystified nonetheless. "I cannot believe Lethridge would be so remiss as to drag your name into it."

"My name?" Zenoria gave a bitter laugh. "No, but then, he did not have to bring my name into it. Everyone knows why he challenged Shelby. That is hardly to the point, dearest cousin. There are letters. Lethridge promised he would get them back for me. Five hundred pounds to buy them back. Felicity, I ask you, was that too much to ask of him?"

Felicity stared at her kinswoman aghast. "Five hundred pounds? Are you mad, Zenoria?"

"No, but I soon shall be. My father, the earl, will not hesitate to cast me to the wolves if he hears of this, or, worse, sends me to my Aunt Hortense in the south of Cornwall. Good God, Cornwall! I should rather die than be forced to live in that beastly place. Indeed, I should even prefer to marry Lethridge, perish the thought. At any rate, I daresay I shall have no choice but to marry him, which is undoubtedly why he initiated that stupid duel. He would have me for his wife. Never mind that I loathe the thought of serving as a broodmare to bear his precious heir, or any other man's, for that matter."

Stunned at that final, unexpected revelation, Felicity stared at her cousin as if seeing her clearly for the first time in her life. "Not bear his heir? And yet you would ask him to purchase your freedom for a king's ransom. And if Shelby dies? What then? Shall you go into exile with the man who has ruined his life for you?"

"Pray don't be such a gaby, Felicity." With a shrug, Zenoria settled herself prettily on the settee. "If Shelby dies, I shall undoubtedly go on as I always have, and Lethridge may go to the devil for all I care. This is all his fault. Shelby, however, will not die," she added tragically. "I should never be so fortunate. Mr. Grantham believes the marquess has taken a turn for the better. Can you believe it? You do see that is why I must find Lethridge."

"You may be sure that I see all too clearly," said Felicity, marveling that she had not yet scratched her cousin's eyes out. "You are afraid that Lethridge has perished from his wound, are you not? And then what will you do? Poor dear Zenoria. The whole world must feel sorry for you, never mind that you have brought scandal, ruin, possibly even death to a man whose only fault was in loving you. You need not come to me for help or consolation, Cousin. It is my devoutest wish you will receive precisely what you deserve when all is said and done."

Zenoria, who had gone from hot to cold during

that telling assessment of her character, rose, white-faced and shaking with outrage, from the settee.

"You do have a gift for plain speaking, do you not?" she pronounced in scathing accents. "Sweet Felicity. I always thought butter would not melt in your mouth. But then, I failed to see the obvious, did I not? You are in love with Lethridge. I daresay you have been wearing the willow for him for ever so long. That is why you have buried yourself in this wretched place. But for your own sake, I advise you to forget all about Lethridge. You will never have him, Cousin. He will always be mine for the asking."

"You may be certain that I am aware of that. I have always been aware of it, more is the pity." Setting the newly potted plant aside, Felicity removed her work gloves and laid them on the table with an icy calm. "Here is Hannah. You will have tea, of course, Zenoria. And then no doubt you will be anxious to be getting on back to Town."

Seeing Zenoria torn between what must have been an almost overpowering wish to make an exit in the grand style and the more basic desire to partake of the generous repast of biscuits, fruit, cold meats, and tea enticingly set out on the tea tray, Felicity smiled ironically to herself. Zenoria and she had been friends once, childhood playmates who had laughed together and shared childish secrets. An only child indulged to excess perhaps could not help being self-centered, grasping, and shallow.

"Oh, botheration," she said, relenting. "Pray do sit down, Zenoria, and take tea. London can wait. You know you grow faint when you miss a meal."

Felicity could only be relieved when, an hour and a half later, Zenoria at last determined she really could not stay a single moment longer. Tea had been delightful, and it was always splendid to enjoy a quiet coze with her dearest cousin, Felicity was breezily informed. As if there had never been an angry exchange of words between them, reflected Felicity, marveling at the ease with which Zenoria put anything unpleasant behind her. But then, she had always had the faculty for shedding responsibility for what Felicity's mama had been wont to call her niece's predilection for mayhem and destruction.

"I do hope you will tear yourself away from your precious cottage and come up to London for at least a se'ennight," Zenoria exhorted gaily through the carriage window. "You know how Mama would love to have you."

"Yes, perhaps I shall," Felicity called, waving, as the carriage jerked into motion. "Give Aunt Elsbeth my love."

"You come and give it to her yourself," drifted back to Felicity from the carriage only just then rounding the turn in the drive. The next moment, it entered the spinney of beech trees and vanished.

Slowly Felicity let her hand drop. It was over, another crisis put safely behind her, she thought, allowing herself a sigh of relief. She turned back to the house—and was made immediately aware of Lethridge, watching her from the summerhouse by the decorative pond where he had apparently been enjoying a cigar.

Instantly her heart sank as it came to her that he was awaiting an explanation for her extraordinary behavior earlier in the withdrawing room. Faith, she had almost forgotten. It had been her firm intention to tell him everything as soon as Zenoria was safely removed from the premises. Unfortunately, in the wake of Zenoria's unsettling revelations, she found herself prey to sudden misgivings.

Or was it only the voice of temptation? she was immediately moved to ask herself, as it came to her that she would hardly be doing William a service to reveal to him that the female who had just pulled away in the carriage was the woman he loved. Hardly had that thought formulated itself in her mind than another, even more insidious, notion presented itself. Considering Zenoria's deplorable lack of the proper feelings, it seemed to whisper, would Felicity not, in fact, be a fool to fling away her one chance at happiness, no matter how fleeting it might prove in the end?

Inexplicably, her heart began to pound as she saw Lethridge toss away the cigar. *What now, Felicity Talbot?* she asked herself as she made herself cross the drive in the direction of the summerhouse. There was something about the tall, masculine figure striding deliberately toward her that warned her. Short of feigning a swoon, she could not put matters off, much as she might wish to have done.

Whatever she had expected upon coming up to Lethridge at the edge of the lawn, however, it was not to have him take hold of her hand and, tucking it in the crook of his arm, begin to conduct her purposefully toward the house. Neither was it to hear him declare, "Come, my poor girl, you have been made to suffer enough unpleasantness for one day. It is time you got out of the house. It is my considered opinion a simple diversion is in order."

"A diversion?" More than a little flustered at this peculiar turn of events, Felicity attempted to come to a halt, only to find herself firmly compelled to continue along. "In case you had failed to notice, I *am* out of the house," she pointed out, having to resort to a skip and a hop to keep up with William's

long stride. "Furthermore, I haven't the least notion
what you are talking about. I have just spent an hour
and a half visiting with my cousin. I fail to see why
you should consider that an unpleasantness. Perhaps
I rather enjoyed it."

At that bald absurdity, William himself came to a
halt. With a hand on either of her arms, he turned
her to face him. "I consider it so because I saw you
with her in the solarium and again just now as you
walked her to her carriage. So pray do not try and
deny you found her visit trying. I know you, Felicity.
And I have seen your cousin's kind before. She is a
spoiled, self-centered beauty who thinks nothing of
using people to her own ends. She can be enor-
mously charming, even generous at times to a fault,
but it is all a sham to obtain whatever it is she thinks
she wants at the moment. You may be sure the object
of her desire will change as swiftly as her mood, which
may ever be depended upon to be quixotic at best.
Unfortunately, one cannot keep from loving her,
even when one is aware of her shortcomings, or from
coming to her aid when her selfish impetuosity lands
her in a coil of her own making. She is, in short, the
most trying of acquaintances, the proverbial bad
penny, the sort that one would do better never to
foster as a friend, a relation, or a lover. I could wish
I had it in my power to keep her from working her
wiles on you, Felicity Talbot. Your generosity of heart
and sympathetic nature must inevitably render you
particularly vulnerable."

Felicity, who must certainly marvel at his acute assessment of a woman whom he presumably had no
recollection of knowing intimately, stared at him with
suddenly narrowed eyes. "You need not concern
yourself on that point, Will, I assure you," she said
measuringly. "As it happens, I am well aware of my

cousin's peculiarities; I have known her all my life. I cannot but wonder, however, how it is you have so precisely detailed them. One might suppose that you are as well acquainted with her as I am."

"Then perhaps I am," William answered with a shrug. "I'm afraid you would know that better than I. I am, if you recall, lamentably deprived of my memory."

Yes, of course he was, reflected Felicity, ashamed of her ridiculous suspicions. No doubt his perspicacity could be attributed to an acute instinct for judging character, which, upon his having been subjected at his first glance into Lady Zenoria's eyes to what Felicity's favorite authoress Lucinda Evalina, who just happened to be the Duchess of Lathrop, was wont to describe as "a blinding flash of sublime illumination," had been rendered ever afterwards impervious to the young beauty's flaws. "I daresay you have met her in the course of events," Felicity replied carefully. "My cousin has long been considered a reigning beauty in London. Perhaps you felt something when you saw her just now. Was there anything about her that struck you in the least familiar?"

"No, nothing," replied Lethridge, without a flicker of emotion. "Save for the distinct sense that I know her type. Should there have been something familiar to me?"

Felicity, wondering at her utter lack of any proper feelings of guilt, could only marvel at the newfound depths of her depravity as, deliberately, she lied to him. "Not necessarily. I only thought that seeing someone you must have encountered at the various social events in London might have jogged a chord of memory."

"I see," said Lethridge, appearing to consider the possibilities. A strange flutter went through Felicity as she found herself staring suddenly into the full intensity of William's eyes. "Perhaps it should have done, had your cousin meant anything to me. As it is, I daresay any association I might have had with her was due only to the circumstance that she is your kinswoman and Bertie's. I can hardly think she would ever have been in my style of female, can you?"

"I should never presume to try and tell you what your style of female might be," said Felicity, feeling a distinct sense of unreality at this sudden turn of the conversation. "On the other hand, how can you know for certain my cousin did not fit in that no doubt august category?"

"I know, my darling girl," replied Lethridge, taking her arm and leading her once more toward the house, "because in my farthest imagination I could never envision Lady Zenoria as my wife, let alone as mistress of my house. She could never be chatelaine of Greensward."

He said it with such utter conviction that Felicity had the uncanny premonition it was naught but the simple truth. But that was absurd, she told herself. He was an amnesiac who, unable to remember anything before the event of his having regained consciousness at Primrose Cottage, was merely extrapolating from what he knew of himself in the present to explain what he could not know of himself in the past. He had loved Zenoria enough to fight a duel for her, and when it did all come back to him, he undoubtedly would have little difficulty picturing Lady Zenoria as both his wife and the chatelaine of his beloved Greensward. What he would find incredible was that he had ever entertained the notion that he was attracted to Felicity Talbot.

And yet he *was* attracted to her, she told herself, with an unconscious jut of her delightfully pointed chin. Indeed, she could not be mistaken in what she had felt as he had taken her in his arms and kissed her. Or, afterwards, in the way he had looked at her, as if she were in truth his darling girl. There had been a warmth in his embrace, in his look, in his voice that had had nothing to do with the sort of affection one might feel for a troublesome little sister. She was not so naive or inexperienced not to realize that he had looked at her the way a man looks at a woman.

An unwitting thrill shot through her at the very thought that, given time, she might even bring him to love her. And why should she not? she asked herself. It was not as if Zenoria had more to offer him than she. And if in the end he could not find it in his heart to love her, what did it truly matter? At least for a few brief days, she would have lived her dream of happiness, and that was a deal more than she had ever dared to hope.

"You might at least tell me where we are going," Felicity said some several minutes later as Lethridge helped her mount to the seat of his curricle.

Lethridge, vaulting lightly to a seat beside her, gathered up the ribbons and the whip.

"I am told Faversham holds a street market, the oldest in Kent as a matter of fact, dating back over eight hundred years." Nodding to Huggins to let go the horses' heads, he set the team of high-stepping bays into motion. "It occurred to me that you might enjoy such an outing as that might be, and it would afford me the opportunity to purchase a few of the necessaries. It would seem I am devilishly poor at packing. But then, no doubt I failed to anticipate that a couple of days would turn into a rather lengthier stay."

"As it happens, Bertie was very nearly certain the highwaymen who held you up must have taken a fancy to your baggage. It is almost certain they took most of it with them," supplied Felicity, who had not before considered that particular when she concocted her original story.

"And my valet?" queried Lethridge, taking the edge off the spirited team of bays. "Presumably I employ one. Is it my practice to travel without him?"

"How should I know?" replied Felicity, who did not doubt that the fiercely loyal manservant must by now be beside himself with worry over his master. Unfortunately, there had not been room in Lethridge's curricle for the valet, nor opportunity for Bertie to obtain a larger conveyance. Lemmings, despite his protestations, had had to be left behind. "Lemmings is getting on in age. Perhaps you did not feel it necessary to require him to accompany you for a brief stay in the country."

"No doubt that was it." Will's brow puckered in a frown. "Lemmings, you say. An exceedingly proper old fellow, who was used to sneak milk and biscuits to my room when I was a lad. Good God, how could I ever have forgotten old Lemmings?"

"You have been made to forget a deal more than Lemmings," Felicity reminded him, her heart sinking at this further sign that his memory was beginning to stir. "The doctor said you were exceedingly fortunate. A mere fraction of an inch to the right would have ended more than your ability to recall your past."

Lethridge smiled reflectively. "Yes, I seem to recall someone observing that I should very likely have lost what few brains I possess." Intriguingly, he noted Felicity's hands tighten convulsively in her lap.

"It is true, you know," she retorted, remembering

all too well the riot of emotions within her breast
upon finding William awake at last after a seeming
eternity of dreadful uncertainty. "You took a terrible
chance. One that might very well have cost you your
life. For a man noted for his unshakable sense of
logic, you behaved in what could only be considered
a wholly irrational manner."

"No doubt in future I shall strive to follow a more
logical course," smiled Lethridge, who, in light of
what he had awakened to discover, could not but
think that he had been irrational indeed to tempt
fate as he had. But then, he might never have realized
the treasure awaiting him, tucked away in the rustic
environs of Kent, had events been otherwise. Now
that he was aware of it, he would gladly risk a deal
more than a glancing blow from a pistol ball in order
to claim that treasure as his own. "Tell me about Bertie. By my calculations, I should have expected him
back in Kent by now. It is hardly a journey of a fortnight to the North Yorks and back."

"No," agreed Felicity, thinking swiftly. She could
hardly tell him, after all, that Bertie and Jerome
French were hiding out in London to avoid being
questioned about their part in an unlawful duel, not
to mention the present location of one of the prin-
cipal parties involved. If they could not be found,
Bertie had pointed out, they would not be forced to
lie. As soon as they had word of Shelby's fate, one
way or another, Bertie would ride *ventre à terre* to Kent
with the news. Still, she had to tell Will something.
"But then, Bertie can never be depended upon to
do anything with punctuality," she said, sacrificing
without remorse her brother's character to the cause.
"I daresay he has been detoured on his return by
notice of a prizefight or a mustering of the Quorn
or some such event. You may be sure he will rather

belatedly recall that he was expected to come immediately back with the reassurance that your parents are well and expecting further news about your recovery, and that is when he will show up at Primrose full of apologies and excuses. If I were you, I should not refine too much on his absence. He will come eventually, you may depend on it."

"I do depend on it," Lethridge replied, neatly feather-edging a blind corner. He could only hope, however, that Bertie would come rather later than soon, he mused grimly to himself. He was acutely aware of the slender woman next to him, and, while he was persuaded that he had made some little progress in dispelling the notion that his interest was on the order of a brotherly affection, he was ruefully aware that he had yet to break through the formidable defenses she had erected against him. He needed time, time that could only be purchased with Bertie's continued absence.

Fortunately, perhaps, any further discussion of Bertie and other matters that Felicity could only find discomfiting was terminated by their arrival on the outskirts of Faversham.

The ancient town of Faversham, boasting a thousand years of recorded history, presented a pleasant aspect of neat timber-framed houses set along sprawling streets. Felicity, glad to turn the talk to a subject that was innocuous at best, did not hesitate to point out Watling Street, which had replaced the old Roman road, or to mention the Arden Theatre, in which the Elizabethan play *Arden of Faversham* could be witnessed in its original setting.

Lethridge, who could not have cared less that Faversham boasted the oldest gunpowder mills, the oldest club, and the oldest brewery in Britain, as well as the most impressive collection of fruit varieties to be

found anywhere in the realm, was content to drink
in his darling girl's animated visage as she instructed
him in the various points of interest to be offered by
the town. And, while he could not but agree that it
was informative to note that James II had been held
prisoner by local fishermen in Number 12 Market
Street, which they had just passed, he found the sun
glinting golden sparks in her hair far more provocative.

No doubt had he not been totally captivated by her
obvious pleasure in the sights and sounds of the bus-
tling street market in full swing, and had he not, further, to attend closely to maneuvering the curricle
through traffic to a safe stopping place, he would not
have failed to notice they had attracted the attention
of a gentleman who, lounging with a shoulder against
one of the pillars upon which rested the Guildhall
beneath and around which sprawled the market, observed their passage with particular interest.

Lethridge, flinging a coin to a grinning youth, gave
the lad the promise of another just like it if he would
walk the horses until their return. Then, leaping
lightly to the ground, he turned to help Felicity
alight. Neither was aware, as they threaded their way
through the milling crowd, that the gentleman, lei-
surely straightening, followed in their wake.

Nine

As a child, Felicity had been used to come often in the summer months to visit her papa's spinster sister at Primrose Cottage. Her Aunt Alice had liked nothing better than to have her nieces and nephews running tame about the place. As it had meant bathing and playing in the shoals, not to mention indulging in alfresco meals of fresh oysters on the beach, even Bertie had been glad to accompany Felicity for a week or two at a time, which was how Lethridge had come to know Primrose Cottage and Aunt Alice. He had spent a fortnight there with Bertie before returning home to Greensward to take up his more serious pursuits of helping his father oversee the estate that would one day be his.

This was not, consequently, the first time that Felicity had been to the street market in Faversham in the company of William Powell. They had come there together, the three of them, when Felicity was twelve and William and Bertie dashing young bloods of nineteen. It was, in fact, one of the most memorable events of Felicity's young life.

The crowded market with its abundance of wares, ranging from fresh fruit, seafood, pickled pigs' trotters, pies, and pastries to such delightful folderols as parasols, bonnets, delicately embroidered scarves, bolts of cloth, hand-painted china, and one particularly memorable stall displaying finely wrought pieces of paste, had seemed a wondrous, magical place to Felicity, who had yet to experience the more sophisticated environs of Bond Street. No doubt her face had lit up at sight of one especially lovely locket enameled in red, green, and purple which opened up to reveal a tiny mirror inside. In Felicity's twelve-year-old eyes, there had never been anything more beautiful, nor ever could be. Despite the fact that she had since been the recipient of her Aunt Alice's collection of fine jewels, not to mention her mother's pearl necklace, diamond pendant, and earrings, and an exquisite emerald necklace that had belonged to her maternal grandmama, the small enameled paste locket to this time held a special place in her jewel case.

Unconsciously, her hand went to the delicate thing hanging on a chain about her neck. Seeing the longing in her eyes, William had bought it for her that day in the marketplace. Telling her it was something to remind her of him always, he had clasped it about her neck, and then, no doubt, had forgotten all about the incident.

Ruefully, Felicity glanced sidelong up at her companion's strong, handsome profile as they strolled through the teeming crowd. She wondered if he had the smallest inkling of what he had done to her that long-ago day with a simple gesture of kindness. She had known then with an utter certainty that he had irrevocably driven a wedge into her heart, leaving an empty space that only he could fill. Nor had it been the extreme case of calf-love that Bertie had teasingly called it.

The lamentable fact of the matter was that she had

never found another whom she could love as she loved William Powell.

The thought was hardly one to give her comfort, as it came to her with a rending pang that he was hardly likely to thank her for the tissue of lies she had fabricated for his benefit, especially as she could not quite dismiss the distinct possibility that she had entertained some unconscious ulterior motive for keeping him in the dark. She was only human, after all. So long as he remained ignorant of the true state of affairs that had brought him to Kent, she could continue to have him near. Might not that be why she had done it?

No doubt that unrewarding reflection had brought a frown to her brow. Certainly, she had been so lost in self-examination that she failed to realize William had spoken to her. It was not until he had recourse to stop and turn her to face him that she was brought with a jar back to the present.

"William," she exclaimed, a hand to her breast. "What is it?"

"I was on the point of asking you that very question," replied William, probing her face. "Perhaps I was wrong to have insisted on Faversham Market. I had hoped you might find it a pleasant diversion. If you would like to return home, however, I shall not take exception."

"No, of course not." Smiling, she shook her head. "I beg your pardon. I am afraid I have been poor company. I was just thinking . . ." She stopped and shook her head again. "Never mind. It is only that the market—being here with you—brings back memories."

His eyes sharpened on her face. "We have been here together before?" A hand lifted to the square of plaster over his temple, a by now familiar gesture. "Tell me. I regret I have no memory of it."

"No. How should you?" She pulled away and turned her head to look up and down the market-place. "I believe it was there. No, there," she said, leading him through the press. "Yes, it was here, I am sure of it." The stall before which she stopped displayed, not paste jewelry, but an assortment of finely woven rugs. Nevertheless, it occupied the same space as that other one long ago. "You and Bertie brought me at my Aunt Alice's insistence. I was only twelve, and you and Bertie seven years older than I, quite the young gentlemen. I was inordinately pleased with myself, I can assure you."

Lethridge smiled, watching her face. "No doubt the company of two puffed-up swells might have that effect on a young miss yet in the schoolroom."

Felicity gave a playful toss of her head. "Actually, you were very gallant, treating me as a grown-up young lady. I believe you made Bertie promise not to bait me, because even he behaved decently, for him. I was made to feel as if the two of you actually enjoyed playing gooseberry to an exceedingly young miss."

"I am relieved I was not so callow as to fail to play the part of a gentleman. I should even go so far as to speculate it was not all play-acting. I suspect you may have been very engaging, even at twelve."

"Hardly. I was all arms and legs, and I had the deplorable habit of saying precisely whatever came to my mind, a practice which was used to cause Bertie no end of embarrassment. I believe you treated me with kindness because you understood how much it meant to me to be out in the company of my elder brother and his dashing friend."

"Dashing, was I?" An appreciative gleam of amusement shone in the look he bent upon her.

"Oh, very, but never more so than when you bought me this, here, at this very stall." She smiled as she touched the locket. "It was my very first gift from a gentleman. I'm afraid it made a very great impression on me."

His eyes lifted to hers, the flicker of a shadow in their depths. "You kept it. All these years. The devil, and I cannot even recall the event. What a sorry character you must think me."

Felicity's hand went out to touch the sleeve of his coat. "I hardly expected you to remember. How should I? You could not even recall your own name. It will come back to you, Will. You must be willing to give it time."

"Time. Yes." But how much time? He was swept with a sudden impatience to be done with it. How much more had he forgotten of his darling girl? He felt like a miser, jealous of every lost memory of her. And of how much else? he wondered. Covering his anger at himself and the unknown gaps in his past with a wry quirk of his lips, he took her arm and led her away from the stall. "With you to instruct me, no doubt I shall remember sooner than late. At least you will serve as my inspiration. What else can you tell me about my misspent youth?"

"That it was never misspent, my lord," she said lightly. "You will no doubt be relieved to learn that, in spite of your lively sense of the ridiculous, you are of a sober disposition. You take pride in those duties that fall to you as the heir to Greensward. You have a deep love for your home and your heritage. The Powells are all noted for their stubborn loyalty to family, their deep affection for one another, and their close bonds to Greensward; and you are no exception."

"And you, Miss Talbot," Lethridge countered.

"What do you hold dear? What led you to take up residence in your beloved Primrose Cottage so far from your home in the Lake District?"

"My Aunt Alice left it to me when she died," Felicity answered simply. "I suppose she recognized in me a spirit not unlike her own. At any rate, having my own house gave me the freedom to stretch my wings a bit. I have found I like determining my own life. And I am close enough to Town that I could enjoy a visit to London on occasion, should I feel like it. Strangely, I have yet to miss the gaiety of the social life in London, something to which I had eagerly looked forward when I was growing up. I daresay three Seasons satisfied whatever yearnings I might have had to take my place in Society, at least for a while," she ended with a shrug.

"Those three Seasons," William said, watching the emotions chase themselves across her face. "Were they all that you had hoped they would be?"

"You mean, was I a success?" She laughed, her eyes dancing up at him. "You will be happy to know I was a *succès fou*. How should I not, with all I had to recommend me? I had a glorious time, and I shall always remember my Seasons with fondness. I found, however, that I am deplorably lacking in any social ambitions. A life comprised of little more than a continuous round of gaiety holds little appeal for me. Do you think me sadly provincial if I confess I prefer the country?"

"Now you are being absurd. How should I think *you* provincial, when I am finding that the longer I am in your company, the more I entertain a similar disposition?"

At the seeming implication in that observation, Felicity felt a warm rush of blood to her cheeks.

"Quite so, my dear." Insufferably, William smiled.

It was at that moment that his glance fell on a shop front that advertised itself as a mercantile house for gentlemen. "Ah, here we are," he said with satisfaction. "Perhaps you would not mind waiting. I promise I shan't be a moment."

"Pray don't give it a thought. I daresay I shall find plenty to amuse me while you are gone."

A single, imperious eyebrow shot toward William's hairline. "Meaning, one must suppose, you do not intend to miss me."

"Not in the least, my lord," Felicity retorted archly.

"Little devil. You have given me back some of my own, have you not?" A sudden frown darkened Lethridge's brow. "Only promise me you won't wander off. I cannot like to leave you unprotected. You did say Steed maintained a house in town."

"Enough," Felicity exclaimed. Laughing, she gave him a small nudge toward the shop. "I shall be fine. What could possibly happen? Not even Steed would dare to abduct me in the midst of a crowd. Now, go. I shall be waiting when you return."

"I shall depend on it," warned William and, shrugging off his momentary feeling of apprehension, left her to make his purchases.

Hardly had Lethridge disappeared into the dimly lit interior of the shop than a glad cry rang out.

"Felicity! Lady Felicity Talbot."

Felicity's head came around to behold a fashionably dressed woman of about her own age making with obvious pleasure toward her. Felicity suffered an immediate sinking sensation. Faith, it had never occurred to her that she would encounter someone she knew at Faversham's street market. And not just anyone, but Eleanore, Lady Braxton, one of the *ton's* leading luminaries. At any other time she would have derived no little enjoyment from just such a meeting.

She and Eleanore, having made their bows in Society in the same Season, had formed an immediate liking for one another, a liking that had deepened over the years into an enduring friendship. Unfortunately, there was not the slightest possibility Eleanore could have failed to recognize Felicity's tall companion in a single glance, and even less chance that she would not have heard about the cursed duel.

Hardly had those thoughts reared themselves in Felicity's head than Lady Braxton descended upon her.

"Felicity," exclaimed the countess, clasping Felicity's hands and delivering her a buss, first on one cheek and then the other. "By all that is marvelous. I cannot believe my eyes. I should never have thought to run into you—here, of all places."

"That is just what I was going to say about you. As it happens, I have set up housekeeping at Primrose Cottage, a short distance from town. The last I heard, you and Braxton were on the Continent. Something about a diplomatic mission. What in heaven's name are you doing in Faversham?"

"Setting up my nursery, what else?" Lady Braxton laughed excitedly at the look on Felicity's face. "We returned from the Continent three months ago, just in time for my lying-in. A girl, Felicity. Lady Jane Olivia Winthrop. Were you to hear Braxton talk, you would think she is the brightest, most extraordinary child ever to grace the face of the earth. Only ask him yourself. He has just stepped across the way to purchase a hobbyhorse for his pride and joy, never mind that it will be months before she is ready to ride it."

Felicity, who could only be grateful that Lady Braxton had apparently failed to take note of Lethridge before he stepped out of sight, and desirous of steer-

ing her friend away from the shop lest he suddenly
reappear, allowed Eleanore to take her arm and lead
her several stalls down to where the Earl of Braxton
was in the process of examining a carved hobbyhorse
for the latest addition to his young family.

Lethridge, keenly aware of the passage of time,
tossed some coins on the countertop and, snatching
up his parcel, strode quickly out into the sunlight.
The devil, he cursed silently to himself. A good twenty
minutes had crept by while he waited for the elderly
shopkeeper to dodder about in search of the few
things he had required. And all the while, he had
chafed with a vague feeling of unrest, which had
grown with each passing second. Another moment
and he would most certainly have walked out without
the things for which he had come.

He stood for a moment, squinting against the sudden glare of the noon sun, and felt a cold prickle at
the nape of his neck.

Felicity was nowhere in sight.

Felicity, promising, now that she knew Eleanore
and Braxton were at the family estate a short distance
from Faversham, she would make it a point to call
on them from time to time, turned to wend her way
back to the shop where she had left Lethridge.

Although she could not have been more delighted
for her friends, Eleanore and Braxton's glowing happiness had yet left her feeling strangely downpin. No
doubt it was because she had been given to see a slice
of life that she was unlikely ever to experience for
herself, she reflected, sardonically amused at herself.
Really, if she did not know better, she would think

she was turning into a sentimentalist—Felicity Talbot, who had been accused of being wholly without sensibilities!

The devil, she thought, angry with herself. She had been rubbing along just fine, with only an occasional hollow pang at the sound of children playing or at the sight of a young couple walking hand in hand along the beach. No doubt she had simply been unprepared to be suddenly exposed to Eleanore's radiant happiness. Nor did it help to be witness to Braxton's doting adoration of his wife for having given him a child, since it served only to enhance that aura of wonder and mystery that new motherhood seemed always to confer on a woman. That sense which new mothers exuded of being possessed of a wondrous secret knowledge that came to one only through giving birth was a powerful and seductive agent to single females, who could not but suffer, upon strong exposure to it, the arousal of instincts and yearnings over which they had no control. Faith, it was little wonder that her chance encounter with Eleanore and Braxton had served to throw her into a fit of the doldrums. It had been practically inevitable the moment Eleanore had announced her news, especially in view of the already tumultuous state of Felicity's emotions.

Felicity had, to her dismay, found herself picturing William in the role of proud papa and herself in the enviable position of being mother to his child. Naturally, the realization had served to bring reality crashing down on her. It was all a pipe dream, and she was a fool to indulge in fantasies that could only confuse matters worse than they already were.

Instantly she took herself in hand. After all, it was not as if she had not had the opportunity to have a husband and a family of her own, she reminded her-

self firmly. There had been Lord Pomfret, a man of
five and forty who was both well to look upon and
possessed of a certain rakish charm, and an exceedingly young Mr. Linton, who had professed an undy-
ing adoration for her. Nor could she forget Mr.
Jerome French, one of her brother Bertie's closest
intimates, who had courted her with a steadfast de-
votion for more than two years. She might actually
have given his offer the consideration it deserved,
had she been able to take him seriously. That she
could not was perhaps due to the fact that, despite
his twenty-seven years, he seemed as far from emotional maturity as he had as an unruly schoolboy of
fourteen. And then, of course, there had been the
grave-mannered Colonel Bixby of His Majesty's Fifth
Infantry. His suit had come the closest to tumbling
the walls of her resistance. Only the timely realization
that her growing attraction to him was due to the fact
that he reminded her of Lethridge had saved her
from making the greatest mistake of her life. She had
liked John Bixby far too well to have saddled him
with a wife who could never love him for himself, but
only for his resemblance to someone else.

On retrospect, Felicity could not but think she had
not done too badly, given the circumstances. Until
only a little over two weeks ago, she had, as a matter
of fact, managed to convince herself that she was
more than contented with her existence. It was, after
all, the one she had chosen for herself. Why, then,
had Lethridge to drop back into her life unan-
nounced? It was really quite unfair of him, especially
as she was rather certain she could never be so contented again.

Having come to that less than comforting conclusion, she was made suddenly and instantly aware of
a rather less than pleasant aroma of garlic and on-

ions, mingled with stale beer, issuing from exceedingly close range. Inexplicably, she was struck by a frisson of warning. Unfortunately, it came too late.

Felicity glanced up—and was met with the sight of a dirty, bewhiskered countenance in which leered a gap-toothed grin that did little or nothing to enhance its bearer's overall lack of aesthetic appeal—and, behind him, three equally unprepossessing specimens of the lower dregs of society.

The next instant a burlap bag was thrust over her head past her waist, effectively pinning her arms to her sides and muffling her cry of alarm, as she felt herself flung like a sack of potatoes over a hard, burly shoulder.

"Make it quick, mate," rasped a rough voice. "The others've been cut off by some crazed devil wi' naught but a single wing. He's like to bring the soldiers down on us. The cap'n won't like it if we lose his fine piece of baggage."

"See to yerself, Brindle," growled Felicity's burly abductor. "Steed'll get his precious booty soon enough."

From the ease with which the villain had rendered her helpless, it was to be supposed that he was not inexperienced in matters of abduction. On the other hand, it was doubtful he had ever encountered a victim on the order of Lady Felicity Talbot.

Mention of Steed was sufficient to arouse her fighting mettle. Overcoming her first stunned immobility, Felicity erupted in a furious struggle punctuated by as much noise as she could muster beneath the suffocating confines of the burlap bag.

She felt her abductor stagger, thrown off balance, and, heedless of her own safety, was inspired to ever greater efforts. Gritting her teeth, she arched her back and kicked down hard with both feet. With no little satisfaction, she felt the pointed toes of her slippers sink into soft, unprotected flesh. Indeed, she could not be mistaken in thinking she had struck an area of extreme masculine sensitivity, as she was rewarded with a blistering oath from the villain and was the next instant flung with a shocking lack of ceremony to the ground.

"Ho, Steddings. The lady too much fer ye? Let me 'ave 'er. I'll take the wind out'n 'er sails soon enough."

Stunned, the breath knocked from her, Felicity yet had the wit to roll in a frantic attempt to evade Brindle's grasping hands. She came up hard against an unrelenting pair of legs.

"Bloody little she-devil," snarled Steddings immediately overhead. Ruthlessly, she was grasped by the shoulders and dragged to her feet. "I'll show yer a thing or two."

Felicity, in no mood to be instructed, took advantage of her bettered circumstances to let fly with a kick straight to the ruffian's shin.

A roar of pain in concert with her forceful release sent her reeling backwards, to stumble and fall once more with a jarring impact to the ground. She lay gasping for breath, knowing with bitter certainty that at any moment one or the other of her abductors would set on her with renewed fury, but too stunned and bruised to do anything about it.

What came next, she could never afterwards say with any clarity. One moment she was overcome with silent despair as rough hands clutched at her, dragging her up again. The very next a chilling voice edged in steel slashed through her rising panic.

"Take your filthy hands off her. *Gently,* mind you." Felicity thrilled to the ominous click of a pistol hammer being thumbed back. "I suggest you be very careful do you value your skin. By God, if you have hurt one hair on her head, you will not live to see another day."

Felicity heard the whistled intake of Steddings's breath, even as her mind registered the fact that William was there. William had come to her rescue.

"Easy, gov'nor." Felicity was left to stand weaving as the hands released her. "We never meant 'er no 'arm."

"Don't listen to him, Will," gasped Felicity, struggling against the stifling confines of the sack. "They meant to turn me over to Steed."

"So you are a liar as well as a lowborn coward."

"Brindle," shouted Steddings. "God rot yer soul. What the devil be yer waitin' fer? Shoot the blighter!"

Felicity thought her heart must fail her at the sudden, deafening explosion of a pistol shot at exceedingly close range. Indeed, she was overcome with a terrible, rending anguish.

The voice crying out was her own. *"Will!* Oh, God, no!"

Blinded by the burlap bag, Felicity sensed rather than saw Steddings swing hard about. Even as Felicity felt her knees buckling beneath her, she heard the crack of a hard fist smash against bone, followed by the sounds of a scuffle.

It was over in seconds, and suddenly someone was kneeling beside her, swift hands dragging the hateful burlap off over her head.

Blue eyes burned into hers.

"Hellsfire, Felicity. Did that devil hurt you?"

Felicity's head swam as her lungs filled with glorious fresh air. Mutely she shook her head, afraid to speak lest she unloose the flood of tears held painfully in check.

She heard William utter a blistering oath beneath

his breath. Only then did she realize, to her dismay, that she had begun violently to shake.

"The—the d-devil," she gasped, her eyes lifting ruefully to William's. "I c-can't seem t-to stop myself."

Grim-faced, William gathered Felicity to him.

Damn Steed and all his breed, he thought. He should never have left Felicity, not for so much as a single moment. He had *known* Steed might be there. It was, after all, why he had thought to bring along the pocket pistol that, presumably belonging to Bertie, William had found in a drawer in his room. Even so, he had nearly lost Felicity. Bitterly he cursed. He, better than anyone, knew how much luck had played a part in bringing him to the alley. A sudden stir of people, a boy gesturing wildly with excitement, a strikingly attractive woman showing sudden alarm, the one-armed man in tatters holding off two ruffians with naught but his fearless presence and a single massive fist—he had seen them all at a glance, like glaring flaws in a tapestry. He felt again the pressure in his chest, which had been overshadowed by cold rage as he burst onto the scene of infamy. The girl's brave front, the brutality of her captors, had caused him a moment the likes of which he could never wish to live again.

His arms tightened about the girl's trembling form. Hell and the devil confound it! He should have killed the vermin.

Felicity, feeling Will's arms tense, forced her head up to look at him. A pang went through her at sight of the hard bleakness in his eyes. He was taking it badly, she thought. Naturally, he would blame himself. The thought gave her the strength to fight back her own lingering fears.

Gravely she smiled, willing her limbs to cease their

shaking. "When the pistol went off . . ." She closed her eyes, remembering the stab of terrible pain. Almost immediately she opened them again. "I thought you were dead."

His answering smile did little to ease the stark coldness from his face. "But here I am, very much alive. And, unless I am greatly mistaken, Steed will think twice before trying something like this again. Now he will know that I shall not hesitate to hunt him down and kill him."

Good God, he meant it, she thought, realizing she was seeing a side of him she had never suspected before, not even when she had heard about the duel. The realization brought a chill to her heart. "Faith, Will. What have I done? I should never have involved you in this."

In disbelief, she felt his hand lift to brush a stray curl from her cheek as if she were something exquisitely delicate and therefore infinitely dear. The fingers trembled ever so slightly. "There is precious little you could have done to keep me from it. I am involved. Now let that be an end to it."

He saw the stubborn light leap to her eyes and felt his tension ease ever so slightly. She was priceless, his darling girl. Plucky to the backbone and game as a pebble, she would never give up her mission to save the unfortunate Annabel. It was hardly in her nature to abandon what she felt to be right. His thoughts turned somberly to her game fight against her two abductors. Nor would she be easily conquered. She was all fire and spirit, and he would be hard-pressed to keep her safe from her own impetuous determination.

He felt a small chill brush his spine. He had almost failed her today. He would not do so again. It was past time he took matters into his own hands.

Felicity's trembling had ceased as the shock of her
recent ordeal gave way to an acute awareness that at
any moment they might be discovered in what could
only be construed as compromising circumstances.
Reluctantly, she stirred and felt an instantaneous
pang of loss as William loosened his arms about her.

"It is time I got you away from here," he said,
grimly aware that the villain who had fled, a pistol
ball in one arm to serve as a reminder of his failure,
might yet return with reinforcements. His glance
flicked over to the still-unconscious Steddings,
sprawled motionless on the ground a few feet away.
He looked back to Felicity. "Do you think you can
walk?"

"Indeed. I am not such a poor creature as to allow
a pair of cutthroats to put me on end." Ruefully she
laughed. "Though I fear I must present a sorry appearance. I lost my hat when that miserable creature
thrust the sack over my head, and I have not a doubt
that my hair is a mess and my gown soiled beyond
salvaging."

Rising, he lifted her to her feet with him and held
her as he studied her face, until at length a bright
tinge of color flooded her cheeks. Satisfied, he nodded to himself.

"You, however, are sound." He felt a warm rush of
gratitude that her harrowing adventure had to all appearances left her spirit unscathed. He was equally
certain she had never appeared more beautiful to
him than she did at that moment with dirt on her
face and the hem of her gown rent where she had
caught her heel in it during her desperate struggle
with the abductors. "You are alive," he said, "and, to
all practical purposes, unharmed." He turned and,
pausing only to retrieve his parcel, led her toward

the mouth of the alley. "That is all that really matters."

"To you, perhaps," retorted Felicity, awarding him a wry grimace. "As it happens, that was a new hat, one I had been saving for a special occasion. Dare I say that narrowly escaping being made the captive of river pirates was not precisely the occasion I had in mind?"

It was a silly thing to say in light of the day's events, and in truth she cared not a whit for the lost hat, new or otherwise. Still, even a lame stab at humor was better than nothing. It served at the very least to cover her confusion, generated by Will's exceedingly odd behavior.

Furtively she glanced up at him as he helped her toward the carriage, his hand beneath her arm supporting her. She had never seen him like this, his features stern, seemingly chiseled from stone, his mouth a thin, forbidding line. Even harder for her to bear than this unfamiliar steely hardness of the man, however, had been the sudden dizzying warmth of his eyes as moments ago he had searched her face for something and had apparently found it.

Really, it was too much, she thought testily. She was bruised and battered, and it seemed that every muscle in her body was aching. How dared he compound her discomfort by unloosing a horde of butterflies in her stomach! With a vague sense of unreality, she lifted a hand to touch her cheek where she seemed yet to feel the tender brush of his fingers. It really was quite unfair that, at the mere touch of his hand, she should have been made to suffer what had given every manifestation of a sudden onslaught of heart palpitations. And as if that were not all or enough, she had had to contend with a melting sensation at that blazing look of concern with which he had greeted her upon freeing her from the odious confines of the sack over her head.

It was all more than she could endure to contemplate in her present state of acute vulnerability. And now what must he do but behave in the manner of an avenging guardian! It was very much too bad of him, she fumed. Indeed, she was very close to being out of all patience with him.

Hardly had that thought crossed her mind than a pair of strong hands spanned her waist and, lifting her with infinite ease, settled her most inconsiderately tenderly on the seat of the curricle. Felicity clasped a hand to her breast in the wake of the unwitting thrill that had shot through her, rather like a bolt of electricity, leaving her head spinning.

Clearly, it was the last straw.

"Enough, Will Powell!" she blurted, as Lethridge, swinging lightly up, settled on the seat beside her and gathered up the ribbons. "You will stop all this—this *nonsense* at once!"

William, understandably startled at that unexpected outburst, allowed his hands to drop, with the result that the bays shot forward, nearly unseating Miss Talbot. Almost instantly he had them under control again.

"I beg your pardon," he said, relieved to note that he had not lost his passenger. "No doubt you will pardon my lack of comprehension. What nonsense, precisely, would you have me stop?"

"You know very well what," declared Felicity, knowing she was perilously close to disgracing herself with a wholly feminine shed of tears and quite unable to stop herself. "I will thank you to stop behaving as if the blame for what happened must be laid at your door. It was my own fault for not paying attention to what was going on around me. I will not allow you

to take it upon yourself to seek out Steed. I will not
have it, do you hear me? It is not your obligation to
exact punishment for what he attempted today. And
pray do stop looking at me as if I were some delicate
piece of china that must be kept wrapped in soft
wool. I am the same Felicity Talbot you were used to
take fishing and whom you once put over your knee
for stealing a ride on Telamon, your prized Arabian
stallion."

Had she hoped by that telling argument to put an
end to his unsettling change in behavior, she was
soon to be disappointed.

"You are all of those things and a great deal more,
Felicity Talbot," said William, neatly passing a
farmer's hay wagon. Maddeningly cool, he glanced
down at her. "You are, after all, the woman I am going to marry."

Ten

Thickening clouds scudded across a quarter moon high overhead as the small skiff worked its way down the Swale. Lethridge, sitting in the bow of the sailboat, drew his borrowed boat cloak close against the chill of the mist and the sea. He did not doubt that he would be treated to a rainstorm before the night was over. The prospect was not one to which he looked forward with any great pleasure. Indeed, he would rather travel by way of a swift horse than in a leaky boat stinking of fish and bilge water. Still, he was aware of a frisson of excitement, a quickening of the blood in his veins, which might be attributed to the hour and the unfamiliar environs, but which he knew more certainly stemmed from the mere fact that he was at last asserting a direct influence on events.

His gaze came to rest speculatively on the huddled form at the tiller. Garbed in yellow nankeens and a worn short coat, a savage-looking cutlass thrust through a leather belt at his waist, Huggins presented more the aspect of a pirate than had Steed and his bloody cutthroats. At least Lethridge could be grateful that Huggins gave the appearance of being a deal more at home on the sea than ever he had in the stable. But then, Huggins had confessed to having earned his scars at the Battle of Trafalgar in a king's man-of-war. Curious, William thought. The man could not be much above fifty, and yet he had witnessed or been a part of every major naval battle in the late wars. The Saintes, the Nile, Biscay, the Copenhagen—Huggins had seen them all from the lower gun deck of one great two-decker or another. No doubt their present endeavor must seem rather tame in comparison, but potent, nevertheless, with dangerous possibilities.

The thought brought a hard glint to Lethridge's eyes, serving as it did to remind him of the circumstances that had brought him to his present damnably uncomfortable position, crouched in an old, weathered skiff, sailing into uncertain waters, a borrowed sword clipped to his belt and a brace of pistols thrust through his waistband.

It had occurred to him in the wake of Felicity's harrowing escape from Steed's hired cutthroats that he could no longer wait and do nothing while Steed laid siege against the women in Primrose Cottage. Felicity had said it herself the day after their excursion to Faversham's street market: "I will not grant Steed the power to rule my life, Will. I care not what you say. I will not be imprisoned in my own house."

It had little comforted him that she had finally been brought to agree to take a man with her on her visits to the various women whose lives she was striving to better. The risks she would run by leaving the protection of the house would still be great. Even so, it had taken further persuasion to convince her to accept the man he had chosen for the assignment—Sergeant Major John Hallows, late of His Britannic Majesty's Royal Marines. Even a man cast ashore because of the loss of an arm was better than a footman reared in the household, if that man was a former marine who had spent most of his life among fighting men.

A faint smile touched William's lips at the recollection of his first unlikely encounter with Hallows. It had been in Faversham at the head of the alley into which Felicity's abductors had carried her. Had it not been for the former marine's timely intervention in what he had seen at once as a "foul deed perpetrated by rogues of obvious ill intent," it was doubtful that Felicity's rescue would have been so happily achieved. As it was, Hallows had divided Steed's unsavory band, cutting the odds William faced by half. William had not waited till longer than the next morning to send a lad in search of the good Samaritan. The man had come at his lordship's invitation with a wariness in his strong, weathered face, a man, who, garbed in the ragged remains of a uniform, no longer could trust either in himself or his fate. It had been moving to William to watch Hallows's bleak weariness change suddenly to a sort of shining hope as it became clear to him just what he was being offered.

"You'll not regret it, milord," said Hallows, his gratitude somehow painful to behold. "I'll not let you down. I've one good arm left, and I know the sort you're up against. Never fear, your lady will be safe with John Hallows."

"I have no doubt of it," William had not hesitated to assure him. "Still, you must have a care that she does not try and give you the slip. She is a lady who values her independence. I fear she has little patience for the sort of caution required in the circumstances."

There had been a gleam of understanding in the look Hallows bent upon his new employer. "She is a lady of spirit, I saw it in her gallant fight against

Steed's bloody pirates. Oh, aye, milord," he added at the sudden leap of interest in Lethridge's eyes. "John Hallows is a man who keeps his ear to the ground. There is something else you should know. A certain young sea captain has been making inquiries about your Mr. Steed. It is my belief he thinks he has found what he was looking for. I know the young firebrand, and I know Mr. Steed. I fear, milord, Captain Trent is sailing blind into the eye of a hurricane."

"Then, Sergeant Major, it would seem someone must stop him."

The words had come easily enough. The deed, however, had looked to be far less certain of accomplishment. Trent had for some time been like a bloody will-o'-the-wisp, seeming to come tantalizingly within reach, only to slip through Lethridge's fingers again—until tonight, that was, thanks to old Huggins, who was in the habit of taking a wetting at the Red Boar, a tavern on the seamier side of the wharfs. It had been while jawing over a tankard with his old seafaring cronies that Huggins had spotted Hiram Bishop, Trent's first mate, in the act of acquiring a substantial supply of beer. It had not taken the old sailor long to surmise that the *Annabel* was being provisioned to put out to sea. Nor had he hesitated to take it upon himself to discreetly follow Bishop from the Red Boar far enough to ascertain the first mate's intended direction.

"I knows these waters like the backs o' me hands, me lord," Huggins had confided to Lethridge little more than an hour later. "There be only one place Cap'n Trent'd anchor his schooner and still hope for steerageway. We'll find him, me lord, never yer fear."

It had been uncanny, the way Huggins had seemed to change before Lethridge's eyes. Given the weath-

ered skiff and a purpose, what had seemed an air of
bumbling uncertainty had suddenly vanished. The
old sailor was in his element.

Lethridge, who was a deal less comfortable in his
unfamiliar surrounds, turned his gaze outboard. The
shoreline, revealing itself in brief snatches as the
moon appeared to move in and out of the drifting
clouds, was otherwise nearly indistinguishable in the
darkness. He could not even imagine how Huggins
was finding his way, let alone how he could possibly
know where they were at any given moment. Bristling
silhouettes of trees on black humps of land gave way
to the pale gleam of beach sliding by or to the reedy
rustle of salt marshes and the flutter of birds startled
from their nesting places. It was a foreign landscape
to one more used to heath-covered moors and grassy
downs. An image of green fields flashed through his
mind, a bourn shining silvery in the sunlight, an
Elizabethan house set on a low hill. Inexplicably, he
felt a rending pang.

"We're almost there, me lord," Huggins warned
in a carrying whisper. "Might be better was yer to let
me do the talkin' at first, bein' as how yer bain't acquainted wi' the cap'n. He can be a mite testy when
he—"

Huggins broke off suddenly with a muttered curse.

Lethridge stiffened, a prickle exploring his spine.
"Huggins, what—"

"H-s-s-t, me lord." Huggins's arm shot up. His
head turned and held stiffly. Slowly he lowered his
hand. "Listen, me lord," he whispered. "Does yer
hear it?"

Lethridge sat rigidly silent, his senses strained to
the sounds around him. Save for the lapping of the
water against the hull, the call of a bird, crickets, the
wind in the sails, he could detect nothing untoward.

Then, indistinctly, he heard it—the metallic creak of rowlocks, the splash of oars.

"Boats!" He looked to Huggins for confirmation.

"Aye." The old sailor's eyes gleamed in a sudden spate of moonlight. "Best pray Cap'n Trent seen fit to post a sharp lookout. Them'll be swarmin' his decks else, afore he can cut his anchor."

"River pirates!" Lethridge clenched his fingers about the grip of a pistol thrust in his waistband. "We must warn Trent."

Felicity sat, curled up on the window seat, her knees clasped to her chest, and stared out at the moving clouds silvered in moonlight. There would be rain before the night was over. She could smell it through the flutter of lace curtain.

The distant chime of the downstairs hall clock told her she should long since have sought her bed. She was tired, her body still sore from her unlooked-for adventure in Faversham only three days before. It was not her bruises, however, that kept her at her solitary vigil, her thoughts unwelcome companions. She knew well enough she could not have slept had she wanted to, and she had not the will to battle her pillows.

Will was out there somewhere in spite of all her protestations to the contrary—alone, with only Huggins to lend support should there be trouble. He might at least have taken Hallows with him. The former marine would have been a formidable ally in spite of his loss of a limb. But old Huggins? Even when he was not three sheets to the wind, the poor man was lost most of the time in a world of his own.

She felt a rush of shame for her uncharitable thoughts concerning her groundskeeper. The fiercely loyal Huggins, like an old and trusted dog, would have laid down his life for her had she asked it of him. It had been that way since the day he had approached her to beg a few coins for food and, taking pity on him, she had offered him employment instead and a roof over his head.

"Not many would've give Chester Huggins a second glance," he was fond of saying. "But then, Lady Felicity bain't of the common mold."

Ruefully, she reminded herself that Huggins had been clever enough to discover what might prove the first solid link to Trent's whereabouts. Certainly, he had surprised them all with his uncanny knowledge of the Swale, the Isle of Sheppey, and the surrounding waters, not to mention his unshakable conviction that he knew the "onliest place" Trent would choose to anchor. Further than that, he was the only one of the household who knew how to sail a boat, John Hallows not excluded. Nevertheless, Felicity could not be easy, knowing that, should they run into Steed's river pirates, Huggins would be of little use in an armed confrontation.

The devil with Will and his adamant refusal to allow her to go with him. She was not inexperienced in the use of firearms. Her brother Bertie, in one of his rare moods to humor his younger sister, had taught her how to shoot when she was fifteen. He had even presented her with a fine pearl-handled pocket pistol when she had shown a natural ability for hitting a target. She had never had occasion to use it or even to remove it from its velvet-lined box until the day after her near-abduction in Faversham. Primed and loaded, it resided now on the table by her bedside, a chilly comfort against the uneasy dreams that haunted her sleep at night.

It had not been sufficient to point out to Will that

there was little reason for Trent to trust a complete stranger, let alone welcome him aboard his schooner. The captain would know and trust her, however. She was, nominally at least, his employer.

"I shall have Huggins to vouch for me," Will had odiously been quick to counter. "And I have no intention of living another moment like the one I experienced upon seeing you in the hands of cutthroats." His hands on her shoulders, he had held her with his eyes. "You will do better here, Felicity, with Hallows to protect you, as shall I without the fear for your safety to distract me."

She had given in in the end because he had so obviously meant what he said—and because the blaze of tenderness in the look he bent upon her had somehow robbed her of all volition.

Botheration, she thought. She was not under his spell now.

Suddenly she bolted to her feet to stand, impotent and angry, her hands clenched against her frustration. How could she have let him talk her into waiting, knowing, as she had, what it would be like to be left behind? Naturally, it was all right for *her* to be distracted with worry over what might be happening at that very moment. That was the lot of a woman, was it not? she thought bitterly. She, however, was no hothouse flower. She had already fought one battle with Steed's pirates. Surely she had proven she was quite capable of holding her own. William Powell had no right to take over the running of her affairs. It was not, after all, as if she were his wife!

It was perhaps unfortunate that she had come to that particular conclusion in her deductive reasoning, as it brought her to the crux of what had really been acting as a spur to her uncertain temper of late.

Will had declared that she was the woman he was going to marry!

Good God, that was the last thing she had expected when she concocted her desperate scheme to keep him safely hidden at Primrose Cottage. She had, through the best of intentions, unwittingly won the declaration that she could never otherwise have hoped to have from him, and now, having been presented with that which she had most desired, she must refuse him! Only she had not done so, at least not in so many words, she reminded herself, the memory bringing a flush to her cheeks.

"I beg your pardon," she had retorted that afternoon on the seat of the curricle, "but I do not recall being asked to marry you."

"I am well aware of that," William had agreed, mirthlessly smiling. "On the other hand, you may be certain that when the time is right, I intend to remedy that omission."

When the time was right? Good God, thought Felicity, flinging herself down on the window seat once more. The time would never be right. How could it, when he could not remember the true state of affairs unless she were to enlighten him?

And now what must he do but embark on an errand that might very well prove dangerous? Even worse, he had done it all for her sake, while she was allowed to do nothing. Nothing, that is, she reflected wryly, but wait and drive herself to distraction with her unrewarding ruminations. Faith, it really was too bad of him. But then, what else should she have expected? William Powell was hardly the sort to turn his back on a woman in a coil, even if it was of her own making. It simply was not in his nature.

Finally, in disgust with herself at her inability to banish the disturbing thoughts of William Powell from her mind, let alone the dire possibilities inherent in his plan to dissuade Trent from the young hothead's ill-considered course, she determined on a practical curative for her nervous state. No doubt a glass of warm milk would not work wonders, she told herself, but at least it would be something to do other than prowl aimlessly about her bedchamber.

Throwing a dressing robe on over her nightdress, she reached for a candle, then hesitated, her glance on the pistol on the night table. But this was absurd, she told herself, deliberately straightening. Things were come to a sad pass indeed if she felt the need to go armed to the kitchens for a glass of milk, she reflected ruefully. Then, telling herself she was doing nothing more than creating a tempest in a teacup, she turned away, only to come to a halt again. "The devil!" she breathed, and, snatching up the weapon, slipped it in the pocket of her dressing robe and let herself out of her room into the hall.

The household having long since retired to bed, the halls lay steeped in silence, disturbed only by the small creaks and groans natural to an old house. Inexplicably, Felicity experienced a chill of unease as she made her way down the stairs. Indeed, she came very near to dropping the candle at a sudden clap of thunder, which heralded the arrival of the storm that had been building all evening. Telling herself she could no doubt attribute her absurd case of the nerves to the crackle of electricity in the air, she willed her heart to cease its pounding and resolutely squared her shoulders. It would be the height of absurdity to allow herself to be thrown into a silly fit of the vapors over something so common as a Kentish storm. She at least had the protection of a well-built house around her. William and Huggins, on the other hand, must surely have been caught out without the smallest hope of shelter.

Hard upon that disquieting thought, the rain came, spattering against the windows on a blustering wind, and suddenly the last thing she wanted was a glass of milk, warm or otherwise. She shivered, feeling the chill in the air penetrate her cotton nightgown beneath the dressing robe, hanging open in the front. Images of Will and Huggins battling the fury of wind and storm in their small boat held her where she was, though she knew she should return to the warmth of the fire in her room.

She jumped, her heart pounding, at a resounding crash somewhere upstairs, followed immediately by a persistent banging. Feeling foolish, she realized that one of the shutters must have been blown open and that, further, she was shivering with cold.

"Enough is enough, Felicity Talbot," she announced irritably to the empty room. "You are letting your imagination run away with you." Chiding herself for a gaby, she shook off the momentary feeling of dread that had gripped her and turned to retrace her steps to the stairway.

Will and Huggins were well able to fend for themselves, she told herself sternly. No doubt, realizing the storm was almost upon them, they had pulled ashore and taken shelter in a house or a barn until the weather should clear. Certainly, it was helping neither of them for her to behave like a silly peagoose over nothing more momentous than a storm, a few creaks and groans, and a banging shutter. She would see to the shutter, and then she would go to bed. It was as simple as that.

The hand came out of nowhere, clamping over her mouth before she could utter the scream that rose in her throat. It dragged her relentlessly backward.

* * *

Lethridge, waiting with tensed muscles as the skiff rounded the point, glimpsed in the sudden flash of lightning the schooner lying at anchor and, gathered around her like hounds for the kill, half a dozen boats filled with men. It was clear in that single glance that, intent on their stealthy approach on the schooner's stern, the men in the boats had failed to note the small sail bearing down on them. It came to him with paralyzing certainty, as well, that any decisions to be made had been made for him. Even he could see that it was too late to change tack. In moments, the skiff would be thrust among the boats.

Deliberately rising to his feet, he drew the pistol and aimed.

"Now, Huggins," he said and braced himself against the pitch and sway of the skiff beneath his feet.

Huggins's stentorian shout rang out. *"Ahoy, the ship! REPEL BOARDERS!"*

Lightning flashed. In that instant, Lethridge fired.

Even as a man, reaching to grapple the schooner, pitched forward into the water, Lethridge drew the second pistol and fired again.

The schooner came alive with shouting men and the crack of gunfire. Against flashes of lightning, Lethridge saw that two of the boats were working to grapple with the schooner. Still, Trent had been given warning. As men swarmed up and over the sides of the ship, they were met by the fierce onslaught of Trent's defenders.

With an effort, Lethridge tore his eyes away from the savage fighting on the schooner's decks. The skiff, carried on the wind and the river's current, was bearing rapidly down on the disengaged boats.

It would be over swiftly, he thought with a vague sense of unreality. What had begun as a simple mission to find Trent and persuade him to a surer means of bringing Steed to justice had altered dramatically. It hardly needed mathematical computations to demonstrate the impossible odds of two men pitted against the dozen river pirates carried in but a single boat.

Tossing both guns into the bottom of the skiff, he drew the borrowed sword from its scabbard. Briefly he tested the balance. Like John Hallows, who had carried it in defense of king and country, the hilt of the sword was tarnished and worn, but the steel of the blade was well made and true. A fine weapon, he thought. A pity it was about to end up on the bottom of the Swale or in the possession of one of Steed's thieving cutthroats.

At last an image of Felicity flashed through his mind. Sweet, courageous Felicity! In light of his present circumstances, he could only be grateful he had taken steps to ensure her safety in the event anything happened to him. John Hallows would see to everything, he had made certain of that.

There was a shout near at hand. Lightning flashed, and a boat's stern appeared to leap out of the darkness at him. Lethridge tightened his grip on the sword hilt as a figure in the stern sheets turned his head, a shout starting from his throat. Then the skiff's bow struck alongside, slamming into oars, and Lethridge slashed downward, sinking the razor-sharp edge into flesh. What had begun as a shout changed to a scream even as Lethridge felt the jar to his wrist, the rasp of steel against bone as he pulled the sword free. Ducking, he struck aside the slash of a cutlass, then thrust between the attacker's ribs. The man sagged, a dead weight dragging at Lethridge's sword arm, even as another savage form scrambled across the stern sheets, an upraised cutlass slicing downward. Lethridge tensed, powerless to stop it.

A flash of movement, the clang of steel against steel—Huggins cackled insanely as he swept the cutlass aside and hacked his blade across a bulging neck. Then at last Lethridge dragged his sword free. He turned to take the thrust of a boarding pike on his sword hilt, knowing it could not go on much longer. Men were crowded against the side, hampered by their numbers and the close quarters, but already figures were balanced atop the gunwales, preparing to leap across. In moments the skiff would be swamped, all hope of defense at an end.

Huggins, hacking and slashing beside him, yelled something indistinguishable in the din of fighting.

Lethridge stared into the muzzle of a cocked pistol. He swept his arm up, smashed the sword hilt into the barrel. There was a blinding flash, a sharp explosion—a blow, like a fist, flung him backward, leaving him stunned and staring up at the sky as the heavens opened up.

Vaguely it came to him that something was not quite what it should be. Then suddenly he understood. It was quiet, save for the rumble of thunder and the howl of wind and rain.

He felt someone kneel beside him and looked up through the splash of rain in his face into Huggins's scarred, homely features.

"They'm goin', me lord. Trent beat 'em off, by God. The storm done the rest."

"For Christ's sake, get me up."

Lethridge, feeling his head hammering, struggled to push himself on to one elbow.

"Easy, me lord." With Huggins's rough hands supporting his shoulders, Lethridge levered himself up to peer over the gunwales. The wind-driven rain had come with blinding swiftness, throwing confusion into the ranks of the attacking boats. The figures of men dropping over the sides of the schooner bore testimony to the success of Trent's defenders. The two boats that had been grappled to the sloop had been cut adrift, and the others were drawing steadily away toward the southeastern reaches of the Isle of Harty.

Their own skiff, adrift in the wind and a receding tide, seemed drawn to the schooner, which loomed out of the darkness over them. Lethridge had time to wonder how Huggins had managed to tie down the rudder and lower the sail in those fleeting moments before the skiff rammed the pirate boat. Then the bow came into jarring contact with the schooner's side, and, as the stern came around, trapping the skiff against the anchored ship, a harsh alarm rang out from topside.

"Hellsfire, Cap'n. There be another 'un."

"Softly, m'lady," whispered John Hallows in Felicity's ear. Carefully the former marine sergeant removed his hand from Felicity's mouth. "There are intruders about to breach the house."

Felicity breathed in sharply. "Who? Where—?"

Hallows lifted a warning finger to his lips. "Four, maybe five, not counting the blighter I laid out by the coach that brought them. They've come for Mrs. Steed, and I expect they'd have taken you if you'd been in your room."

Felicity, drawing in a steadying breath, swiftly gathered her wits about her. Steed had come with Lethridge away. *Steed had known,* seemed to ring like

an alarm in her head. Hallows had been the one variable that Steed could not have anticipated.

Quelling a shudder, she turned to face Hallows,
reassuring, somehow, in the flickering light of the
candle. "How did you know?"

"His lordship isn't the sort of man to leave things
to chance. Before he went, he gave orders to stand
watch. Old Goliath here's got a keen ear, m'lady."

A low whine and the shock of a cold nose against
Felicity's bare hand brought Felicity down to one
knee, her arm going around the dog's neck.

"Goliath," she murmured, pressing her cheek
against warm fur.

"Even so," Hallows remarked, "I expect I'd have
caught wind of the blighters. They're a scurvy lot."

"But what of Annabel?" demanded Felicity, coming quickly to her feet. "Faith, I have been thinking
only of myself when we should be doing something
to save her from Steed's men."

"Not to fear, m'lady," said Hallows, opening the
withdrawing room door a crack to peer out into the
foyer. "His lordship took the precaution of removing
Mrs. Steed belowstairs to the cellars. Had me fix it
up all cozy-like with rugs and a cot, a table and lamp
and such. He was a mite worried about you, miss,
knowing you'd likely not take to the idea of being
asked to hide out—in a cellar or anywhere else.
Which is why old Goliath and me have been patrol-
ling the grounds. It was somewhat ticklish when I saw
your light moving about downstairs at the very moment those blighters began scaling the wall to Mrs.
Steed's room. But as it turns out, I expect it was lucky,
you being downstairs while they are searching the
rooms up there."

"Searching!" Felicity's hand went out to Hallows's
sleeve. "But then, they are still here, and the entire

household is in danger! They will not stop until everyone is dead or they have discovered Annabel in the cellar."

"At the moment, m'lady, that is not my concern. His lordship's orders were to see to your safety, and that is what I mean to do. They won't find Mrs. Steed. They'll never make it past the door to the cellar. Once I have you safely out of the house, I will see what is to be done about—"

"And I mean to see these felons leave my house, Mr. Hallows," Felicity interrupted in measured accents. "Now, before they are able to do any mischief." Drawing the pocket pistol from her dressing gown, she stepped firmly past Hallows to the door.

There was a moment of hesitation as Hallows appeared to assess this unexpected turn of events. Then quietly he cleared his throat.

"I beg your pardon, ma'am," murmured the former marine, his weathered features impassive, "but if you're set on taking on four men with that little gun, I expect I should come along with you."

Felicity awarded him a grateful look. "I should be most happy to have you, Mr. Hallows."

Noiselessly, Felicity slipped through the withdrawing room door into the foyer, the gun gripped tightly in her fist. She was ruefully aware that her heart was pounding in a most unsettling manner and that her mouth was most uncommonly dry. Worse, she had not the smallest notion how best to proceed. Bertie had taught her how to shoot a gun; unfortunately, he had seen little reason to instruct her in the finer art of stalking intruders in one's house.

"Might I suggest a rear action, ma'am?" Hallows said quietly as she hesitated, her gaze searching the head of the stairway. Beside her, Goliath gave vent to a low growl sufficient to cause the hairs to rise at the

nape of her neck. She could feel Hallows tense with
the knowledge that the intruders would almost certainly be making their way to the lower quarters
within minutes. "They will be searching the rooms
upstairs, including the attic, and will soon be certain
you and Mrs. Steed are somewhere below, in hiding.
The servants' stairs would seem to offer a strategic
advantage."

An instinctive protest rose to Felicity's lips, her first
thought being that Hallows was trying to direct her
away from danger. Then it came to her. Here, they
were most certain to be discovered with no option
but an unavoidable confrontation, which she and
Hallows were ill prepared to meet. The servants'
stairs at the very least offered the opportunity for
maneuverability.

"We can get Hannah and the others out," she said,
coming at last to the gist of the matter.

"You'd have made a good officer, ma'am." Hallows
grinned. "Might I suggest we hurry? Old Goliath,
there, seems a mite anxious."

Goliath, as a matter of fact, appeared to be in the
sway of an almost irresistible impulse to launch a ferocious attack up the darkened staircase. Clearly, he
was held back only by the warring instinct to stay and
protect his mistress.

"I know, Goliath," murmured Felicity, reaching a
hand down to calm the bristling dog. "But you must
stay with me. Come, Hallows. Let us go."

The servants' stairs, located at the back of the
house, gave access to all the floors, but, most importantly in the circumstances, to the servants' quarters.
The household staff were quickly aroused and told
to retreat at once to the stables where they were to
wait until they were summoned—only it seemed that
everyone, from Mrs. Bickford, the cook, to Freddie,

the seventeen-year-old footman, wanted to stay and take up defenses against the "bloody fiends, beggin' Lady Felicity's pardon." Felicity, greatly moved but aware that at any second they must soon be discovered, firmly refused each and every one of them.

"Hurry and go now," she whispered for the ninth time as she nudged Daisy and a disapproving Hannah out into the rain, which, thankfully, had abated to a gentle drizzle. "Mr. Hallows and I shall be along directly, I promise."

Hardly had the last of the servants been shooed out the kitchen's service entrance, a process which had consumed a good ten minutes but seemed an eternity longer, than Felicity felt Hallows's hand close on her arm in silent warning.

"They're close by, ma'am," murmured Hallows, his eyes pointedly on Goliath.

Goliath had gone ominously still and, despite the dog's resemblance to a dust mop of gigantic proportions, left little doubt that his entire body was quivering with an instinct for danger. A low growl rumbled deep in his throat.

"Annabel!" Felicity breathed, grasping the former marine's sleeve. "Quick, Hallows! We must go to her."

Upon those final words, Felicity dashed from the kitchen into the pantry at the end of which was the stairway to the cellars. Goliath lumbered at her heels. Hallows was given little choice but to hasten after them down the curving stone steps to the cellar door.

"Annabel!" exclaimed Felicity. "Hurry. Unlock the door!"

She felt Hallows at her back stop and turn.

"It is too late, m'lady." Deliberately, he placed himself between her and the stairway.

Felicity's nerves tingled to the soft scrape of shoe

leather against stone, the threatening growl of the dog.

Knowing it was useless, she yanked down on the door handle. A startled gasp burst from her lips at the click of the latch. The door gave way before her.

"Annabel!" she called, lifting the candle above her head.

The flickering light cast grotesque shadows about the newly refurbished cell. A neat cot with a blue counterpane, a chair and a small table with a lamp, a braided rug—all leaped out at her against the racks of bottled wines. Her stomach clenched with a terrible hollow sensation.

"Annabel!" she called again, knowing it was pointless.

The cellar was empty.

Behind her, Goliath gave vent to a ferocious snarl. Hallows braced himself. Felicity came around, her hand fumbling for the gun in her pocket.

A leering face loomed into the faint circle of light. Hallows lunged forward, driving his fist into the bewhiskered jaw, then, catching himself, rammed his shoulder hard into a second villain's midriff. His arm clasped about the man's waist, Hallows drove the man backward up the stairs. With a growl, Goliath hurtled past the two grappling men. A scream of mortal terror rent the air at the head of the stairs and echoed down the staircase.

Felicity stood in stunned silence, her eyes fixed on the ruffian who shoved himself up off the cellar floor where Hallows had felled him. Clasping the pistol tightly, she held the weapon straight out before her.

"I suggest you turn around and go back up those stairs," she said very carefully. "Otherwise I shall be forced to shoot you."

Dismayed, she saw that her hand was shaking.

The ruffian saw it, too. Grinning to expose yellowed, crooked teeth, he started toward her.

Eleven

Lethridge, sinking gratefully into a worn leather chair, allowed his gaze to travel curiously over the schooner's stern cabin. It was small, the deck beams overhead so low that he had been forced to bend his shoulders to keep from hitting his head, but there was a certain charm about the cabin nonetheless, he decided. The graceful slope of the stern windows with the padded seat beneath them must allow for a splendid view, and the desk, chairs, and other furniture, while showing much use, were neatly arranged to provide the maximum benefit from the limited space.

He let his gaze rest speculatively on the youthful captain who lived and worked here, presumably planning every detail of sailing this sleek lady. Tall and slim, his black hair falling over his forehead, he looked much as Lethridge had imagined. He noted the slender hand tapping impatiently against the side of one leg and guessed that Captain Trent was not so calm in the wake of his encounter with Steed's river pirates as he would like Lethridge to believe. But then, there was about the man a sense of reckless energy only just contained beneath the surface. Like a green, spirited colt, he would take careful handling if Lethridge were to have any hope of winning his trust, let alone his cooperation in the venture he had in mind.

Suddenly Lethridge was made aware that Trent's blue, restless eyes were trained speculatively on his uninvited guest.

"May I offer you a drink, my lord?" Trent said, reaching for a decanter and two glasses. "You have the look of a man who could use one." Pausing in filling the glasses, he added, "Perhaps you should have someone see to that wound on your head. I've a man who is not unfamiliar with such things."

Lethridge, touching his fingers gingerly to the crust of dried blood over his temple, smiled mirthlessly. The graze from the pirate's pistol ball was little more than an inch above the healing scar of that other one. Strange that it should have left him feeling peculiarly clearheaded, more so than he had felt since he had awakened a fortnight ago to Goliath perched on his chest and Felicity Talbot staring down at him, her lovely eyes dark with anxiety.

He shrugged. "It is nothing, but thank you for your concern." Accepting a glass, Lethridge gave a sweeping gesture encompassing the length of the ship. "She is a fine vessel, Captain Trent. It would have been a shame to lose her."

"Aye, my lord. She was bequeathed to me by my grandfather. It is all I have left of that other life." The blue eyes hardened. "All I want of it." He turned swiftly to Lethridge. "And it would seem I have you to thank for it. What are you doing out here, my lord? You haven't the look of a seafaring man."

Lethridge smiled wryly. "You are right, Captain. I am better suited to a fast team of horses than a seagoing vessel. If I ever step foot in a leaky boat again, it will be too soon. It was, however, necessary. You are a cursedly difficult man to meet, Captain Trent."

Restlessly Trent's fingers tapped the hilt of the sword at his belt. "I'm a hunted man, as you've just seen. And now I've the additional worry of excisemen to occupy me. I haven't much time, my lord. If you hadn't asked for this interview, I should already have weighed ship for open sea."

Lethridge eyed Trent steadily. "And if I were to tell you how you can rid yourself of Steed once and for all *and* clear yourself with the excisemen with the same stroke, what then, Captain?"

Lethridge saw the slender fingers clench on the sword's hilt.

"Then, my lord, I'd say you were either a magician or a liar."

Lethridge felt as if his arms must pull from their sockets as he climbed down the chains and dropped stiffly into the skiff. Huggins was already before him, his hand on the tiller, a grin on his face.

"Us'll make a sailor of yer yet, me lord," he said, bringing the sail around to take the wind as Lethridge shoved them free of the schooner's side. "Even Cap'n Trent were impressed with the fight yer put up agin that scum."

Lethridge, squinting against the dull throb in his skull, sank wearily down in the bow. "If you say so, Huggins. No doubt I should make as good a sailor as you do a coachman, given practice." As Huggins gave a low chuckle, Lethridge deliberately turned his gaze on him. "I believe I must thank you, Huggins," he said quietly. "For saving my life, and for a great deal more besides."

Even in the darkness, Lethridge sensed the man's startled pleasure. "All in a day's work, me lord."

"Yes, no doubt," murmured Lethridge, feeling his

tiredness like a weight bearing him down. "All the same, I shall be glad to be quit of this vessel."

His thoughts drifted to Felicity and the news he must tell her. Meggie was alive and closer than either of them had deemed possible. Trent had discovered the child quite by accident in the care of an oysterman and his wife. Even dressed in rags and covered with filth, the little girl, with her black hair, ivory complexion, and blue-violet eyes, had stood out among the couple's brood of seven hopefuls like a white rose in a field of yellow buttercups.

"Tell Annabel, when you see her, that her Meggie's safe with my sister Laura. Tell her I . . ." But Trent had not finished it. Turning away, he had stared out the stern windows, his frame taut with what he could not bring himself to say. Lethridge thought he knew what was in the young firebrand's heart. It could not be easy loving another man's wife.

Still, the trap was to be laid—not a ship secured at anchor, but a warehouse full of contraband. Trent had more than done his part. Using threats and bribes and paid informants of his own, he had broken the Gentlemen's code of silence and in so doing had traced Steed's underground smuggling and pirating network, from the porters and batmen who ran the illicit crops of goods inland, to the "hides"—barns, cellars, abandoned houses—anywhere contraband might be concealed until it was sold and dispersed throughout the countryside. Young Leftenant Wilkers was about to become something of a local legend, Lethridge thought with grim amusement. Tonight, when Wilkers raided the warehouse, he would have all the evidence he needed to put Steed out of business for good.

Not that it would have much of an effect on the free trade in Kent, he reflected cynically. Lethridge suspected there would always be smuggling; for too long it had been a way of life along the coasts of England ever to change now. Trent, from this day forth, would be a marked man.

Lethridge, fighting to keep his eyelids from drooping, smiled faintly to himself. He believed he had come up with a solution to Trent's problem, if the stubborn young fool did not get it into his head to up anchor and run before Lethridge could implement it. Trent had given his word to be waiting at the rendezvous. It remained only for Lethridge to do his part to make certain Wilkers was on hand to play his crucial part in the plan and, equally important, to draw Steed into the snare.

Nothing must go wrong, he thought, forcing himself to go over every detail in search of some variable he had missed. In the event that the plan misfired, Trent, at least, must be protected. The captain was taking the greatest risk of all, setting himself up as the bait. He did not deserve to end up in some alley with his throat slit. It would be well to send the letter immediately, thought Lethridge, pressing his fingers gingerly to the throbbing groove at his temple. But for now he was aware of a nagging impatience to reach Primrose Cottage and Felicity.

Annabel would have her Meggie back before the day was through, and by the time the night was over, Steed would be finished. Then at last there would be nothing to keep him from focusing all his energies on the one thing that really signified.

Lethridge had only to close his eyes to see her—the crinkle of her eyes when she laughed, the lift of her head when she was moved to anger, the tilt of her chin when her mind was set on a thing, which was too often for his own peace of mind. And yet he would have had her no different. She was Felicity, his sweet, impossible, darling girl.

The bow struck sand, and he jerked his head up and rubbed his eyes. He felt gritty from lack of sleep, and the wound over his temple throbbed. A hot bath and a shave would work wonders for him, he decided, thinking of everything that had yet to be done. The first probing fingers of dawn were driving back the darkness. With relief, he recognized the old, rotting pier, the abandoned fisherman's hut standing a short distance away from the beach, the rising knoll from which he had watched Felicity keep her appointment with Trent. He shoved himself up and swung his leg over the side. It would not be long now.

The walk up the hill and through the cherry orchards served to revive him, the perfume of cherry blossoms bringing back memories of the picnic he had shared with Felicity, his mounting despair at his inability to remember his past, the nagging feeling that his angel was keeping something from him. Was it really only two weeks ago? he wondered. It seemed as if he had lived a lifetime in that short span, as if whatever had come before held little of importance in light of what he had awakened to, he thought with a bemused smile. Unconsciously, he quickened his step.

She must have been watching for him. Hardly had he stepped free of the cherry orchard, his eyes seeking the house on the hill, than he glimpsed the slender figure hurrying toward him, skirts billowing about her legs. Instantly his weariness was forgotten, replaced by the sudden grip of apprehension.

"There he is, Hallows!" Felicity exclaimed, pointing from the balcony. "He is all right! Thank God, he is all right."

The next instant she had turned and, picking up her skirts, was running down the stairs, heedless of the gaping servants. She did not stop running until, reaching him, she flung herself against his tall frame, her arms about his neck.

"Will, you have come back! I have been so afraid I should not see you again."

Startled, Lethridge clasped her to him. He felt a chill grip his heart. She was weeping uncontrollably, Felicity, his dauntless, wholly sensible girl! The devil, he cursed. What had occurred in his absence to so break her defenses?

Grim-faced, he held her, his hand slowly stroking her hair, until at last he felt her shudders give way to a tremulous sigh, followed by a hiccough. Will, feeling her stir in his arms, instantly loosened his hold on her.

"The devil," sniffed Felicity, suddenly and abashedly aware that she had utterly disgraced herself. "I detest females who cry. It is so damnably feminine. What a peagoose you must think me."

"A peagoose indeed," William agreed, drawing forth his handkerchief and dabbing at her cheeks. "I should even go so far as to say you have become a veritable watering pot."

Felicity, startled into a watery gurgle of laughter, snatched the handkerchief from him. "Wretch!" she said, blowing her nose. "How dare you poke bogey at me when I have had a devil of a time. You know very well that in the norm I am not such a poor creature."

Lethridge, relieved to see the color returning to her face, was yet aware of a mounting pressure in his chest. Something had occurred to break her reserve. "I collect I am mistaken," he observed soberly. "And now, suppose you tell me what has happened."

"Oh, nothing much," Felicity said on a gasp, "save that I have shot a man, and Annabel is missing. I fear she has gone back to Steed; indeed, she must have done. Will, however shall we get her back again?"

Lethridge, attaching his signature to the bottom of the page, laid the pen aside and quickly folded the sheet of paper. For a moment he hesitated, dwelling on the implications of the letter, exploring his reluctance. If only there were more time, he thought, ruefully aware how little he felt ready to put his fate to the touch. But there *was* no more time. Annabel Steed's disappearance had made that patently clear. Even if he survived the night, he could hardly afford to put things off any longer. There were too many others now to consider.

Suddenly he was angry with himself and the vague sense of foreboding that had brought him to the study to write the letter, a dread that he did not doubt was due as much to fatigue as anything else. Impatiently he took up the candle and dripped wax on the seam of the letter. With an air of finality, he deliberately pressed his signet ring into the wax. Bloody hell, it was long past time he put his affairs in order.

Shoving himself up from the desk, he crossed quickly to the bell pull and rang for the stable lad, then stood staring out the window, his back to the room until the youth entered.

"Please see that the letter on the desk is carried to London at once. You will change horses at the posting inns. There is a purse to defray the expenses," he said with only a cursory glance over his shoulder. Consequently, he did not see the boy's eyes, round with curiosity, as he took in the sword and the loaded pistol laid out on the desk, or how they widened even further as Lethridge told him the direction on the missive.

"Very good, m'lord," replied the youth. Turning smartly, he left his lordship to his ruminations.

At least, thought Lethridge, the letter would provide Trent with an alternative to living his life on the run. It might even offer a solution to Annabel's dilemma—if, that was, Annabel was not already dead because of her fool-headed gesture. And he did not doubt that that was what it had been, in light of the previous night's events.

With everyone of the household trying to speak at once, it had been some time before Lethridge was able to piece together all the events that had led overnight to the cellars being filled with felons, one of whom had sustained a bullet wound to the foot and another of whom, while not greatly injured, appeared to have developed an unnatural dread of Old English sheepdogs. It was the latter who, when faced with the prospect of being left alone in Goliath's company, was to prove the most eager to divulge to an ecstatic Leftenant Wilkers everything he knew about Steed's pirating and smuggling enterprises.

"There, you see, Leftenant Wilkers?" Felicity had been unable to resist saying. "Captain Trent, far from being a smuggler or a pirate, is an honest sailor who has been maliciously maligned by the man you should have been after all along. I know you will want to make amends to the captain by immediately calling off your pursuit of him. After all, he is sticking his neck out to bring Steed into your custody."

"You may be sure of it, ma'am," replied the young leftenant, doffing his hat to her. "My lads will have strict orders to see to Captain Trent's protection."

"Splendid," Felicity applauded, seeing Wilkers to the door. "And please feel free to drop by for tea anytime. You will always be welcome at Primrose Cottage."

With Wilkers having been made aware of his role in the night's planned proceedings, there had been only one task left to be done to set matters into motion. Steed's henchman, whom Hallows had rendered insensible outside the house and who subsequently had been kept separate from his fellows, was to be blessed with unexpected good fortune. Not only was he to manage an unlooked-for escape, but he was to be given to overhear Huggins and John Hallows obviously in their cups, discussing with no little jubilation Steed's failed attempt on "Cap'n Trent's" schooner. More importantly, he was to learn of Trent's boast that he would wreak a suitable vengeance that very night for Steed's bloody raid.

"Cap'n Trent are a bold 'un, matey," Huggins had chortled, helping himself to a drink from a flask which exuded fumes strongly suggestive of rum. "Mark me words, come t'morrow Steed'll not know what hit 'im."

"Maybe," Hallows had replied somewhat doubtfully. "Steed's storage house in Faversham will be well guarded. Trent will need more than brass to clear it out. He'll need a hand from Lady Luck herself."

"A guinea on Trent, matey," Huggins had ventured daringly. "The cap'n'll strike nigh on to midnight and be gone afore Steed can muster so much as a by yer leave."

Hallows shook his head ponderingly. "I hate to take an old Jack's money, but you're on. Much as I'd like to see Steed get what's coming to him, I daresay Trent'll never get away with it."

"What's an old bullock like yer know?" Huggins had scoffed, lifting the flask with a flourish. "Chester Huggins'll be drinkin' to Cap'n Zachary Trent by this time t'morrow. Yer can wager yer bloody boots on it."

In spite of the fact that his carefully constructed plans would seem to be progressing with an ease he could not have foreseen, Lethridge was yet conscious of a nagging feeling of dissatisfaction.

Had it not been for Annabel's disappearance, he did not doubt he would have been content to play a minor role in the final act of bringing Steed to his long-deserved justice. All logic and reason cried out against a needless display of heroics. It would have been enough to be the architect of Steed's destruction without having to wield the actual sword that felled him, especially as there could never be any sort of guarantee in an armed conflict who would come out the victor. Coldly, Lethridge acknowledged a powerful aversion to the mere possibility that Josiah Steed might cut his stick for him. Such a realization did not bring into question either his manhood or his courage. He knew he was not averse to taking a calculated risk—*for a strong purpose.* Killing a man like Steed, however, was akin to ridding the world of a blight. It was a necessity, not a question of honor.

Annabel, however, had changed all that. It was the height of irony that, in choosing to sacrifice herself unnecessarily, she had made a confrontation with Steed unavoidable for Lethridge.

Damn the wench! Just when it had seemed that nothing stood in the way of the realization of the one goal that mattered to him, he was to be faced with a fight he neither wanted nor needed. How much greater the irony when set against the bittersweet moments he had experienced only hours ago at the hands of his darling girl!

It had been just after Felicity's unwonted surrender

to tears, followed by her startling revelations concerning the night's adventures. Only after having given way to relief at seeing Will safely returned to her, especially in the wake of a night to try the hardiest of souls, had she truly looked at him.

It had almost been worth the nagging pain in his skull to see the swift blur of concern in his darling girl's eyes.

"Will," she had exclaimed, reaching hesitantly up to touch the wound over his temple. "Faith, you are hurt!"

It had done him little good to assure her that it was only a scratch and that, indeed, his brains were still intact. She would not be consoled until she had him seated on a straight-backed chair in the parlor, a bowl of warm water and a clean cloth near to hand.

It had been exquisite torture to sit still while she, hovering over him, ministered to his wound. The fiery sting of the ointment applied to the cut had been nothing compared to the sweet torment of her fingers' gentle touch or the featherlike brush of her bosom against the side of his face as she reached across him for the square of court plaster. It had taken every ounce of his considerable willpower to remain outwardly unmoved as his senses were assailed by the feminine scents of lavender water and perfumed powder, not to mention that tantalizingly indefinable woman's scent that was uniquely hers. And all the while, he must be aware too of the barely contained turmoil within her breast, evidenced by the telltale throb of her pulse in the slender column of her neck, the discernible tremble of her fingertips as she had probed the wound for foreign particles that might later have invited the onset of poisoning.

No doubt he should feel ashamed that he had derived a perverse sort of gratification at the realization she was experiencing the horror of how near he had come to death, but he could not bring himself to regret it. It had affected him like potent wine, the knowledge that she could care so much.

And at last he had been driven beyond the bounds of forbearance as, glancing up into her face as she had finished affixing the court plaster in place, he had seen into her eyes.

Almost without conscious volition, he had clamped his hand about her wrist. Even now he could not but marvel at the current of emotion that had flowed, quivering like something alive, between them. Rising, he had pulled her to him, and she had come willingly, her mouth lifting to meet his. He could not be mistaken in that, any more than he could be wrong in thinking she had returned his kiss with a fiery sweet abandon quite unlike anything he had ever imagined before in a woman. He had known in that moment that she was his.

Staring blindly out the study window at the gathering darkness, he thought of her upstairs, asleep at last.

"Felicity," he said.

Then, turning, he picked up the loaded pistol off the desk and, thrusting it through his waistband, reached to strap the sword around his waist.

Pausing only to fling on his greatcoat and hat, he strode without a backward glance out the door and from the house to his mount, saddled and waiting.

"What do you mean he has gone? When?" Felicity demanded, her gaze going from one to the other of the two men standing before her in the foyer. "Gone where?"

Huggins shifted his feet, his eyes studiously avoiding those of his mistress. "It were at the end of the second dogwatch," he said unhappily. "Before the sun were down. He made us promise not to tell yer, me lady. We give our word."

"Your *word*," repeated Felicity in no mood to be conciliatory. "Your word. A pox on your word. He has gone after Steed on his own, has he not? Hallows, you will tell me. He has gone to fetch Mrs. Steed back before Trent launches his raid on the warehouse, hasn't he? If he is not killed in the trying."

The side of a fist to her mouth to quell a tumultuous gasp, she paced a step, then halted, her eyes on the hall clock. Nearly half past eleven. She had slept without moving for six hours, only to bolt awake in the grip of some formless sense of dread. She had known before ever she descended the staircase that Lethridge had gone, impelled by his cursed sense of duty. And now Trent and his men would be making their approach on the warehouse with Leftenant Wilkers and the excisemen positioned and ready to leap into the fray. Damn Lethridge and his noble intentions! How dared he risk his life again for something that was not his concern? No one had asked him to do it.

Carried on a wave of panic, she turned on John Hallows and the squirming Huggins. "The devil," she gasped. "How could you have let him go by himself?"

"His lordship's a stubborn man, milady," Hallows observed quietly. "He said our duty is to you now."

"Your duty is whatever *I* tell you it is. I am ordering you to take me to him. Huggins, you will bring the carriage around. At once, do you hear me?"

"It would not be strategically wise, ma'am," Hallows calmly insisted. "We could not possibly reach his lordship before he has already done what he set out to do. Begging your pardon, milady, but try and see it through his lordship's eyes. Mrs. Steed will have gone home, to the house in Faversham. It is all she would know to do. If Mrs. Steed is still alive, she will be little better than a hostage. You know what Steed is as well as I do. What do you think he would do to her if he saw armed men riding up to his front door?"

"He would kill her," Felicity said bitterly. "Then make his escape by boat down Faversham Creek to one of his ships. The warehouse and his men would be taken, but he would be free to continue on somewhere else. The trap would have been rendered meaningless."

Felicity looked away, remembering Lethridge in those last moments before he had sent her upstairs to her bed—the way he had held her, his hand running over her hair with a tenderness that even now made her heart ache. And all the time he was bewitching her, silencing her protests and soothing away the last of her lingering fears, he had *known* what he had meant to do. Faith, *why* had she not seen it before?

"He will not wait for Steed to go to the warehouse," she continued dully, seeing it the way Lethridge must have done. "He will confront him in his home, knowing Steed's men will all be at the docks, waiting for Trent to come. It will be his best chance to take Steed without harm to Annabel."

Hallows's steady gaze met hers. "One man, alone, milady. It was the only way. His lordship knew that better than anyone."

Felicity, overcome with a helpless sense of despair, had failed utterly to hear the front door open. Nor was she aware of the quick, light step behind her.

"His lordship knew what better than anyone?" demanded a familiar masculine voice at her shoulder.

"What lordship? Why the devil does everyone look so glum? Damme, Felicity, don't say Will has cut his stick now that Shelby has left the country, for I won't stand for it. And neither, I daresay, will Lord and Lady Bancroft, here. Stands to reason, after all. He's their son."

"Bertie!" breathed Felicity, who had turned to regard her brother with no little astonishment. She was a deal more than astonished, however, to discover, standing just inside the door, a distinguished-looking gentleman and a lady who, despite the care and weariness writ plain on her face, was remarkable for her fair good looks and trim, upright figure. Both of them, in the wake of Bertie's less than tactful outburst, were studying her with an air of grave apprehension.

Felicity felt the world seem to tilt and turn. There was, however, no disputing the evidence of her own eyes and ears. Shelby, it seemed, had survived his wound. Further, by some quirk of fate, he had been persuaded to sail from England. Lethridge was free of the threat of self-imposed exile. And now the Earl of Bancroft and his lady wife had come in search of their eldest son.

It came to her with stunning certainty that her brief dream of happiness had come to an end. And yet how insignificant it all seemed now!

The charade was over, but Lethridge might already lie dead.

Felicity felt a cold, hollow space open up inside her.

The house facing North Lane and, beyond it, the pond which gave access to Faversham Creek had not the look of a pirate's stronghold. The imposing wealden house with its projecting wings of timber frame

and red tile cladding might have belonged to a prosperous merchant, reflected Lethridge, tethering his
horse to the ironwork fence in front. But then, Steed
was undoubtedly prosperous, and the house, a pro-
jection of the pirate chieftain's vanity, provided at
least the facade of respectability. Further than that,
it furnished a possible clue to the man's character,
and to the motivation, perhaps, behind his ruthless
obsession to reclaim his wife for the sole purpose of
putting a period to her existence.

Grimly, Lethridge recalled the arrogance and
loathing in Steed's look, the unconcealed contempt
in his eyes. Lethridge did not doubt that the man's
antipathy for all that was represented by the privi-
leged classes was surpassed only by his envy of that
which he could never hope to attain. Rank, privilege,
social position—the manner in which these were
taken for granted by persons who regarded them as
theirs by right—all these he would despise simply because, by birth, they were denied to him. How much
greater must be his obsession for a wife whom he had
been unable to break and whom he could never fully
possess because her heart had long since been won
by another! Ironically, that was the one aspect of the
man's character that gave Lethridge any hope that
Steed had not yet done away with her.

Steed's vanity had demanded that his wife be returned to him. With any luck, his need to degrade
and break her to his will was keeping her alive. And
perhaps, just perhaps, Steed's overweaning arrogance would be sufficient to gain Lethridge the time
he needed.

Time, he thought, going over it all again in his
mind. By the time Lethridge had left the cottage,
Steed must already have been informed of Trent's
supposed intentions. Presented with the opportunity

to rid himself once and for all of the man who not only had stood between himself and the unattainable Annabel, but who had become a dangerous thorn in his side, Steed would have begun immediate preparations to put his own trap into place. Then would come the waiting.

Steed would be inside the house now with Annabel, taunting her with the imminent demise of the man she loved. Lethridge knew it as surely as he knew Steed would not leave the girl alive when he departed for his final rendezvous with Trent. Annabel's fatal error had been to think Steed wanted her, when all he would ever desire from any woman was to realize a total subjugation of her will to his. That, Annabel had given to him when she returned willingly to his house. Having achieved his purpose, Steed would have no further use for her now, save to torment and hurt her for his own pleasure.

Lethridge bent his head to peer at his watch. Half past eleven. It was time.

Deliberately he walked up to the front of the house.

The butler who admitted him viewed Lethridge's tall, aristocratic bearing with studied impassivity belied by the flicker of surprise behind the guarded eyes. Negligently Lethridge tossed him his hat, followed peremptorily by his greatcoat.

"You may inform Mrs. Steed that Viscount Lethridge is here to see her." Lethridge paused in removing his gloves to direct his gaze at the servant, who had remained unmoving. *"At once,"* he said coldly. "And do not tell me she has retired for the night. I know she has not." He slapped the gloves down inside of his hat. "On second thought, you may take me to her."

"I'm afraid, m'lord, that is quite impossible. Mrs. Steed—"

Lethridge came quickly around. "Nothing is impossible, save for any hope for your continued well-being do you fail to do as you are told." For a moment he let his words sink home. Then, satisfied, he casually straightened his cuffs. "Now," he said, feeling the bored mask of the Corinthian slip into place, "you may direct me to Mrs. Steed."

The butler visibly swallowed. "Of-of course, m'lord," he said, a distinct quiver in his voice. "If you would be so good as to follow me."

Steed, it was soon obvious, enjoyed being surrounded by luxury, as was evidenced by the heavy brocade and satin upholstery, the damask drapes and thick Oriental rugs, all lending to the impression of unbridled opulence, done in sultry crimson and gilt. As he followed up the staircase in the butler's wake, Lethridge was aware of the profusion of objets d'art, which served to add to the oppressiveness of the place.

He eyed the slight figure in front of him, the narrow shoulders compressed with uncertainty, and grinned mirthlessly. He had not liked stripping the man of his dignity, but it had been patently necessary. Having his presence announced would hardly have served his purpose. Steed might have used the warning to put a swift end to Annabel. Briefly he wondered if he had already come too late. The cursed house seemed shrouded in brooding silence, like a bloody mausoleum.

He was soon to have his answer. From beyond a closed door issued a woman's low-throated cry, swiftly silenced. Lethridge clenched a fist on his sword hilt. Before him, the butler hesitated, his head turned over his shoulder to Lethridge so that the fear shone stark in his eyes. Lethridge guessed the man had heard it all before, knew what was going on in that closed room and the sort of man he served. With a curt nod, Lethridge dismissed him, then, without waiting for the man's scuttering retreat back the way they had come, reached for the door handle.

Even knowing what he might find did not prepare Lethridge for the sight that greeted him beyond the open door. Steed, standing, one knee propped on the edge of the bed, a shoulder rising and falling as he slammed a fist down with calculated savagery, and, beneath him, the jerk of the woman's slight body, pale against the blood-red velvet of the bedcover.

In a single stride, Lethridge was in the room, his hand snaking the sword from its sheath.

"Steed!" he uttered chillingly.

Steed, feeling the cold touch of steel against the throbbing vein at his neck, went deathly still.

"Leave her," Lethridge commanded, his voice cutting through the sudden silence. Carefully he backed away as Steed slowly straightened.

On the bed, the woman stirred, a low moan escaping through her lips. Lethridge kept his eyes on Steed, moving warily beneath the sword point pressed against his throat. Out of the corner of his eye, he glimpsed the woman's nakedness, the marks like obscene brands on her body, and felt the sickness in his throat burned away by a hot, mounting rage.

"I have known some mean, cowardly bastards in my time," he said, measuring each word, "but none to compare to you. And I cannot think of a reason why I should not run you through right here and now—save for one." In a single swift movement, he smashed the sword hilt hard into Steed's face, snapping his head to one side and ramming him to his knees. Deliberately Lethridge flung the sword aside. "It would be too bloody quick for you."

Steed, realizing he had been granted a reprieve, lifted his head up. The green eyes stared at Lethridge with chilling coldness. He lurched to his feet to stand swaying slightly, his chest heaving with each breath. Contemptuously he ran the back of a hand over his smashed and bloodied lips. "Then you're a damned fool," he growled and launched himself at Lethridge.

Lethridge felt himself in the grip of some terrible madness that swept away all caution and reason. Feeling his lips part in a wild grin, he met Steed head on, oblivious to everything but the need to drive his fists into that smashed and bloodied face. Seemingly impervious to the hammering of Steed's blows, he drove the man relentlessly backward about the room, until at last he saw the leap of fear in Steed's eyes. Then, and only then, did he end it.

Drawing his arm back, he slammed his fist into the man's jaw, the whole force of his rage behind it.

Steed went down with a jarring crash and did not move again.

Dazed by the savagery of his own emotions, Lethridge stood, swaying, over Steed, his breath coming in quick, shallow gusts. Only then, as he felt the anger, along with his strength, drain out of him, did he become aware of the woman's shuddering gasps in the silence.

It was not over yet, he reminded himself. If things were progressing as planned, Trent and his men would be preparing to walk into Steed's trap. A grim smile played about his lips. It would be a shame if Steed were to miss his own party, he reflected. Clearly, it behooved Lethridge to make certain that did not happen. But first he must see to the girl.

Twelve

Felicity, confronted with the unavoidable reality of Lethridge's mama and papa in her foyer, their faces expressive of the misgivings fostered by her brother Bertie's unfortunate outburst, felt her heart go out to them in spite of her own anxieties.

"Bertie, how could you!" she declared, awarding that worthy a withering glance. Quickly she closed the distance between herself and her unexpected guests. "Pray pay my brother no mind, Lord and Lady Bancroft," Felicity hastened to reassure them. "Lethridge is away at the moment, that is all. Indeed, you will be glad to know his lordship has all but recovered from his wound. Physically, he is just as you remember him."

"Physically?" repeated the earl doubtfully, his alarm, rather than being allayed, appearing to increase exponentially.

Felicity bit her bottom lip in consternation. Faith, it was going to be more difficult than she had imagined. "What I mean is he has quite regained his strength," she hurried on, acutely aware that she was making a complete mull of things and somehow unable to stop herself. "You see, he was wounded in the head . . . well, not *in* the head precisely," she hastened to amend at the sound of Lady Bancroft's sharply indrawn breath. "He was struck a glancing blow to the temple, which put him in a coma for some little time. We were all quite concerned for him. He came out of it, of course, for which we are all very grateful. Indeed, he has since made a remarkable recovery." She hesitated, hardly knowing how to put the true nature of his condition into words. "The thing is, he has not quite been himself."

"Not himself? Good heavens, my girl," exclaimed the Earl of Bancroft. "What, precisely, are you trying to tell us? Will is not—not—"

"But of course he is not, William," said Lady Bancroft, who had been studying Miss Talbot with a calm, penetrating gravity strongly reminiscent of her eldest son. "Come, my child." Taking Felicity firmly by the arm, she led her past the gaping Huggins and John Hallows and through the open withdrawing room doors straight to the settee before the fire in the fireplace. "You must think us dreadfully rag-mannered, arriving like this. I must apologize for the lateness of the hour, but you see, having learned from Lady Braxton that Lethridge was seen in Faversham, we simply could not constrain ourselves from coming straightaway. It was purely by chance that we encountered Bertram upon our arrival at the Ship Hotel. When he informed us Lethridge was here with you, I fear we did not think beyond our concern for our son. Still, it was unconscionable for us not to have sent word ahead that we were arriving. You have been under a deal of strain, have you not, and here we are adding to it."

"No, of course not, Lady Bancroft," Felicity said, recalling somewhat belatedly her duties as a hostess. "Please, won't you have a seat? Bertie, be so good as to ring for a tray, while I relieve Lord and Lady Bancroft of their things. I daresay you must all be famished after your journey."

"I, for one, could not eat a thing," observed Bancroft, allowing Felicity to take his greatcoat, hat, and gloves. "But about William—"

"All in good time, my dear," Lady Bancroft gently admonished, sending the earl a meaningful look. "Miss Talbot has already assured us that William's health is excellent, and she is quite right. We have come a very long way. I think we should all benefit from a dish of tea and a moment to catch our breath."

"Or perhaps something somewhat stronger than tea, what, my lord?" suggested Bertie, who, having seen Lady Bancroft's glance, was beginning to apprehend what must have been obvious to the countess almost from her first close scrutiny of Felicity. It occurred to him that the girl was looking rather pinched around the gills, which was deucedly unlike his normally mettlesome kid sister. More than that, she appeared peculiarly nervous, continuously glancing at the mantel clock as if she expected someone to come bursting into the house at any moment. Deucedly odd it was, to his way of thinking. And where the devil had Lethridge gone off to in the middle of the night? He had the uneasy suspicion that there was trouble afoot and that for once in her life his little sister might need him to help her. The devil of it was he couldn't for the life of him think how.

Going to the decanter on the sidetable, Bertie poured two glasses and handed one to his lordship, who stared at it for a long moment as if questioning why it was there in his hand. It was obvious to Felicity, watching him, that Bancroft feared the worst for his eldest son. How could she possibly tell him that, aside from suffering from an acute case of amnesia, Lethridge might even then be lying dead? With a

sense of helplessness, she glanced at the mantel
clock. A quarter past midnight. How could she go on
pretending, she wondered despairingly, when her
thoughts were all in Faversham?

Emmaline, Lady Bancroft, seeing that look, was
made immediately aware of the feeling of being
caught up in some sort of bizarre nightmare that
must soon come to an end. Had anyone told her as
little as four days ago that she would find herself trav-
eling nearly the entire length of England in the old
family travel coach in search of her firstborn son,
who, having recklessly engaged in a duel and report-
edly been wounded, had apparently dropped off the
face of the earth—indeed, unbeknownst to herself,
had been missing for all of three weeks—she would
have been more than a little incredulous. Lethridge,
of all her children, she would have said, would be
the last to so abandon all sense of duty and rationality
as to risk his life in a meeting at dawn at twenty paces.
She might have believed such a thing of Timothy,
who, even as a child, had ever demonstrated a tendency to give way to a proud, passionate nature.
Faith, she would have come sooner to believe it of
Francie, her impetuous, daredevil tomboy, than of
William, who in temperament and intellect was the
one who took most after her dearest, eminently rational Bancroft. But then, she could not but admit
that she had always known that, of all her sons, William was the one in which the water ran deepest.

Indeed, she had given the matter a great deal of
consideration in the past five days since Lucy and
Phillip had returned without prior warning to
Lathrop to prepare them for the possibility that the
heir to Greensward had succumbed to a fatal wound.

How dared her meddlesome brood keep something like that from their parents! she thought, as

close as she had ever been to being out of all patience
with her numerous offspring. And yet how very like
them, she immediately sighed to herself. She was perfectly aware that their motives had sprung from a
deep and abiding affection. Still, she found it difficult
to forgive them for the nearly three weeks that had
been lost, which might have been spent in trying to
find William. Nor had it helped to learn to what
lengths her children and their spouses had gone to
try and discover his whereabouts. Strangely enough,
everything that was brought to light had seemed to
point to Faversham and Miss Felicity Talbot, and yet
in each instance what had seemed promising had led
apparently to a dead end.

Mrs. French, in a flutter of pleasure at finding the
Marchioness of Leighton in her Egyptian withdrawing room, had confided to Florence that her son
Jerome had for some time entertained a deep affection for the Duke of Breverton's only daughter, a connection that could not but please the Right Reverend
French and his wife, and that, further, Jerome had
accepted an invitation to the home of Lord and Lady
Braxton outside of Faversham solely for the opportunity to be near Miss Talbot. Emmaline did not
doubt that Lady Braxton had been more than a little
startled, not to mention inordinately pleased, to have
none other than Paul Francis Moberly, the Marquess
of Leighton, arrive at her front door while she was
giving a houseparty. Jerome French, however, though
he had indeed been given an invitation, was not
among those present. As for Miss Talbot, Lady Braxton had no news of her friend's whereabouts, since
she herself along with her husband had only taken
up residence in England a little less than three
months earlier.

It was Josephine who, while attending Lady Fon-

tesquieu's ball, had overheard speculation that Lady
Zenoria Eppington had at last met her just desserts.
The young beauty, it was rumored, having failed to
bring Viscount Lethridge up to scratch in the wake
of the scandalous affair of the duel, which simply everyone knew, no matter what clever ruse the viscount
had employed to wrap it up in clean linen, had been
fought over her, was to be sent in disgrace to Cornwall to live with an aging relative. The lady herself
had been heard to deny the rumors, even going so
far as to claim she would soon be in a position to
disprove all such allegations. She had hinted that,
only recently while on a visit to Kent to the home of
her cousin Felicity Talbot, who, as everyone knew was
a close childhood friend of the viscount's, she had
been pleased to receive word that Lethridge intended to call on her as soon as circumstances per-
mitted. No doubt, Lady Zenoria declared with
haughty self-assurance, shortly following that greatly
anticipated event, there would be an announcement
sent to the *Gazette*.

It was not true, Josephine had said, greatly agi-
tated, to her dearest Ravenaugh. William would not
send word to Zenoria and leave his family in ignorance of his well-being. He, of all people, would know
how worried they must be.

And that was the crux of the matter, thought Emmaline, watching Miss Talbot pour tea. It was not the
duel that troubled her so much as Lethridge's silence. Closing her eyes, she could see her dearest
William, his grave, sensitive features so like his father's. No matter what evidence there might seem to
be to the contrary, Lethridge simply was not the sort
to rush headlong into danger in the heat of the moment. On the other hand, she knew her son too well
not to realize that, given the right circumstances, he

was perfectly capable of placing himself at risk with calculated, well-reasoned deliberation, which led her to believe there was a deal more to his meeting with Shelby than lay immediately at the surface. Still, he had to all intents and purposes survived the duel. Why, then, had he not sent his family word to that effect?

Her gaze went to her young hostess. That would seem to be something only Miss Talbot could tell them, and she appeared most peculiarly distracted, not at all like the calm, composed young woman Lady Bancroft had come to know on the two or three occasions they had met—which was why the countess, moved by compassion, had intervened on the girl's behalf. Obviously, the child had needed a few minutes to collect herself.

Unfortunately, it would seem that Lady Felicity had little profited from the respite, reflected the countess, observing the hand that wielded the tea server display a tendency to shake—so much so, in fact, that, at the sudden chime of the clock striking the half hour, Felicity gave a jerk, sending tea sloshing over everywhere.

"Oh! I beg your pardon!" she exclaimed, nearly upsetting the dishes in a mortified attempt to blot up the spill. "How very clumsy of me. What a gudgeon you must think me."

"I say, old girl," Bertie interjected, taking the tea server from her before she could inflict any more damage. "If I didn't know better, I'd say you were three sheets to the wind. Better sit down before you convince Lord and Lady Bancroft of it."

"The thought never once entered our minds," kindly declared Lord Bancroft, who, having had a hand in rearing four daughters, was able to recognize all the signs of a female on the verge of tears. "Your sister is clearly overwrought, and I daresay it is all our fault for barging in on her in the middle of the night. My dear, you must not mind us. After all, we owe you a debt of gratitude which we can never repay. William, as you must be aware, means a—a great deal to us. Here, you tell her, Emmaline," he said abruptly with a helpless gesture of a hand. "I daresay it would be better coming from a woman."

"Bancroft is right," Emmaline said, patting Felicity's hand sympathetically. "I fear you have been put to a great deal of trouble for which we can do little in return—save to say thank you for saving our son's life." She gave vent to a small, twisted smile. "It is all quite inadequate, I know, but there it is. And, now we are forced to impose even further on your kindness."

"Not at all," murmured Felicity, making a valiant effort to smile in return. "Naturally, you are more than welcome. Did you say Lady Braxton told you where to find Lethridge? I'm afraid I don't understand. How could she possibly have known?"

"Well, actually, it was our daughter Florence who first directed our attention to Faversham. I daresay it will be no surprise to you to learn that Lethridge has been the object of a rather extensive search. It seems that Florence was given the distinct impression from Mrs. French that she entertained certain . . . shall we say 'expectations'? . . . regarding their son Jerome and the Duke of Breverton's only daughter."

"Can't see why," said Bertie. "Told Jerome m'self his case was hopeless. Daresay Felicity will never love anyone, but Le—"

"*Bertie,*" Felicity pointedly interrupted. "Be so good as to make yourself useful. Kindly finish pouring the tea, if you will. I beg your pardon, Lady Bancroft. You were saying?"

"Yes, well," said Emmaline, who appeared much struck by that little byplay between brother and sister. "The possibility that Mr. French was to attend a houseparty at Lady Braxton's led Leighton to Faversham. Unfortunately, Jerome was not there, and at that time Lady Braxton had yet to know you were in Kent. I daresay it was little more than a day or two later that she saw Lethridge driving you away from Faversham and immediately sent word to that effect. Which is how it is that we find ourselves your uninvited guests."

Felicity deliberately met the other woman's eyes. "You are wondering," she stated flatly, "why Lethridge or I did not send you that pertinent information. There is a reason for it, though I fear you may not like to hear it."

"On the contrary, my dear," interposed the earl, "we should be most grateful to have it at last out in the open. It has something to do with William's— er—condition, does it not? What did you say? That he is 'not quite himself'?"

Smiling into Felicity's eyes, Lady Bancroft gave Felicity's hands a small squeeze of encouragement. "Pray don't be afraid to speak plainly, my dear. Now that we know Lethridge is alive and on the road to recovery, you may be sure Bancroft and I are perfectly able to bear up under anything you have to tell us. After all, we have not reared seven children without learning how to deal with adversity. Bancroft is fond of saying that having possession of all the facts is far better than tormenting oneself with all the imagined possibilities. I daresay we shall feel better knowing what Lethridge is going through, if you could simply tell us what his condition is."

Already laboring under the fear that, far from saving the life of Lady Bancroft's son, she had contrib-

uted in no small measure to placing Lethridge once
more in the gravest peril, Felicity found Lady Bancroft's sympathetic manner more than she could bear
with fortitude. Indeed, she was keenly aware that she
was mortifyingly near to a fit of the vapors.

Before she could stop herself, Felicity bolted to her
feet.

"I'm afraid, Lord and Lady Bancroft," she said,
standing rigidly before Lethridge's mama, her hands
clasped tightly before her as though braced to receive
a mortal blow, "that there is no easy way to say it."
Nervously she began to pace. "You must understand
that Viscount Lethridge was very ill for several days.
He was considerably weakened by fever. And then
there was the trauma of the wound itself." She
stopped to face the others in the room. "When he
came out of the coma, he was unable to recall even
the smallest detail of his past. He is, I'm afraid, an
almost total amnesiac."

"An amnesiac," uttered Bancroft on a gusty
breath.

"Good Lord," said Bertie.

"But his other faculties are intact?" persisted the
earl. "He is able to function quite well?"

"Indeed, my lord. Save for the unfortunate loss of
memory, he is in every way the man we have always
known. Unhappily, that is not all or the worst of it."

Felicity drew in a sharp breath as the clock on the
mantel struck one. It was most assuredly over, whatever events had transpired at the house and on the
docks in Faversham. Lethridge and Trent, not to
mention Leftenant Wilkers, might very well lie dead
or wounded. And poor Annabel—what of her?

To those present, she visibly paled, and Lady Bancroft was both alarmed and filled with pity to note the
expressive eyes appeared most peculiarly haunted.

With an effort, Felicity made herself continue; indeed, the words began to pour from her as if she could no longer contain them, or her anguish.

"At first I did not write to let you know of his condition because I told myself it was necessary to keep him hidden until there was word of Shelby's fate. Lethridge was hardly in any case to take care of himself, let alone avoid the possibility of arrest should Shelby perish of his wound. I could not be sure there were not already soldiers searching for him, in which case there would seem every possibility they might intercept any messages I might try to send to you. At least that was what I kept telling myself. In light of what has come of it, I really cannot be certain if I was not simply lying to myself out of purely selfish motives."

"The devil, Felicity," spoke up Bertie, who thought he knew where his sister was leading, and who, indeed, had a very good notion of what had put her in a quiver. "You were only doing what I told you. No need to make more of this than it is. Only protecting Will, after all. Daresay if anyone is to blame, it's me. Now, enough said. Let's just leave it there."

This unexpected championship from her older brother when she might have expected something altogether different was almost too much for Felicity.

"But I cannot leave it there," she insisted. "Indeed, I cannot bear the—the deception a moment longer." Deliberately she turned her gaze on Lady Bancroft and the earl and drew a deep breath. "Lethridge is laboring under the false impression that he—he loves me, when in reality his heart belongs to my cousin Zenoria. And it is all my fault, because I dared not tell him the truth for fear that in his weakened state he would do something foolish, like insisting on leav-

ing at once for London or—or coming to the conclusion he must marry me because of some stupid
notion of honor or—or any number of other things
that, in his peculiar state of vulnerability, would have
threatened his well-being. And then, later, when I
might have done, there seemed always something to
keep me from it, though I cannot in all conscience
be certain I did not keep silent only because I—I . . ."
She left it unfinished, unable to say it aloud in front
of Lady Bancroft and the earl—that she loved
Lethridge and could not bear the thought that, because of her and what might be construed as her
selfishness, they might all have lost him. She rushed
on, wanting to get it over with before her nerve utterly failed her. "First there was the raid by excisemen, followed by Zenoria's unheralded visit, upon
which I was nearly abducted by smugglers. Then, just
when I had determined it could not go on one moment longer, Will returned home wounded from his
encounter with river pirates. And now what has he
done but taken himself off to fight a duel with a man
who is as unscrupulous as he is ruthless, which is precisely what got Will into trouble in the first place.
Only, this time I have no one to blame but myself.
So you see, you have very little for which to thank
me and a great deal for which to condemn me. Faith,
I shall never forgive *myself* if he is . . ."

Unable to bear the stunned looks on their faces,
she turned sharply away, the side of her fist to her
mouth to stifle the tearful gasp that was rising to her
throat. And now she froze, her eyes fixed in disbelief
on the tall figure limned in the doorway.

His fair hair was more disheveled than was strictly
acceptable even for the windswept. His clothes
showed the stains of travel, and, in addition to the
lines of weariness at the corners of his eyes and

mouth, there was a gash on his cheek and a distinct bruise on the side of his jaw, but he was in all ways her beloved William.

He was alive, and he had come back to her—she could see it in the look in his eyes. And then it came to her that, when he knew the truth, his look would change to disgust. The sudden unutterable relief at seeing him alive, coupled with the inescapable realization that she must very soon be beneath contempt in his eyes, was too much for her. With a gasp, she did what Felicity Talbot had never in her life done before. Crumpling to the floor, she fainted.

Felicity lay listlessly in her bed, aware that she had slept well into the afternoon and yet unwilling to rise and dress. She felt utterly drained of feeling, as if nothing could ever touch her again. Not even the knowledge that she had utterly disgraced herself before Lord and Lady Bancroft, not to mention her older brother, or that she was sadly neglecting her duties as their hostess, served to arouse so much as a flutter of butterfly wings in her stomach. She wondered vaguely how one could go on about the daily business of living with a terrible empty place right through one's middle.

Gradually, in spite of everything, she became aware of a gnawing sensation in the pit of her stomach and realized she could not recall the last time she had eaten anything. Even worse, she soon discovered that, no matter how she positioned herself, she could not relieve the nagging ache in her back or the beginnings of a crick in her neck. At last, unable to bear another moment of her body's protest at her unwontedly protracted stay in bed, she flung aside the bedcovers.

It seemed, she mused ironically, that no matter how she herself might feel about it, her body was determined to go on with the demands of living.

Resolutely she rang for her abigail.

It was not her lady's maid, however, who arrived at her bedchamber door some few minutes later, but Josephine, Lady Ravenaugh, the youngest of the Powell hopefuls, carrying a tray and wearing a cheerful smile on her lovely face.

"Thank heavens, you are awake at last!" Setting the tray on a table, Josephine hurried to take Felicity's hands in her own. "I am so glad." Eagerly her blue-violet eyes scanned the other woman's face. "You have no idea how long I have been waiting to see you. Devon had almost to physically restrain me from breaking in on your rest."

"Ravenaugh is here with you?" said Felicity, aware of a sinking sense of impending doom.

"But of course he is. He would never let me come by myself. But then, everyone is descending on Kent. The proprietor of the Ship Hotel in Faversham is fairly bursting with a newfound sense of importance. After all, he can hardly claim to have a duke, a marquess, three earls, and a viscount, not to mention their respective wives, plus Thomas and Lady Juliana, engage rooms beneath his roof every day of the week. We have, I fear, taken every suite on the second and third floors as well as all the private sitting rooms."

"No, have you?" Felicity smiled a trifle wanly as she struggled to grapple with this new turn of events. Josephine had said a viscount, which meant that William had not wasted any time in removing himself from the cottage. But then, she could hardly blame him. It would be remarkable if he ever wished to lay eyes on her again.

"Pray do not let it distress you, Felicity. They only

came because we have all been so concerned about William. Naturally, they will wish to thank you for what you have done, but only when you feel you are ready. Believe me, the last thing we should wish is to overwhelm you with the entire Powell clan at once." Suddenly she stopped, a sympathetic smile tugging at her lips. "My poor Felicity. You have been having a difficult time of it, haven't you? But things will be better now, I promise. Now, enough. You must come sit down and eat while I tell you everything that has been going on while you have been asleep."

Felicity, seeing the futility of protest, soon found herself settled in a chair with the tray across her lap, while Josephine regaled her with all the news, which was considerable.

No doubt it was perfectly natural, in the circumstances, that she should begin with Shelby's recovery, followed almost immediately by his hasty departure for parts unknown. It seemed that the marquess, unlike Felicity, had not been spared the daunting experience of having the entire Powell clan, or at least the adult male portion of it, minus Timothy, who was with his regiment in India, and Lethridge, who for obvious reasons had not been available, descend upon him in full force. To be confronted by the Duke of Lathrop and the Marquess of Leighton must surely be unsettling, but to have the Earls of Ransome and Ravenaugh in addition to Lord Thomas Powell in their company would be enough to send anyone fleeing the country. The contingent of some of the *ton's* most influential gentlemen, it seemed, had convinced Shelby that there could be little advantage to remaining in England where he would be barred from every private gaming club, ostracized by his peers, and revealed to the world as a conscienceless womanizer, a cheat, and a blackmailer. Aside from the obvious repercussions of social ruination, no doubt he had little welcomed the prospect of being challenged, one after the other, in order of seniority, by every Powell son and son-in-law to take to the field of honor. Clearly, even were the odds of survival not overwhelmingly against him, the time it would take to satisfy so huge a demand would have occupied a major portion of his remaining years, laughed Josephine.

"They accused him of blackmail?" queried Felicity, intrigued in spite of herself. "But how could they possibly have known about Zenoria's letters? I cannot believe she would have told anyone."

"I know nothing of any letters," Josephine answered. "And Lady Zenoria, you may be certain, was never mentioned. I understood from Devon that it was Mr. Jerome French whom Shelby was trying to squeeze. Something about Shelby's having seen Mr. French leaving an inn in the company of a young, unmarried female of gentility. It was apparently all very innocent, according to Mr. French, although the world could not be depended upon to so view it. It was all a matter of a practical joke that went awry because of a runaway horse in a rainstorm and the carriage having suffered a broken axle." Josephine faltered at sight of her friend's seemingly stricken expression. "Felicity, dear, what is it? You have gone as white as a sheet."

Felicity shook her head. "It is nothing. Only, Jo, are you certain? It was Mr. French and not Zenoria whom Shelby was blackmailing?"

"Quite certain, Felicity. You have only to ask Devon. Or Lathrop, for that matter. He was the one who found out about it only yesterday evening. Some sort of missive, which led to the confrontation with Shelby. But why do you ask? Is it important?"

"In truth I hardly know," replied Felicity, a frown darkening her eyes. Then, forcing a smile, she set the tray aside. "Pick out a gown for me, will you, Jo? I believe I shall get dressed."

Thirteen

The house seemed strangely quiet. Empty, thought Felicity as she prowled the rooms in the wake of seeing Josephine and Ravenaugh to their carriage. She chided herself for feeling a little hurt by Josephine's insistence that they could not stay the rest of the afternoon but must get back to the family waiting for them in Faversham. It had made her feel suddenly rather forsaken and very much alone, which was patently absurd, she told herself. She had lived in the cottage for almost a year without feeling in the least lonely. And besides, Bertie was about somewhere, probably out tramping the grounds, renewing old acquaintances. There was a girl, she remembered, whom he was not averse to flirting with when he was here.

She thought of her promise to join Jo and the others later for dinner at the Ship Hotel and wished she had had an excuse to cry off. Briefly she considered sending a note pleading a headache, but immediately dismissed the notion as churlish in the extreme. They would all know why she had done it, and that she could not bear. There was no getting around it at any rate. She would have to face Will eventually, if not at the Ship Hotel, then somewhere, sometime when she was least expecting it. It would be better to have it over with, she told herself, and was not in the least comforted by the knowledge.

At last, unable to bear the confines of the house any longer, she threw on an old cloak she was used to wearing on walks along the beach and let herself out of the Blue Salon's French doors into the rose garden, but even that was not enough to still her disquiet. Beyond the protective walls, the wind blustered inland, tossing the grass in undulating waves like windswept water—like the restlessness that had driven her from the house.

She opened the ironwork gate and stepped through. An image of Steed flashed through her mind, the man's arrogance as vivid as that day he had accosted her there. She had learned enough from Josephine to know that Will had saved Annabel and that Steed had been taken in the raid, badly beaten but alive. It was certain that Steed would stand trial and be hanged for his crimes, and then Annabel would be free at last. She thought of Trent, of Annabel and the child Meggie and wondered what would happen to them now. Surely there was nothing any longer to keep them apart, save, perhaps, Trent's stubborn pride.

The dog's rumbling bark brought her head up, her eyes searching the down. Goliath, a great, lumbering mass of white fur, bounded joyfully out of the cherry orchard and up the hill to her. A paw landing on either of her shoulders, the dog nearly bowled her over.

"Down, Goliath, you dreadful beast," Felicity scolded, pushing the dog away, then laughing as she knelt to rumple the animal's fur.

To her surprise, Goliath lunged from beneath her hands and, running a short distance, paused, his head turned to her with a look of canine expectancy.

He whined deep in his throat, his nonexistent tail wagging ecstatically.

Felicity went quite still, her gaze going beyond Goliath to the tall figure of the man walking steadily toward her. He was hatless, his greatcoat billowing around him in the wind. In something like despair, she thought he had never looked more formidable— or more compelling.

Felicity caught her bottom lip between her teeth. He had not, as she had believed, left without waiting to see her. He had stayed, biding his time until she was alone. No doubt what he had to say to her could not be said in front of others. As she came to her feet, a hand pressed to her heart, she felt a wild urge to turn and flee into the house.

Somehow the very absurdity of such a notion helped to steady her nerves. Whatever she had done or why she had done it, she was still Felicity Talbot, and he was William Powell. Surely that must account for something.

The look in his eyes, however, would seem to discount that rationality. They burned through her with a fierce, smoldering intensity that seared her heart and scattered her defenses.

"Will, pray don't look at me like that!" Felicity uttered on a rising note. "I know how much you must despise me for the lies. Indeed, I should not blame you if you cannot forgive me. I cannot forgive myself, but in truth I never meant to—"

"Hush," William uttered thickly. Ruthlessly he pulled her to him. "I could never hate you." Before Felicity could voice a protest, he covered her mouth with his.

While it might be true that she had been kissed before, by Thaddeus Wilcox and Sir Andrew Parks and even by Will Powell himself, she had never experienced anything remotely like the fierce, tender hunger with which Lethridge embraced her, his lips moving over hers with an aching urgency that rendered her breathless and trembling with emotions she had never before known she had. Even Lucinda Evalina's unparalleled descriptions of the powerful feelings evoked between a man and a woman destined to an all-consuming love for one another could not compare with what Lethridge aroused in her. And, still, she could not silence the small, persistent voice of conscience that cried out against giving into a lie.

"Will, no," she gasped, pulling away at last. "You mustn't." Drawing in a long, tremulous breath, she made herself say the words. "I know they have told you the truth about e-everything. And even if you cannot yet perfectly remember it for yourself, you soon will." She forced herself to look at him. "Zenoria is waiting for you. You must let nothing deter you from going to her."

Lethridge stared at her, his eyes dark with barely contained passion. With a seeming effort, he controlled his breathing. "Yes, of course, Zenoria," he agreed, watching the nervous flutter of her hand. "And you, I suppose, must simply go to the devil."

"I should hope not, my lord," replied Felicity, schooling her features to reveal nothing of the longing in her heart. "I shall close up the cottage and go to Breverton for a time. After that, I shall return to London to oversee the establishment of my hostel for unwed mothers. And the school, of course. I daresay I shall be happily occupied for a long time to come."

"Oh, I daresay. And I, in the meantime, am to be left to a loveless marriage with a woman who has made it plain that she is as faithless as she is selfish, is that it?" returned Lethridge, clasping her by the arms. "I'm afraid I cannot think much of this plan of yours. As a matter of fact, I most heartily object to it."

"I wish you will not be absurd, my lord," said Felicity, stung by his harshness. How dared he persist in believing he must marry her out of some mistaken notion of honor! She had known he would despise her when he learned the truth, but she hardly expected him to accuse her of being faithless and selfish. Really, it was too much. Indeed, she would not have it. "Pray don't be absurd, Will Powell," she said, turning away to hide the hurt that must be plain in her eyes. "You will marry Zenoria, the woman you have always loved. She has made it clear to the world that she views your suit with favor. She will not turn you down when you offer for her."

"No, she would not dare," declared his lordship with an odd twist of his lips. "After the fiasco with Shelby, she would hardly survive the scandal. And neither will you, my dearest Felicity. We have been alone together in this cottage for three whole weeks."

"And nothing happened," Felicity uttered on a gasp. "It means nothing. You owe me nothing."

"After three weeks with you," Lethridge stated firmly, as if she had not so rudely interrupted him, "I am more convinced than ever that I cannot countenance such a future as you have described. I want you for my wife, Felicity, and I warn you I am in no mood to take no for an answer. We will be married by special license with as great dispatch as possible."

Felicity's head came up, her eyes sparkling dangerously. "You are mistaken, my lord. I should rather embrace scandal than to marry simply to satisfy your notions of honor. That would be the greatest disgrace of all. You are free, my lord, to marry Zenoria. *Why* do you not go to her?"

"The devil, Felicity, why do you think?" demanded Lethridge, clasping Felicity to him. "It is because I am free, free of my damnable illusions, free at last of Zenoria. I love you, Felicity Talbot. Heaven knows why it took a bullet to the skull to make me see it, but I can only be grateful that I have at last had the scales stripped from my eyes. It was never Zenoria. It has always been you who held my heart captive."

"Stop it. I will not listen to any more of this. Do you think I am without feelings? I have loved you for as long as I can remember, and I am perfectly aware I was wrong to deceive you these past weeks, wrong to allow you to go on believing you were simply Will Powell, my cousin once removed, when you are Lethridge, the man who fought a duel over my cousin. You do not have to pretend you do not despise me for the deception."

"Despise you?" Felicity almost quailed before the sudden leap of his eyes. "Good God, Felicity, how can you think so? I have been driven mad with the certainty that you could never forgive me for deceiving you. The truth is it has been some time since I have been William Powell, your cousin once removed, whom you so generously took into your care. You may be certain that the man who declared he would have you for his wife knew precisely who he was, and that, furthermore, he was perfectly lucid when he made his declaration."

Felicity, stunned by that unexpected announcement, stared at him with dawning enlightenment. "When he—you . . . The devil, Will Powell, what are you saying? That you have known all along who you are?"

"More importantly, I have known for some little time who *you* are—a delightfully stubborn, maddeningly independent female who has driven me half mad with worry over her insistence on flying into the face of danger. You really must marry me, my dearest Felicity. I love you far too much ever to think of allowing you to embroil yourself in another of your madcap schemes without me to see to it that nothing ill befalls you."

Felicity felt the walls of her resistance tumble before the fiercely tender light in his eyes. Will Powell loved her, had loved her without knowing it for no little time. Strange that she had not realized he was far too rational a creature ever to have fought a duel over her cousin's indiscretions. She should have known him well enough to guess there was a deal more to it than that. Still, she could not resist punishing him just a little for his deception before she gave free rein to the happiness welling up inside her.

"Then of course I will marry you, my dearest Will," she said, leaning her palms against his chest and gazing up at him with twin imps in her eyes. "For if you must know, it has come to my attention that a band of white slavers has been abducting young girls from the countryside and selling them to London's most loathsome bordellos. I am convinced that, with you to help me, I shall be able to put an end to the enterprise. And besides," she added quickly, seeing the warning glint in his eyes, "I have come to suspect it was never my cousin Zenoria who lured you into that ridiculous duel. You did it for me, did you not? Because Jerome played that miserable trick on me, pretending to lose control of his cattle in the hopes that I should swoon in his arms. Only he did not plan on there being a rock in the road sufficient to break the axle and leave us with little choice but to seek help at a certain country inn. An inn to which Zenoria had just happened to steal for a tryst with the Marquess of Shelby. They saw me with Jerome, did they not? And Zenoria told you about it. My dearest, most noble-hearted Will, was Shelby really blackmailing poor Jerome because of that silly, unfortunate incident? Is that why you did it? Pray do not deny it. I know it had to be you who wrote Lathrop informing him of Shelby's loathsome attempts at blackmail."

"That, and to ask Lathrop to engage Trent's services in his shipping business. Your young captain and his Annabel, along with Meggie, are already on their way to Canada, where they will begin a new life under my brother-in-law's auspices. I had to make sure you and your friends would be protected if—"

Quickly Felicity touched a fingertip to his lips. "If Steed put a period to your existence. For that I shall not soon forgive you. The devil, Will. Why did you not tell me you had recovered your memory?"

Lethridge, closing his fingers around Felicity's wrist, pulled her hand down between them. "Because, my darling girl, I had only brief snatches of things, like the occasion you played your stunt on Rutherford. Over time, I had glimpses of the past, images of you, of Bertie, even Zenoria and finally Greensward. It was not until I found myself staring down the muzzle of a pirate's pistol and felt the shock of the ball crease my skull that so much more came back to me. I remembered, Felicity Talbot, that I had been waiting all those years for you to grow up. Unfortunately, you seemed to do it all when my back was turned. That day I awakened from my coma to you, I fell in love with a beautiful woman, but it was the captivating little girl with freckles and eyes too big for her face who first won my heart."

"But Zenoria—?" Felicity interjected, struggling to

digest this startling new revelation. "Everyone knew you were head over ears in love with her."

"On the contrary, Miss Talbot," Lethridge humorlessly smiled. "People saw what Zenoria wanted them to see. My error was in befriending Bertie's cousin with the intent of smoothing the way for her first Season in London. She did not hesitate to make it seem a deal more than it ever was. For your sake and Bertie's, I allowed people to think what they would in the hopes she would one day fall victim to one of her own intrigues. And now it seems that she has. Say you will marry me as soon as all the arrangements can be made, my darling girl. You will be doing me the greatest of favors. With you as the future chatelaine of Greensward, I shall at last be happily free of Lady Zenoria Eppington."

"My dearest Will," said Felicity, her eyes shining up at him, "I have been waiting since I was ten years old to become your bride. You may be sure I am not in the least prepared to wait a moment longer than it takes to obtain a special license. Besides, I am reliably informed that my future in-laws are to celebrate their thirty-second wedding anniversary in little less than a week. It would be a shame, would it not, if we caused them to delay their trip to the South of France by holding out for a formal ceremony?"

"Good God," exclaimed William, clearly torn between elation and consternation, "the new family travel coach! I completely forgot."

"But of course you did," said Felicity, laughing. "You were, after all, an almost total amnesiac. For your sake, I suggest you remain one for a few days longer—only promise, my dearest Will, you will not forget me."

That he could never do, thought William, gazing down into his darling girl's laughing eyes. Even deprived of his memory, his heart had known what his mind had not. She was Felicity, his dearest friend, his life, his happiness, his only love. But, more than that, she was the future of Greensward.

ABOUT THE AUTHOR

Sara Blayne lives with her family in New Mexico. She is the author of eight traditional Regency romances and two historical romances set in the Regency period. Sara is currently working on her next historical romance set in the Regency period—look for HIS SCANDALOUS DUCHESS in October 2000. Sara loves to hear from readers and you may write to her c/o Zebra Books. Please include a self-addressed stamped envelope if you wish a reply.

BOOK YOUR PLACE ON OUR WEBSITE AND MAKE THE READING CONNECTION!

We've created a customized website just for our very special readers, where you can get the inside scoop on everything that's going on with Zebra, Pinnacle and Kensington books.

When you come online, you'll have the exciting opportunity to:

- View covers of upcoming books
- Read sample chapters
- Learn about our future publishing schedule (listed by publication month *and author*)
- Find out when your favorite authors will be visiting a city near you
- Search for and order backlist books from our online catalog
- Check out author bios and background information
- Send e-mail to your favorite authors
- Meet the Kensington staff online
- Join us in weekly chats with authors, readers and other guests
- Get writing guidelines
- AND MUCH MORE!

**Visit our website at
http://www.zebrabooks.com**

More Zebra Regency Romances

Put a Little Romance in Your Life With
Constance O'Day-Flannery

Merlin's Legacy

A Series From
Quinn Taylor Evans